"I w　　　　　　　　　　*r said*

He　　　　　　　　　　e one kiss and I'll do everything I can to get you the interview."

Rory thought that her heart might just beat out of her chest. Kissing this man might be the biggest risk she'd ever take. But she wanted the kiss. Desperately. What could it matter? She dared herself to do it.

"One kiss," she agreed.

He backed her up against the mirror. "Last chance to change your mind."

"I'm not going to change—"

Before she could even finish her sentence he'd lowered his head, drawn her up on her toes and covered her mouth with his.

There was such heat—glorious waves of it. And each movement of his hands, of his tongue seemed to throw fuel on the fire. She arched her body, straining against him, but it wasn't enough. She had to—

"I want you." His voice was a rough whisper in her ear.

No, she told herself to say.

"Yes," she said. "*Yes.* Please hurry."

Blaze™

Dear Reader,

Writing a miniseries about triplet sisters Natalie, Rory and Sierra Gibbs has allowed me to create three very special women who find the courage to risk it all to get what they want. As they came alive on the page, I found myself admiring each one of them. But if I had to pick a favorite, I'd lean toward Rory—perhaps because she lacks the confidence of her more focused sisters.

Wannabe magazine writer Rory Gibbs has always thought of herself as the "muddled in the middle" triplet. Her sisters are tall, beautiful and successful; she's short, still trying to figure out what she wants to be when she grows up, and as unlucky with men as she's been with jobs. However, her latest plan—to land an interview with reclusive businessman Jared Slade—will allow her to prove to herself, her boss and everyone else that she's finally found a career she's good at. Problem number one is she can't get past Hunter, Jared Slade's handsome and dangerous bodyguard. Problem number two is she doesn't want to get past him—she wants to make love with him!

I hope you'll enjoy reading about how Hunter and Rory dare to take the greatest risk of all. And I hope you'll want to read Natalie's and Sierra's adventures, as well—in *The Proposition* (May) and *The Favor* (July). For excerpts, contests and news about my future books, please visit www.carasummers.com.

Happy reading,

Cara Summers

CARA SUMMERS

THE DARE

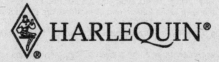

HARLEQUIN®

TORONTO • NEW YORK • LONDON
AMSTERDAM • PARIS • SYDNEY • HAMBURG
STOCKHOLM • ATHENS • TOKYO • MILAN • MADRID
PRAGUE • WARSAW • BUDAPEST • AUCKLAND

To my cousins, the Kansier women: Jane, Kathy, Mary, Margaret, Amy and Debbie. I admire your strength, your courage, your love of adventure—and especially your unfailing sense of humor. You inspire the kind of women I try to create.

Thanks.

ISBN 0-373-79192-5

THE DARE

Copyright © 2005 by Carolyn Hanlon.

Prologue

Summer 1999

IF HE FAILED, the drop to the alley below would kill him. Harry Gibbs stood on the roof of the Hotel L'Adour Paris and glanced at the gap between the two buildings. He felt the familiar rush of adrenaline and grinned.

He didn't allow himself to look down, or to take in the picture-postcard view that the roof of the hotel offered. At 3:00 a.m., the Eiffel Tower and Notre Dame were still bathed in light, but Harry focused all his concentration on that dark narrow space—ten feet at the most. He'd paced off the distance in the alley that morning. Just in case the robbery didn't go quite as planned.

And it hadn't. He'd gotten the necklace out of the safe, but he hadn't had time to close it and replace the tapestry before Madame Cuvelier had awakened in the next room and rung for her maid. There was only one route from the maid's quarters to Madame's bedroom, and that was through the salon he'd been standing in.

Madame Cuvelier, a resident of the small hotel for the past ten years, was a restless sleeper. That information was in the dossier he'd compiled on her. That made the theft riskier.

And more fun. Instead of exiting through the door, the

way he'd come in, he'd had to hurry out onto a balcony and climb to the roof.

When the sound of sirens pierced the night air, Harry turned and strode to the far end of the roof. Then, he did what he always did when the stakes were high. He dared himself to make the leap. As he crouched down into the position of a sprinter, he thought of his daughter, Rory. He'd been thinking a lot about her lately. Tonight, he promised himself. He'd write to her.

Clearing his mind, he murmured, "You can do it, Harry. *Dare you!*" Then he ran, lengthening his stride as he raced across the roof. Fifty yards became forty, thirty, twenty, ten. He prepared for the jump, felt his right foot hit the parapet. Then he leapt.

For a prolonged second, he was arcing over the alley, his body slicing through the air. If something happened to him…

Before he could complete the thought, his foot came down hard and he tucked and rolled across the roof. Lungs burning, blood singing, Harry got to his feet and ran toward the door. It took him less than three minutes to finesse the lock. The sirens were still blocks away.

He was whistling as he stepped into the stairwell.

AN HOUR LATER, Harry stood on the balcony of his apartment in Montmartre and swirled cognac in a glass. Now that the excitement of the heist was over, his mood had turned melancholy again as he once more thought of Rory. Dammit, he missed her. He had three girls, triplets, and lately, he'd been missing all of them.

More than that, he'd been feeling an urgent need to talk to them. That was impossible, of course. They'd been ten years old when he and his wife, Amanda, had forged their agreement. She'd wanted a normal life for the girls, and so had he.

For the first ten years of their lives, he'd done his best to give them one. But he'd become bored with their "normal" life in the suburbs of D.C. He'd missed the adventure, the risk taking, the thrill of pulling off a perfect heist.

Amanda had been firm. At ten, the girls idolized him, and she didn't want them idolizing his profession. Therefore, he could leave and resume his former profession as a master jewel thief on the condition that he didn't see his girls or communicate with them until their twenty-sixth birthday.

Harry took a sip of his cognac. He'd made a mistake— the biggest one of his life—by agreeing to those terms. He and Amanda should have found another way. Two weeks ago, the girls had celebrated their twentieth birthday, and six more years had begun to seem far too long. Time could easily run out for him before that. It nearly had tonight.

Turning, he strode toward the desk in his study. On the night of their birthdays, he'd written a letter to his oldest daughter, Natalie.

But it was Rory, the second born, he'd thought of on that roof tonight. Each of his daughters had inherited something from him. Natalie had inherited his gift for picking locks and his talent for disguise. Sierra, the youngest, had inherited his curiosity and his analytical brain.

But it was Rory who'd inherited his love of taking risks and his inability to refuse a dare. Even as a toddler, she'd been the most impetuous of the three, and he'd always thought of her as his little daredevil. Natalie had worked hard to suppress any reckless streaks in her nature. And Sierra had naturally preferred to think things out, to plan.

Rory had always chosen to throw herself into situations, making things up as she went along.

Earlier he'd opened an album to his three favorite photos of his middle daughter. In one, she was running over the finish line in a race. Harry smiled. Of the three girls, she was the one who always rushed headlong through life.

In the second, she was at her senior prom. And she was beautiful. When she was a little girl, she hadn't believed that. She'd always felt that her sisters had inherited the "beauty" genes, as she'd called them. He couldn't help but wonder if the years had brought her more confidence.

In the last picture, his favorite, she was on horseback, leaping over a fence. She'd been nineteen, and no doubt she'd dared herself to do it. That was what she'd always done when she was little. Rory had always been an excellent horsewoman. He recalled the times they'd ridden together, just the two of them, and rubbed the heel of his hand against the tight little band that squeezed his heart.

He had taken those photos himself. He might have promised Amanda that he wouldn't contact them, but that hadn't kept him from being there at important events over the years.

Harry set down his glass of cognac. He might have a pictorial history of his girls' lives, but he didn't have them. Reaching for a paper and pen, he shook off the nagging feeling that his time was running out. He might have to wait six years to deliver the letter in person, but he could write to her tonight.

To Rory, my darling daredevil...

1

WHY COULDN'T SHE EVER PLAN ahead?

Rory Gibbs gave herself a mental kick as she pushed her way through the crowd in the waiting area of the Blue Pepper. When she'd made the urgent call to her sisters to join her for dinner, she'd totally forgotten that Tuesday night was singles' night at the popular Georgetown bistro. Now, as usual, she was going to have to depend on her luck to get a table. Rising to her tiptoes, she scanned the crowd trying to spot one of the owners.

George, a gentle giant of a man, would be busy at the bar, but his partner, Rad, should be somewhere near the reservation desk. Skirting a group of preppy-looking men, Rory climbed the four steps that led to the bar and once more scanned the crush of people. Or tried to. It was just hell being short.

"Excuse me." Rory smiled up at a tall man as she wedged herself a path between him and the brunette he was talking to. He didn't even glance down at her. Neither did another man whose elbow she jarred as she attempted unsuccessfully to duck beneath it. Halfway to the reservation desk, she finally bumped into Rad as they both were squeezing their way around a group of three women.

"Rory, Rory, Rory, Rory." In spite of the crush of people, Rad managed to grasp her hands and kiss the air near her left cheek. Then he stepped back to give her a critical once-over. She returned the favor, noting that tonight his hair was white-blond and spiked. Rad changed his hair color almost as frequently as he changed his ties.

Before he'd bought the Blue Pepper, Rad had studied fashion design in New York City, and he'd appointed himself fashion policeman for the Gibbs sisters. He'd convinced her older sister, Natalie, to experiment with new colors and to start wearing her hair down.

For a full minute, Rory held her breath, hoping that the outfit she'd decided on met with his approval.

Rad had insisted she develop her own signature style. But like everything else she did, she was never quite sure how she was doing. She'd gotten the idea of pairing the faded, low-slung jeans with a vintage organdy-and-lace shirt from one of the layouts in *Celebs* magazine. She'd made the look her own by tying the shirttails beneath her breasts and adding strappy, high-heeled sandals, along with cascades of thin Italian gold hoops in her ears.

Finally, Rad beamed a smile at her, then leaned in and pitched his voice to be heard above the clatter of glasses and snatches of conversation. "A very nice variation on the Sarah Jessica Parker look! And I love the little gold bar in your navel. Veerry sexy."

"Thanks." Rory tried not to think about the fact that the only men who ever used that word to describe her were gay. No negative thoughts tonight, she reminded herself as she beamed a smile at Rad. "Tell me my luck's holding and you can find me a table."

Rad's brows shot up. "On a Tuesday night? You're lucky to have two sisters who plan ahead and call for reservations. Detective Natalie paged me at noon."

That figured, Rory thought. Natalie took her responsibility as the oldest very seriously, and as a cop, she was good at thinking ahead.

"Dr. Gibbs beat her by calling this morning," Rad said.

That figured, too. Sierra was a meticulous planner. She was forever making lists on blue note cards, and it had certainly paid off. She'd recently accepted a tenure-track position in Georgetown's psychology department, and she ran her life with the same smooth efficiency that she wrote her books and taught her courses.

A little sliver of envy ran through Rory. Despite that they were triplets, she and her sisters were as different as two suns and the moon, and she wanted to be more like them. For starters, Natalie and Sierra had inherited the "planning" genes while her own approach to life so far could best be described as seat-of-the-pants.

She envied them in the looks department, too. Both Natalie and Sierra were tall like their father while she was short like their mother. Natalie was a smashing redhead; Sierra was a cool Gwyneth Paltrow–type blonde; and she was a plain brunette. But what was beginning to bother Rory most of all was that at twenty-six, her sisters were settled on their career paths and she was still trying to figure out what she wanted to be when she grew up.

Those days were history, she reminded herself. If everything went well tomorrow, she would no longer be the "muddled in the middle" triplet. She would be a reporter with a staff job at *Celebs* magazine. Nerves knotted in her stomach. If everything went well…

"Dr. Gibbs and Detective Natalie are waiting for you out on the patio," Rad continued.

Sierra and Natalie had also inherited the "title" genes. She was just plain Rory.

"I've already put in an order for the appetizer special." Rad turned her in the direction of the patio and gave her a nudge.

Food. That's what she needed to settle her nerves. Usually, she chewed bubble gum, but she'd run out—a result of bad planning, of course.

No negative thoughts, she lectured herself again. As she nudged, ducked and generally bulldozed her way through the crowd, Rory tried to organize her thoughts and screw up her courage. After all, she was about to have one of life's defining moments. She was going to open the letter her father had sent to her.

One month ago, she and her sisters had gathered here at the Blue Pepper to celebrate their twenty-sixth birthday, and Natalie had dropped a little bombshell into their lives.

After not seeing or hearing from Harry Gibbs for sixteen years, they'd each received a letter from him—a letter that had been held in trust by their father's attorney for six years after Harry had died. They'd only been twenty when they'd lost both parents within months of each other.

Even now, it was hard for Rory to let herself think about her father without feeling a few pangs of pain and resentment. She couldn't quite forgive him for walking out on them when they were ten. Neither could her sisters. Shortly after he'd left, they'd stopped calling him Dad and started referring to him as Harry.

Coming up short behind a solid wall of people who'd gathered to watch the salsa band, Rory edged her way along, looking for an opening. Just the thought of opening that letter had the nerves dancing in her stomach. Natalie had opened her letter a month ago, and the advice Harry had given her—to trust in her talents and risk everything to get what she wanted—had changed Natalie's life. Not only had her older sister decided to say yes to the adventure of a lifetime, but she'd also found love. Since Natalie had found Chance Mitchell, she'd positively glowed.

But then Natalie had always had a lot of talents to trust in. Rory couldn't imagine what Harry would say to her. Wiping damp hands on her jeans, she gave up on finding an opening in the wall of people. Instead, she ducked her head, twisted to the side and muscled her way through the crowd. After spotting her sisters, she shot across the dance floor, and finally dropped into a chair between them. Martinis were waiting, along with a platter of the Blue Pepper's famous finger food. Rory reached for a stuffed mushroom and popped it into her mouth. Then she said around it, "Thanks for coming."

"You don't have to do this if you're not ready," Natalie said.

Sierra tapped the blue note card on the table in front of her. "We only agreed that you would be the one to go second. You can take all the time you want."

Rory swallowed and drew in a deep breath. "I've waited long enough." Slipping the letter out of her pocket, she set it on the table. "I need Harry's advice." There. She'd said it, and the words eased some of the flutters in her stomach.

"What's up?" Natalie asked.

Rory glanced at Natalie. Of course, her perceptive older sister would know that something besides the letter was bothering her. She drew in a deep breath.

"I've finally chosen a career."

Natalie smiled gently. "I understand why you feel like it's important you make a decision, but you don't have to put so much pressure on yourself, you know, Rory," Natalie said.

Rory glanced down at the white envelope with her name scrawled across it. Yes, she did. Her conversation with her boss that morning clinched it. She was sick and tired of the self-doubts that had plagued her all her life. "You guys were born knowing what you wanted to do. I've changed jobs six times in four years. That must be some kind of a Guinness record."

"Who says everyone has to be like Sierra or me?" Natalie asked.

"And who says that we'll stay at our jobs forever?" Sierra peered at her over the rims of her glasses. "Research shows that most people in our age group will have to change their career paths three or four times in the course of their lifetimes. You'll be much more prepared for those changes than either Natalie or I will."

She could always depend on her sisters for unflagging support, but it didn't change the fact that she'd never felt the kind of confidence that they'd always felt about their career choices. Bottom line—she was tired of being the "muddled in the middle" sister.

Her gaze dropped to the envelope again. "I can't help thinking that if I'd only been as focused on a specific career as you both were, Harry could have come home sooner. I bet Mom was worried that I would have taken up after Dad if he'd become part of our lives again."

Natalie took one of her hands and Sierra the other. "You can't blame yourself for a decision that our parents made. And if you want to blame someone for the fact that Harry went away, blame me. I'm the one who inherited his knack for cracking safes. I'll bet that's what freaked Mom out."

Sierra squeezed Rory's hand. "Children always feel a certain amount of guilt when they're abandoned by a parent."

Rory stared at her. "You, too? What could you possibly feel guilty about?"

Sierra smiled wanly. "I was always sick. I figured that the reason Mom didn't want to go with him was because of me."

"No," Rory protested.

"Not true," Natalie said at the same time.

Then Natalie straightened her shoulders. "I think we have to come to an agreement. We aren't to blame for what they did. And we certainly aren't to blame that Harry died before he could come back and deliver his advice in person." She raised her martini. "Let's say goodbye to guilt."

Rory and Sierra raised their glasses, and then they all sipped their drinks.

"Easier said than done." Rory set down her glass.

"It's a good first step," Sierra said.

"Here goes." Rory picked up the letter from her father. After opening the flap, she pulled out a single sheet of paper.

To Rory, my darling daredevil,
Your mother and I were both twenty-six when you girls came into our lives, and we agreed that you can open this letter on your twenty-sixth birthday in the event that I'm not there to talk to you in person.

Remember when you were little and I used to warn you that you could only trust in your luck so far? Well, I was dead wrong to tell you that. That was what your mother always told me. She was afraid that some day I'd take one risk too many, and because you were always so impetuous, she worried about you, too. I hope that you will listen to me now. Trust in your luck all the way—and be willing to push it. And never be afraid to take risks. You can do anything you want if you dare to take a shot at it. Most important of all—don't be afraid to stay in the game.

If I'd followed that advice, I would never have left you and your sisters. I will always regret that I didn't dare to stay in the game.

Love,
Harry

Rory forgot to breathe as she reread the words. Had he really thought of her as his darling daredevil? The thought had her heart swelling a bit. She drew in a deep breath and let it out. "Well."

"Look at the pictures," Sierra urged.

Rory pulled three photos out of the envelope. There'd been three in Natalie's letter, too. Moisture pricked her eyes again as she noted that one picture had been taken at one of the races she'd run in high school, and another was at her senior prom. The third was one of her on horseback jumping a fence.

Memories stirred in her mind. When she was little, Harry had encouraged her to ride. He'd seen to it that she'd had lessons, and he'd never failed to be there on the side-lines, telling her that she could do anything she dared to do.

She'd forgotten all about that. Perhaps she really had inherited a daredevil trait from him. Studying the picture more closely, she pinned down the time to her freshman year in college. The equestrian team had won a blue ribbon at the state finals that year, and the meet had taken place less than a year before Harry's fatal accident.

He'd been there, just as he'd been at every other important event in their lives. An old familiar ache settled around her heart. "I miss him."

"Me, too." Natalie sighed.

"Ditto," Sierra added.

For a moment, silence stretched between them.

Finally, Natalie cleared her throat. "Okay. Now we want to know why you need Harry's advice tonight of all nights. Did you and your boss at *Celebs* come to a parting of the ways?"

"No." Rory shook her head. "This isn't about another career change. I still want to be a reporter. I think I can be good at it. But my current job hasn't turned out to be what I expected. What it boils down to is I'm really just a research assistant to Lea Roberts, one of their star reporters. I've written some pieces, but I haven't gotten a byline yet."

Even as she explained the situation to her sisters, Rory recalled the scene that had taken place in Lea Roberts's office that morning.

Lea was a tall, stunning brunette with a slender build who was always relaxed and perfectly controlled. But that morning, Rory's boss had been pacing behind her desk.

"You've been asking to do some fieldwork," Lea had said, waving her into a chair.

"Yes."

Lea circled the desk and rested a hip on its corner. "I'm going to tell you up front that I'm not sure you're ready to handle this. But I'm desperate. I can't do it myself because I have to interview Elizabeth Cavenaugh, the chief justice's wife, at her apartment in New York City tomorrow morning, and I can't postpone it. All you have to do is snap a picture. That's it."

"I can handle it," Rory said, wishing that Lea didn't sound so much like she was trying to convince herself of that fact. "Who is the person I'm supposed to take a picture of?"

Lea leaned closer. "You're not to mention this to anyone, understand?"

Rory nodded.

"I've received a tip that Jared Slade is going to be checking in to Les Printemps tomorrow morning. I want you to get a picture of him. One picture. Can you do it?"

"Sure," Rory said, a surge of excitement moving through her. She knew just about everything there was to know about the reclusive businessman who ran Slade Enterprises. She'd been researching him for Lea for two weeks, and the thought of meeting him in person...well, the man just plain fascinated her. "Is that all? Shouldn't I try to get an interview?"

Lea stared at her for a moment. Then she threw back her head and laughed. "An interview?"

Emotions tumbled through Rory. Beneath the hurt and the humiliation, she felt a little flame of anger begin to burn.

"An interview," Lea repeated as she struggled to get her laughter under control. "Slade has never granted an interview—to anyone. He loathes all reporters. You'll be lucky if you can get a picture. Just focus all your attention on that. This could be a real coup for the magazine, and I'm depending on you. If you can get the photo, I'll recommend you for a staff position."

The staff position had been her dream from the moment she'd accepted the job at *Celebs*. She should have been thrilled. But try as she might, Rory hadn't been able to forget that Lea had laughed out loud at her idea to get an interview with Jared Slade. Even now as she waited for her sister's reaction to her story, she wondered if her boss was aware that her laughter had been tantamount to a dare. Pushing the thought temporarily aside, Rory focused her full attention on her sisters.

"She offered you a staff job? That's wonderful," Sierra said.

"And it doesn't surprise me one bit," Natalie added.

When her sisters raised their glasses, Rory shook her head. "It's not a done deal yet. First I have to snap a picture of Jared Slade."

Frowning, Natalie tapped her fingers on the table. "Jared Slade…isn't he that mysterious business tycoon, the recluse?"

Rory nodded. "I've done some research on him. The *Wall Street Journal* calls him the twenty-first-century version of Howard Hughes. He's also been dubbed 'the man with the Midas touch' when it comes to business. His companies run the gamut from five-star hotels and golf courses to high-end retail clothing stores. He's absolutely fascinating."

"He's had his share of trouble lately," Natalie said. "There was a food-poisoning incident at his hotel in Atlanta and a fire at a factory of his in upstate New York."

Rory stared at Natalie. "How did you know all that?"

"He's been in D.C. twice in the past month. Part of my job is to try to keep tabs on high-profile people who might bring trouble here with them. His office always refuses to let us know where he's staying."

Rory picked up a strip of green pepper and gestured with it. "He's like a phantom. No one knows what he looks like. I'm beginning to wonder if he even exists. Maybe he's just a made-up figurehead like Betty Crocker."

When her sisters aimed two blank stares at her, she said, "You know, that was the housewife that General Mills created out of whole cloth to promote their products. She was just a picture they put on their cake mixes and stuff. It could be that 'Jared Slade' is an imaginary person that a very enterprising CEO is using to create a certain mystique about Slade Enterprises."

"You'll have to have some kind of plan if you're going to take a photo of someone who's never been seen and who might not be real at all," Sierra commented.

Rory reached for a cube of cheese and stuffed it into her mouth. Her younger sister had a steel trap of a mind that always got to the heart of the problem. Rory didn't have a plan—exactly—at least not one she could jot down on a note card.

Swallowing, she said, "It's pretty simple. Lea Roberts received a tip that Jared Slade will be checking into Les Printemps tomorrow morning. I'm going to be in the lobby waiting. I figure I'll snap the picture when Mr. Slade registers at the desk."

Natalie frowned. "It sounds risky to me. Celebrities have been known to resort to violence when their pictures are taken by the paparazzi."

Rory met her sister's eyes. "I'll be in the lobby of an exclusive hotel. And I ran hurdles in high school, remember? If worse comes to worst, I'll just make a run for it."

"I still don't like it," Natalie said.

Rory leaned forward. "I've got to do this, Nat. I want this staff job more than anything. It's my way of proving to everyone including myself that I can be successful at something."

"I think this is even more than that," Sierra said. "It's personal. You're intrigued by the man himself."

Rory turned to stare at Sierra. It never ceased to amaze her that her younger sister always saw more than anyone expected her to.

Natalie's eyes narrowed as she shot Sierra a look and then turned to study Rory. "I thought you'd decided to swear off men."

"Real men. I'm on a sabbatical from them since Paul the jerk dumped me. Jared Slade is merely a mystery I'm interested in solving. What makes a man want to hide from the world the way he does?"

Natalie held up a hand. "Let's clarify one point. I don't think that Paul the jerk qualifies as a 'real man.' He used you to help pay the rent while he made it through his last year of law school. The day he walked out was the luckiest day of your life."

"I'll drink to that," Sierra said, raising her martini.

Rory raised her glass and bemusedly toasted her good fortune. "It's not like it's the first time I've been dumped. I'm kind of getting used to it. The way I see it, I don't have good luck with men. That's why I'm not having anything to do with them until my ideal fantasy man comes along."

"A fantasy man?" Sierra grabbed a fresh note card out of her canvas bag. "I'm doing some research on female sexual fantasies. What's he like?"

Smiling, Rory drew a finger down the stem of her martini glass. "He's tall, dark and handsome, of course. And he's a little dangerous looking. He has this tough outer shell, but he's really a sweetie underneath. And when he smiles, he has a dimple—just one—in his left cheek."

Rory warmed to her theme, grateful that the conversation had veered away from the riskiness of her plan to photograph Jared Slade. "But the best part is my fantasy man thinks I'm incredibly sexy. I drive him nuts." She leaned closer to her sisters. "He has the most incredible hands."

"And you know this because…?" Natalie asked.

Thoroughly at ease, Rory selected a stuffed mushroom. "There's not much sense creating a fantasy man if you're not going to engage in some hot fantasies with him."

"Paul really did a job on you if you're reduced to having fantasy sex," Natalie said.

"Do you see me complaining?" Rory licked her thumb. "The great thing about fantasy sex is that there can be more variety than with just one real man."

Sierra glanced at Natalie, who'd grown quiet and grinned. "I don't think our big sister agrees with you. I think she's found her fantasy man. Maybe if you push your luck, you'll find yours, too."

Rory dubiously glanced down at her father's letter. "I'll be happy if I'm lucky enough to get an inter—a picture of Jared Slade."

Natalie frowned. "I'm not going to talk you out of this plan of yours, am I?"

"No, so why don't you wish me luck?" Rory grabbed another cheese cube to ease the nerves that had just returned to her stomach. She hadn't revealed the whole of her plan to her sisters. The picture was just step one.

"Well, I can't argue with following Harry's advice," Natalie said. "It got me Chance."

Rory grinned. "Maybe it will get me my fantasy man."

"Then let's drink to it." Sierra raised her glass.

"And to luck," Natalie said.

"And to Harry." Rory sipped her martini. Tomorrow, she was not only going to snap a picture of Jared Slade, she was also going to get him to agree to an interview. She could do it. She was a daredevil, wasn't she?

LEA ROBERTS STARED OUT the window of her office, but she wasn't taking in the view of the Washington Monument. She was too worried that she'd made a mistake in the way she'd handled Rory Gibbs.

The laughter might have been a bit harsh, but she didn't want Rory even to think about asking for an interview. She would be the one to do that. Jared Slade would be furious with Rory for taking his picture. That would allow Lea to step in and play good cop to Rory's bad cop. Her plan was to offer to trade the picture for an interview.

Turning from the window, Lea began to pace. She really hated to give up the reins of control, but what else could she have done? She couldn't risk taking the photo herself. If Jared Slade was really Hunter Marks, the man might recognize her.

She'd made the right decision. Rory was smart and inventive. Those qualities could work in her favor. Hell, she should be able to snap that photo and get away before Jared Slade could blink.

The problem was Rory Gibbs was also impetuous and hard to predict. She was forever doing something unexpected. Lea raised her hand and pressed two fingers against the headache that had begun to throb behind her right ear. If Jared Slade turned out to be Hunter Marks, it would be her ticket to what she'd always dreamed of: a Pulitzer and most certainly a six-figure book contract.

In her mind, it was still a big *if.* Her anonymous informant seemed certain, but Lea wasn't so sure. Was it really possible that Hunter Marks had reinvented himself as a man who owned and ran a multimillion-dollar corporation? It would be the scoop of a lifetime.

Oh, breaking the story about the scandal that had nearly destroyed a town had gotten her a job with the *Boston Globe* for a while. But the story had become old news as soon as Hunter had disappeared. And after a few months at the *Globe,* she'd been eased into covering the society page and eventually she'd taken the job at *Celebs.* Had there been a way to play her cards differently?

After moving to her desk, Lea fished out an aspirin bottle and downed two tablets without water. One snapshot. Then she'd be able to tell if Jared Slade was the man she'd known ten years ago as Hunter Marks. If he was, she'd have the leverage she'd need to finally get everything she wanted. This time she'd play her cards right.

Hunter Marks had secrets to hide, and Lea knew them all.

2

THIS WAS DEFINITELY her lucky day! Rory Gibbs barely kept herself from dancing a little jig. The sketchy plan she'd had when she'd entered the hotel had worked like a charm. The bell captain had bought her story. Now all she had to do was snap the picture. She gave her bubble gum three quick chews.

One of the two men at the registration desk *had* to be Jared Slade. She was sure of it. But which one? She needed a moment and it wouldn't do to be caught staring at a guest. Taking two quick steps to her right, she ducked behind a potted palm tree and peered through the branches at the two men.

Was it the handsome, preppy-looking blonde? Or was it the shorter, tougher-looking dark-haired man who stood next to him?

Nerves simmering, Rory blew out a small bubble, then used her teeth and tongue to draw the gum back into her mouth. The dark-haired man had given the name Jared Slade to the reception clerk, but the blonde was the one signing the registration form. Rory was betting on the blonde.

Still, it could be the shorter, darker one even though, with his horn-rimmed glasses, he looked more like an accountant than a man who ran a company. Rory blew another bubble.

The way she'd pictured him in her mind, Jared Slade had been larger and drop-dead gorgeous. And in spite of the almost picture-perfect good looks, he had an aura of danger about him. In fact, he'd looked quite a bit like her fantasy man.

Neither of the two men standing at the desk looked particularly dangerous. Rory licked another bubble off her lips. She'd lived long enough to understand the huge chasm that existed between fantasy and reality. The studious-looking accountant was probably the real Jared Slade.

As she dug in her bag for her camera, she took a quick glance around the lobby. A third man had come through the revolving doors with Jared Slade. She'd been too intent on watching the other two at the desk to pay him much heed, but she did so now. He was a large man with dark hair, wearing black jeans, a leather jacket and dark glasses. Rory blinked and stared. He definitely had fantasy-man possibilities.

At that moment, he lifted the dark glasses and shot a quick look in her direction. She felt her heart skip a beat and her mouth go dry. Then as those dark eyes locked on hers, she felt a little punch of something hot right in her gut and her mind simply emptied.

It was only when he turned back to talk to the bell captain that Rory remembered to breathe. And it was only as she drew in a second breath that the oxygen reached her brain and she began to think again.

Well. She'd never reacted that way before to any man. But then, this one was remarkably like the fantasy man she'd created in her head—tall, dark, and handsome in a rough-edged sort of way. She began to chew on her bubble gum again. Would he have a dimple in his left cheek when he smiled?

Time for a reality check, she reminded herself. Mr. Danger was probably a bodyguard with valet duties, since he seemed to be sorting out the luggage with the bell captain. When he glanced over in the direction of the registration desk, Rory scrunched herself farther down behind the palm tree. The last thing she needed was a run-in with Jared Slade's bodyguard before she snapped her picture.

She should have worn something green, camouflage fatigues. For one long moment—even through the palm fronds—Rory felt the large man's eyes on her again. It felt like a mild sort of electrical shock along her nerve endings. She averted her own gaze and willed herself invisible. Her red boots would be hidden, but not the red cap. Since she'd started to develop her signature style, her sisters had teased her about being a slave to fashion. Was she about to pay the price?

HUNTER MARKS FROWNED as he watched the woman in the red hat and boots squat behind a tall potted palm. Who was she and what in hell was she doing?

He scanned the lobby again, but she was the only person there who seemed out of place. Lately, he'd been more paranoid than ever when he checked into a hotel. Small wonder since someone was threatening his company. The procedure was that his two employees—Michael Banks and Alex Santos—checked in while he scoped the lobby for possible reporters. The system had worked well for several years. So far no one had been able to print a photo of Jared Slade. No one, aside from his most trusted employ-

ees, even knew what Jared Slade looked like. And *no one*
knew that Jared Slade used to be Hunter Marks.

But the person who was sending him threatening notes
knew. And more and more, Hunter was becoming convinced that the threat to Slade Enterprises was coming
from within. He'd come to D.C. to get to the bottom of it.

Hunter returned his gaze to the woman behind the potted palm. His eyes had been drawn to her from the moment
he'd walked into Les Printemps. One glance had him thinking of pixies and elves. And that was not the usual turn his
mind took when he looked at a woman. He prided himself
on being practical rather than fanciful when it came to the
female of the species.

This particular specimen had been seated on one of the
settees, not sipping tea or a cocktail as the other occupants
of the lobby were. Instead, she'd been scanning the crowd
while she blew a huge bubble. When the bubble burst, he'd
watched in amusement as she pulled it off her cheeks and
nose and poked it back into her mouth.

He'd taken the time to study her face then. The cherry-
red lips had drawn his attention first, and he'd found himself wondering if they would carry the flavor of the bubble
gum. The errant thought along with the tightening and
hardening of his body surprised him.

Strange, because women never surprised him. And the
pixie with the bubble gum was a far right turn from the type
he usually dated. For starters, she looked too young. Of
course, the slight build could account for that, along with the
hair. From what he could see of it—a few wisps that peeked
out from beneath the red cap—she wore her dark hair shorter
than most men. He shifted his gaze down the black jean jacket
and jeans to the red boots and felt his body go even harder.

Then she glanced his way and for one long moment his gaze held hers. He felt a punch of desire so strong that for a second he couldn't breathe. Then his mind filled with images of her and what he'd like to do to her.

"Here you go, sir."

With some effort, Hunter dragged his mind back to reality as the bell captain handed him three tickets. His reaction to this odd woman was unprecedented.

"The briefcase and the laptop will be taken up to the Presidential Suite for Mr. Slade," the man said. "I'll handle it personally. And the suitcases will be up shortly."

"Appreciate it," Hunter said as he slipped a folded bill across the narrow counter. Then he leaned closer to the bell captain. "Do you see that woman over there, the one behind the palm tree?"

The bell captain took a moment to scan the lobby casually. Les Printemps was a small hotel that prided itself on calling each guest by name. Hunter had researched it himself. The management catered to a very select clientele, a mix of foreign diplomats and celebrities, who paid premium prices because they valued their privacy and expected the hotel to protect it at all costs.

"That's Miss Rory Gibbs, sir," the bell captain said, a wide grin spreading across his face.

"Is she staying here?" Hunter asked.

"No."

Hunter frowned. "I thought only registered guests were allowed in the lobby."

"She's meeting her fiancé here. She said her father brought her here for high tea once, and she wanted to relive the moment with her husband-to-be. Sweet little thing. She reminds me a bit of my daughter."

Hunter returned his gaze to Rory Gibbs just as she pulled a camera out of her purse.

Shit, he said to himself as he strode toward her. Perhaps she was a reporter, after all. He prided himself on having a sixth sense where the press was concerned. But this one had fooled him.

There were only three people in his organization who'd known he was checking in to Les Printemps. Ms. Rory Gibbs was his ticket to finding out just who the traitor was.

RORY'S HEART WAS BEATING so fast that she was sure the two men at the reception desk could hear it. One at a time, she wiped her damp hands on her jeans. She couldn't afford to drop the camera. Dammit. She could still feel Jared Slade's bodyguard/valet watching her and he was having the oddest effect on her whole system.

Focus, she told herself. No one had ever taken a photo of Jared Slade. She needed this picture. Once she had it, she could negotiate step two of her plan—an exclusive interview with Jared Slade.

"We want you to enjoy your stay at Les Printemps, Mr. Slade," the neatly groomed woman behind the desk said as she pushed a key across the counter.

Rory noted that the dark-haired man picked it up. But it was the blond man who said, "Thank you."

They would turn around any minute and she would finally be looking at Jared Slade. Which one would he be?

Turn. Rory concentrated on sending out the message telepathically. But the blonde was asking about the health club facilities. Jared Slade was reputed to be a health nut.

So the blonde was Jared.

"Where's the best place to take a run?" the dark-haired man asked.

Or maybe the runner was Jared. And still they didn't turn around. So much for her telepathic powers.

Raising the camera, she pressed the button on the zoom lens and found herself viewing a close-up of a palm leaf. She pushed it out of her way, only to discover that the two men were moving away from the desk. She could see their faces in profile now. The darker haired man was tough looking and built like a boxer. The blonde had the long, rangy body of a swimmer.

If she'd had to bet money, she still would have placed it on the blonde. But this was too important to trust in her luck. She had to be sure. Edging her way out from behind the palm tree, she aimed the camera and said, "Jared Slade?"

The blond man turned first, and she had three quick shots of him before someone behind her said, "Stop right there."

Whirling, she saw the fantasy man—Mr. Danger—striding toward her. He looked every inch the bodyguard now. In fact, the combination of sunglasses, black leather jacket and black jeans had her thinking for one giddy moment of the Terminator. Rory froze.

She wasn't sure if it was the sheer size of the man that intimidated her for a moment, or perhaps that odd little punch to her system threw her off. The only thing she was certain of was that all of his attention was totally focused on her. She could feel his purpose, feel *him* in every pore of her body. He was the Terminator personified.

When he was still a few yards away, he held out his hand. "I'll take that camera."

She clutched it tight to her chest. She wanted to run. The old Rory would have chosen that option in a nanosecond. Did she dare to stay? Tucking her gum into the side of her cheek, she said, "I'll trade. You can have the pictures, but I want an interview with Jared Slade."

He took one step closer. "Not a chance. Just give me the camera."

Time to rethink her options. He was a lot bigger up close than he was from a distance, and he'd probably be able to outrun her. But if she handed over the camera…

Stay in the game. Even as the words slipped into her mind, she feinted to the right, then darted behind the palm tree. Once she'd cleared the branches, she raced for the lobby door.

HUNTER SWORE under his breath. By the time he skirted the damn potted palm, the little pixie had pushed her way through the front door.

"Stay here," he called over his shoulder to the two men who'd been at the registration desk. Then he ran toward the hotel entrance and made it out to the street just in time to see her turn the corner. By the time he reached it, she was nowhere in sight. She couldn't have reached the next corner, so she had to be in one of the shops.

Deliberately, he slowed his pace, allowing the other pedestrians on the street to flow past him. The first shop he passed had designer chocolates in the window. A quick glance inside told him that his quarry wasn't there, and there was no obvious place to hide. The second shop had lingerie displayed in the window, and he spotted her moving quickly toward the back of the store with an armful of lace and satin in tow.

Hunter glanced up at the name over the shop door and smiled slowly. This was his lucky day. Silken Fantasies was the very shop he'd come to D.C. to buy. Its location in the same block as Les Printemps was one of the reasons why he'd decided to stay at the small hotel. A quick glance at the tall, strikingly attractive woman behind the counter confirmed that she was the owner. At fifty, Irene Malinowitz was looking to retire so that she could spend time with her grandchildren. And Slade Enterprises was looking to turn Silken Fantasies into a very profitable chain.

Slowly Hunter backed out of the flow of pedestrian traffic. He had to hand it to Rory Gibbs. She had a good plan. All she had to do was hang out in one of the dressing rooms until whoever was chasing her gave up.

Except he'd never given up in his life—even before he'd become Jared Slade. Added to that, she'd had the bad luck of running into a shop where he knew the owner. When Rory had disappeared into one of the dressing rooms at the back of the shop, he moved closer to the window and considered his options. He wanted to talk to Rory Gibbs. He also wanted that camera, he reminded himself. The best way to fool her into thinking she'd taken a picture of the real Jared Slade would be to destroy the film.

Then he would ask her how she'd known that Jared Slade was going to be checking into Les Printemps. Very few people in his organization had known that. Denise Martin, the chief administrative assistant in his Dallas office, and the two men he was traveling with—Michael Banks, his executive assistant, and Alex Santos, his accountant. Up until now, he'd trusted all three of them. But now, he was sure that one of them was a traitor. Even worse, one of them knew his past and wanted revenge.

The problems at Slade Enterprises had started three months ago. There'd been an episode of stomach poisoning in his hotel in Atlanta and a fire that had caused some damage in a factory in upstate New York. He'd flown in to deal with each crisis personally. And both times he'd received notes with the same message: *No matter what you do, soon the world will know who you are and what you did ten years ago.*

Hunter was sure that the person sending the notes had to be connected in some way to the scandal that had nearly destroyed not only his family's business, but the town he'd grown up in. A scandal that he'd been blamed for. A scandal that had the power to destroy Slade Enterprises.

Ms. Rory Gibbs might very well know who the writer of those notes was.

Hunter took out his cell phone. Little did she know it, but Ms. Rory Gibbs had just walked into a trap.

RORY LEANED BACK against the closed door of the dressing room and drew in a deep breath. She'd taken a risk when she'd chosen this store. Luckily, it had a place where she could hide. For the moment.

Her last glimpse of the Terminator had been when she'd turned the corner. There'd been no sign of him when she'd ducked into the shop. When he couldn't see her on the street, he'd have to give up.

If her luck held. Crossing her fingers, she drew in another breath. The air was scented with lavender, and classical music poured out of a speaker that hung directly above her dressing room. In a minute, her heart rate would subside, she'd be able to breathe without panting, and her nerves would settle. And then she could figure out what to do next.

"I don't think you have the right sizes."

Rory jumped at the sound of the feminine, well-modulated voice behind her. "What?"

She peered through the slats in the door and made out the red suit of the woman who'd welcomed her to the shop when she'd dashed in.

"The sizes," the voice said. "In your rush, you grabbed large, and I think you'll find that petite will fit you better. I've brought you the same designs. Why don't we switch?"

As she opened the door, Rory glanced down at the bits of lace and satin she was clutching to her chest. She hadn't paid any attention to what she'd scooped up when she'd dashed in. The Terminator had been on her tail.

"Who recommended this shop to you?" the woman asked as they exchanged garments.

"No one," Rory replied. "I just came in—on impulse."

"Ah." The woman smiled at her. "I get some of my best customers that way."

Rory took a moment to look at the items for the first time. Lingerie—tiny bras and what looked to be thongs—in various shades of the rainbow.

"Wow," she said as she spread petite sizes out on a nearby bench. "These don't cover much."

"That's the whole point, isn't it?"

"I've never been able to quite figure out the point." Rory leaned down to finger the lace on one of the thongs. "I mean, no one sees this stuff."

The woman's brows rose. "A lover would see it."

Rory shot her a look. "Not for long. Mostly, they're just interested in getting me naked."

The woman's laugh was low and infectious. "You need to look for a new lover. The first step would be to wear something like this." She moved into the room, and lifted a cherry-red thong and matching bra from the bench, then handed them to Rory. "You'd be amazed at the difference something like this will make in a relationship. Wearing these next to your skin, you'll feel sexier, more attractive, and much more confident about the way you appeal to men."

"Yeah, well, finding a new lover is pretty low on my to-do list right now."

"That could change if you met the right man."

The Terminator flashed into Rory's mind and she felt her body go soft and hot as if something inside of her were melting.

"Try these on," the woman said. "What have you got to lose?"

Rory fingered the silky lace. The truth was she had nothing to lose. And this seemed to be her day for taking risks.

"Red is definitely your color."

Rory glanced up to find the woman smiling warmly at her. She smiled right back, and held out her hand. "I'm Rory Gibbs. And you're a very good saleswoman."

The woman shook Rory's hand. "Thanks. I'm Irene Malinowitz. Let me know if there's anything else I can bring in."

As Rory closed the door of the dressing room, she gave the red scraps a speculative look. She'd never worn red underwear in her life. Black, yes, when she was in the mood to feel a little "sexy" or when all of her white underwear were in the dirty-laundry hamper.

It wasn't that she didn't like to spend money on clothes. She did. Her maxed-out credit cards were a testimony to her weakness for fashion. But she preferred to part with her hard-earned plastic for what went on the outside—like the red boots or the jaunty little hat she was wearing.

She fingered the red lace of the thong—what there was of it. What would it feel like to put on? Considering, Rory chewed on her gum and blew out a bubble. What the heck. It was kind of like taking a dare. And she had some time to kill. The one thing she knew about the Terminator was that he never gave up. She could picture him walking up and down the street, peering into shops.

But first, she was going to find a place to hide the film so that he couldn't just grab it from her. Pressing a button on the camera she was still clutching to her chest, she wound the roll to the end, took it out, and glanced around the tiny room for a hiding place. The only piece of furniture in the room was the bench. Wincing at the grossness of it, she removed the gum from her mouth, and then kneeling, she stuck the film container to the bottom of the bench.

Cloak-and-dagger was not her specialty, but she could rise to the occasion—probably because she'd read so many Nancy Drew and Hardy Boys mysteries when she was a kid. And then there were all those late-night TV movies she'd watched that offered a thousand and one tips for foiling dastardly villains.

And the Terminator had *dastardly* written all over him. Just thinking about him made her feel as if a little electric current were running along her nerve endings. She pressed a hand to her stomach. There it was again—that hot, fluttery feeling. He was still stalking her. She was sure of it.

And she was going to be prepared. Fishing a new roll of film out of her purse, she reloaded her camera and took four quick shots of the lingerie. If he was waiting outside when she left the shop, and he wanted the film, at least she'd be ready. She'd run from him once. Not again.

In the meantime… Rory glanced down at the red thong

again. Standing, she slipped out of her jacket. Trying on a
red thong should be no big deal. No one had to see her in
it. She tugged off her jeans.

Long ago, she'd decided that the "sexy" part of the
Gibbs legacy had also gone to her sisters.

Was Irene right? Could the simple act of wearing red
underwear change her image of herself?

"Lea, it's been a pleasure." Elizabeth Cavenaugh, wife
of Supreme Court Justice Henry Cavenaugh, extended her
hand. "I know you went out of your way to fly into Manhattan, but I just detest summers in D.C. Thank you."

Lea took Elizabeth's hand in hers. During the hour-long
interview, the charm of Mrs. Cavenaugh's southern accent
had begun to wear thin. And the glowing report she would
have to write up on the woman's latest philanthropic project was the kind of article that Lea detested writing. But
she managed a smile. "You'll remember to e-mail me the
recipe for those scones?"

"I'll have Delia write one up for me this afternoon. But
she got it from her mother. Don't be surprised if it reads a
pinch of this and two dashes of that."

Lea brightened her smile. "I'll give it to my cook. That
kind of recipe is right up her alley. And thank you again for
the interview. I don't know when I've enjoyed one more."

As the door closed behind her, Lea pulled out her cell
phone and barely kept herself from running to the elevator. One glance told her that Rory hadn't called yet.

Damn. She glanced at her watch. Noon. Not time to
panic yet, she told herself. After punching the button for
the lobby, she leaned against the wall and tapped her foot.
The interview had been a dead bore. The piece on Eliza-

beth Cavenaugh's work in battling adult illiteracy would be typical of the kind of reporting she'd been doing for *Celebs* magazine for the past five years. She could write it in her sleep. It was the kind of article that made her want to scream.

No matter, she told herself. Her ticket to what she'd always dreamed of having was within reach. By this evening, Rory Gibbs was going to bring her the means to a story that would free her from ever having to write another boring article on politicians or their spouses.

Lea stepped out of the elevator and strode across the marble-floored lobby. When the doorman pushed open the glass door, a blast of moist heat struck her with enough force to have her almost wishing for the coolness of Elizabeth Cavenaugh's penthouse apartment. Almost, but not quite. Instead, she hurried to the curb and raised her arm to hail a taxi.

Two passed her by before a third pulled up.

"Kennedy Airport," she said as she climbed in. "And could you turn the air-conditioning up to high?"

With a nod, the cabdriver pulled into the busy traffic. Leaning her head back against the seat, she closed her eyes. But she couldn't relax, not until she heard from Rory Gibbs.

The air in the taxi had gone from hot to tepid when her cell phone rang.

"Rory?" she asked.

"No. It's me."

Lea's hands tightened on her phone as she recognized the voice of her anonymous informant. This was only the second call she'd received, but she still couldn't pin down whether the voice belonged to a man or a woman. The two things she was sure of were that she'd never heard it before and it was cold. Bone-chilling cold. "Yes?"

"Do you have the pictures?"

"Not yet. It's only noon."

"He's checked in to his suite."

Lea's heart stilled. If that was true, she should have heard something from Rory. "The photographer I sent hasn't reported back yet."

"I trusted you to get those pictures. I won't be happy if you failed."

Lea couldn't repress a shudder even though her temper flared. "Look. I told you I had another commitment. Besides, he might have recognized me. So I sent someone who's as hungry to get those pictures as we are. I can guarantee I'll have them for you by the end of the day."

"You'd better."

"Look, I don't like to be…" She knew that her caller had clicked off, but she said the word anyway. "Threatened. I don't like to be threatened." But even in the still-hot taxicab, she shivered. She couldn't shake off the feeling that whoever was feeding her information on Jared Slade was dangerous.

Pushing the feeling away, she reminded herself there might be one hell of a story here. Besides, she'd dealt with all kinds of anonymous tipsters before. It was ridiculous to let this one frighten her.

And if Jared Slade turned out to be Hunter Marks as the anonymous caller had promised, she'd break the story of the year. Lea managed a smile. Who better to write it than the reporter who'd broken the original story that had caused Hunter Marks to disappear off the face of the earth?

3

HUNTER STEPPED THROUGH THE DOOR of Silken Fantasies. A little bell jangled over his head, and the woman behind the counter glanced up with a smile.

"Welcome to Silken Fantasies."

"Irene Malinowitz?" he asked, taking out a card as he moved toward the counter. The shop was small, but elegant. He noted with approval the plush carpeting, the accents of glass and chrome, and the merchandise displayed gracefully on mannequins and arranged artfully on tables. He'd seen photos, but this was his first trip to the store itself. There was a scent in the air and the muted tones of Chopin floated out of the speakers. He also knew that Irene Malinowitz had built her clientele mostly by word of mouth, and that since she'd launched her catalog, her net profits had risen to just over five million dollars a year.

"Yes?"

Hunter handed her the card. "I'm Mark Hunter, one of Jared Slade's executive assistants." Mark Hunter was the name he used when he traveled and when he dealt personally with clients.

Irene glanced at the card and then met his eyes. "I don't believe we've met."

"No." Hunter seldom spoke with clients directly. Voice

prints were as individual as fingerprints. The more successful Slade Enterprises had become, the more effort he'd put into protecting his anonymity.

"What can I do for you, Mr. Hunter?"

"Mr. Slade has just checked in to Les Printemps, and he would like to have you sign the contracts now in his suite, if that's convenient. He'll want to review them personally and there's something else that demands his attention this afternoon."

A flicker of a frown passed over Irene's face. "I'm sorry, but I have a customer in the dressing room right now, and my assistant is at lunch. Perhaps in a half hour or so?"

Hunter smiled at her. "That's why Mr. Slade sent me in person. I'll be happy to cover for you."

A phone rang on the counter behind Irene.

"That will be Mr. Banks now. He'll verify who I am."

Irene picked up the phone. "Hello?"

Hunter counted five beats until the smile appeared on her face.

"Yes, Mr. Banks."

His executive assistant, Michael Banks, had handled all of the negotiations with Silken Fantasies, so Irene would be familiar with his voice. Michael was bright, and he was good with clients, especially the female ones. Being a man's man, Alex Santos was better with males, and he was a whiz at crunching figures.

Irene was still smiling when she hung up the phone. "My customer is in the dressing room. I should—"

"She'll be fine," Hunter said. "I'll take good care of her."

THE FIRST THOUGHT THAT CROSSED Rory's mind as she studied herself in the three-way mirror was that she had to get to the gym more often and do some of those exercises that promised to lift her rear end. Then she shifted her position and backed away two steps so that she could study herself from the front only.

The image staring back at her from the mirror nearly had her laughing out loud. She'd left only her boots on, and now she wore nothing else but the lacy red thong and the merest excuse for a bra. It seemed that this was her day for really being daring.

And it felt good.

She picked up her jean jacket from the floor and slipped it on over the red bra. Then she walked back and forth in front of the mirror. No one looking at her would know what she was wearing beneath the jacket. But she would know. And the secret knowledge made her feel sexy. Really sexy. As if she could have any man she wanted.

She took off her jacket and then traced her finger along the waistband of the thong. She sighed. There was no way that she could afford this pricey little number, but she really had to add it to her fantasy life. An image of the Terminator tumbled into her mind. What if he saw her in this? Closing her eyes, she let herself imagine just how he might look at her—those dark eyes filling with hunger. And those hands. Oh, he definitely had her fantasy man's hands. The one that had reached out to take her film had a wide palm and strong-looking fingers. They wouldn't be gentle when they touched her. No, they would be hard, calloused, demanding, as they moved over her breasts. Her insides clenched as she imagined those hands trailing down her skin to the thin strap of lace at her hips and then lower—

When she heard the bell on the shop door ring, she jumped. Then with a hand pressed to her heart, she made herself breathe. It was a customer. This was, after all, a store.

Her heartbeat had just returned to normal when above the piano music drifting out of the overhead speaker, she heard a deep voice. A man's voice. With a sinking feeling in her stomach, Rory whirled away from the mirror and dropped to her knees. Then she jiggled the slats in the door to get a look. Black boots, black jeans and the bottom of a black leather jacket. The Terminator.

He'd come for her.

Her mind racing as fast as her heart, she rose and pressed her back against the door. A plan. That's what she needed. Maybe there was a back way out of the shop. She opened the door and took a quick look. He was facing Irene across a glass-and-chrome counter, and she was talking on the phone.

Just looking at him in profile had that strange little zing of awareness shooting along her nerve endings again. *Escape,* she reminded herself. *You're looking for a way out.*

A quick look in the other direction dashed any hope she had of getting away. The back of the shop was a solid wall. Ducking back into her dressing room, she leaned against the door.

And then it struck her. She was thinking of running away, and that wasn't what she wanted to do. This was her chance to negotiate that interview.

To calm her nerves, she focused once more on her image in the mirror. To her surprise she looked even sexier. Her skin was flushed. Somehow, she looked taller, her legs appeared to be longer, her breasts fuller.

In short, she looked like a woman who could get what she wanted.

And she wanted more than the interview. She wanted the Terminator. The awareness that she'd felt the moment she'd looked into his eyes was back—and it was growing. Her insides had begun to melt the moment she'd seen him again. And there was a growing ache right in her center. Rory pressed her hand against her stomach.

Get a grip, she told herself. This was no time to let some pricey undergarments turn her into a nymphomaniac. Nor was it time to become muddled about her objective. The interview. She had to talk to the Terminator and convince him to set up the interview with Jared Slade.

She grabbed her jeans—but first she had to get dressed.

The bell over the shop rang.

Dropping the jeans, Rory tensed, holding her breath.

He was leaving. She had to stop him. She moved to the door, opened it and stepped out.

But it wasn't Irene Malinowitz's back that she saw at the door to the shop. It was the Terminator's.

"I'll take care of everything, Irene," he said.

She heard the door close, the lock click. Then he turned to face her.

For the second time in one morning—perhaps in her life—Rory felt her mind go perfectly blank. She couldn't identify one thought—there were too many sensations cartwheeling through her. Heat. Cold. Nerves. And an electric spark of lust. He was walking toward the dressing room with the same purposefulness in his stride he'd had when he'd moved across the lobby.

He was coming after her.

This time she wasn't going to run.

THE MOMENT HE TURNED AWAY from locking the door to Silken Fantasies, Hunter Marks felt his body go absolutely still. She was standing right outside the dressing-room door, and as his gaze raked over that creamy, porcelain-smooth skin, those wispy bits of red lace, and the incredibly long legs, he felt his head begin to spin. He moved then, almost as if he were being drawn by a magnet.

There was something about her. He'd thought of her as an elf or a pixie. But standing there right now, she looked like an exotic dancer in a high-priced strip club. Was it the elf or the sex goddess who was drawing him?

Or was it something else? She wasn't trying to escape; she hadn't even made a move to cover herself. And there'd been that moment in the lobby of Les Printemps—just before she'd bolted—when her gaze had met his and he hadn't seen a trace of fear in her eyes.

Courage was a rare commodity, and Hunter had always admired it when he saw it. Was that why she pulled at him? As he drew closer, he ran his eyes over her again. Or was his attraction to her merely an incredible trick of chemistry? Whatever caused it, he couldn't look at her without wondering what it would be like to touch her—to taste her and touch her until she was slick and wet and hot for him.

His body heated, hardened, as he imagined what it might be like to slip inside of her and feel her close around him like a moist, tight fist.

Hunter stopped short when he was still a few feet away from her. For one chilling moment, he realized that if he allowed himself to get any closer, he would touch her. Kiss her. Pull her to the floor of the shop and—

Ruthlessly, he shoved the images out of his mind and tried to replace them with some semblance of rational thought. Even as a voice at the back of his mind whispered, *Take her,* he struggled to recall why he'd followed her in here. What did he want from Rory Gibbs?

"I'll give you the film on one condition," she said.

The film. Hunter's eyes narrowed. His brain was starving for blood while hers was clicking along at full speed. He watched her chew on her bottom lip.

Nerves. It gave him some satisfaction to realize that the sex goddess wasn't quite as cool and pulled together as she appeared to be. This close, he could see that her eyes were a deep, golden amber, the color of well-aged whiskey. He could see the flicker of nerves there, too. And he could smell the faint scent of cherry-flavored bubble gum. He managed to keep his gaze from returning to her lips.

"Don't you want to know what the condition is?" she asked.

The condition. Once more, Hunter found himself admiring her for keeping her mind on business. She didn't even seem to be conscious of the fact that she was conducting negotiations while wearing next to nothing. But she wasn't indifferent to him. Through the sheer red fabric covering her breasts, he could see that her nipples were hard little berries. And a pulse was beating at her throat. Thoroughly intrigued, he let himself wonder for a moment—what might it take to taste her right there?

But that wasn't what he'd followed her into Silken Fantasies to do. Annoyance flared—not with her but with himself. He'd dealt with a lot of women in his life—family members, business acquaintances, lovers, and even some enemies—but he'd never met one who could cloud his mind the way this particular one could.

"What's your condition?" he asked.

She briefly chewed her bottom lip again, then said, "I work for *Celebs* magazine, and I want an exclusive interview with Jared Slade."

Not going to happen. And nothing she could have said would have more quickly catapulted him out of the fantasies he was building. She was a reporter, Hunter reminded himself, and he felt his body and his mind finally begin to cool.

He extended his hand, palm upward. "I'll take the camera."

She hesitated. "He hasn't agreed to the interview yet."

"First, I'll develop the film and see what you've got to negotiate with," he said.

She frowned at him. "If you take the film, I won't have anything to negotiate with. You'll have the pictures."

He shot a dry smile at her and saw her eyes widen suddenly in surprise...or fear? "What is it?"

She licked her lips. "You have a dimple."

"Yeah." No, it wasn't fear that was in her eyes. "Now that we've settled that, give me the film. We both know that all I have to do is walk over to the bench, dump your purse and take the camera. You won't be able to stop me."

The pulse fluttered at her throat again, and it took all of his concentration to keep himself from reaching for her. To his surprise, he found himself saying, "I'll give you my word that I'll talk to Mr. Slade and put in a good word for you. Under one condition."

When she licked her lips, Hunter dropped his hand, fisted it at his side, and reminded himself that he was dealing with a reporter.

"What's the condition?" she asked.

"Who told you that Jared Slade would be checking in to Les Printemps this morning? And don't give me any crap about protecting your sources. I want a name."

There was a trace of a frown in her eyes when they met his. "I don't have a name. My boss received a tip and she sent me to take it because she had an interview she had to do in Manhattan today. I told her I could get it. That's all I know."

"Your job was just to snap a picture?"

"Yes."

"What about the interview?"

"That was my idea."

Despite that he considered the words *reporter* and *liar* to be synonymous, his gut instinct told him that she was telling the truth. There was an innocence in those amber-colored eyes that contrasted sharply, irresistibly, with what she was wearing. Or wasn't wearing.

She ran a hand through that short dark hair, and his fingers itched to do the same thing. He could anticipate what the silky texture would feel like beneath his hands.

"Look, getting an interview with Jared Slade will get me a staff job at *Celebs*. And I need the job. I need to prove myself. Can you understand that?"

Hunter said nothing, but he did understand. Perfectly.

"Tell him he can do a Wizard of Oz thing and sit behind a curtain. I only took the pictures because I thought they would give me some sort of leverage to get the interview. You can have them."

She moved to the bench and extracted the camera from a gigantic purse. When she turned back to him, his gaze shifted for a moment to the image of her backside in the three-way mirror. His mouth went suddenly dry. Except for two pieces of red lace, she was nude. The only sign of the thong from the angle was the thin red fabric that dipped low from her waist.

"Here," she said.

As he dragged his gaze back to hers, he was vaguely aware that she'd handed him the camera and he slipped it into his pocket. He could also see her mouth was moving. She was obviously saying something. But he couldn't hear her. He wasn't sure he could even think.

"One kiss," he said.

Rory glanced up. Her throat dried, and her body seemed to be experiencing a meltdown. She couldn't possibly have heard him correctly. But his eyes were so hot that she could feel them on her skin. She licked her lips. "What did you say?"

"One kiss. I want to taste you." He took a step toward her. "One kiss and I'll do everything I can to get you the interview."

One kiss. Rory thought that her heart might just beat out of her chest. One part of her mind—the daredevil part— was thinking yes. What could it matter? But there was another part of her that knew it would matter a lot. Kissing this man might be the biggest risk she'd ever take.

He wasn't moving. In spite of what she could see in his eyes, the decision was going to be hers.

She wanted the kiss. Desperately. She wanted him. But… She felt her old fears swamping her. Where was the confidence that she'd felt just moments ago when she'd looked in the mirror?

Never be afraid to take risks. As the words from Harry's letter streamed through her mind, she suddenly remembered the first jump she'd ever taken on a horse. Her father had given her a little pep talk before she'd ridden out into the ring. "Just dare yourself to do it, kiddo. That's all you need to do. It works like magic."

She'd made the jump. And she was going to kiss this man.

"One kiss," she agreed.

Hunter wasn't sure how long he'd waited to hear her answer, but it had seemed way too long. In the interim, he'd tried to tell himself he was making a mistake. It had been years since he'd done anything this impulsive, this rash. Oh, he'd been plenty reckless before he'd changed himself into Jared Slade. And he'd paid the price. Even in his incarnation as Jared Slade, he'd played some long shots—but only in business and only when he felt confident that his luck would hold.

Right now luck didn't matter to him. Nothing seemed to matter except this hunger that demanded to be quenched. He wasn't even aware that he'd moved until her back was against the mirror, and he was close enough to feel the heat from her body. He touched her, drawing one finger over the pulse that was beating at her throat. Her breath hitched, her skin heated, and the pulse beneath his finger quickened.

"Last chance to change your mind," he managed to say.

"I'm not going to change it."

He placed his hands on either side of her head, noting that her hair felt every bit as soft as he'd anticipated. Then lowering his head, he drew her up on her toes and covered her mouth with his.

It was the heat that hit him first. In that split second before his lips had touched hers, he'd seen the flame light in her eyes. But the shock of it as it shot through his body in an explosive rush surprised him. He thought of the wildfires he'd seen as a child—the kind that devoured everything in their path. Only this one left a hard, unrelenting need in its wake.

The second surprise was her taste. Oh, it was sweet at first, but that was only the first layer of flavor. Beneath that, he tasted heat and spice. What other flavors would he find?

When she nipped at his bottom lip, another arrow of heat

shot through him. He ran his hands down her body and drove his tongue deeper. And all the time he marveled that her mouth, her tongue, her teeth were every bit as aggressive as his. He'd never been so aware of a woman before. Of those small sounds she made when he nipped at her bottom lip, or rubbed his thumb over her nipple.

Her skin was smooth and hot and growing damp beneath his hands. He wanted to taste every inch of it. Her body was small and supple and strong. He wanted it beneath his, bucking and straining.

And he could have her. She didn't seem to believe in holding anything back. Her hands were racing over him—over his shoulders, down his arms—just as his were exploring her. He felt them slide beneath his jacket and move down his back to knead the muscles at the base of his spine. It wasn't enough, not nearly. He wanted the pressure of those fingers, the scrape of those nails, on his bare skin.

He wanted her. One kiss was not going to be enough. He wasn't sure that anything would be enough to stop the ache inside of him. He had to have her. Images flashed through his mind, of driving himself into her on some moonlit beach while waves pounded on the shore. Of carrying her to the nearby bench and letting her ride him. Or merely opening his zipper, then lifting her and taking her against the mirror where they stood. His hands moved down to cup her buttocks and pull her up. He said her name, which turned into a groan, when she wrapped her legs around him. Then he very nearly sank to his knees when she pressed her heat against his and began to rub against him.

Slamming one hand against the mirror to steady himself, he dragged his mouth free and tried to think. First he had to breathe. The sudden rush of air burned his lungs. There were reasons why he shouldn't do this. Couldn't do this. Then he made the mistake of looking at her. Her lips were moist and parted, still swollen from his kisses. Her eyes were huge and the deep golden color was misted. He wanted—no, he needed—to see what those eyes would look like when he entered her and filled her. He leaned forward and took her mouth with his again.

Rory sank into the kiss, eager to drown herself in it, in him again. There was a greed in him that matched her own. Never had her fantasies been this sharp, this real. Never in her wildest imaginings could she have conjured up the sensations shooting through her. There was such heat—glorious waves of it. And each movement of his hands, of his tongue, seemed to throw fuel on the fire. She'd known hunger before but never one this desperate, this enormous.

His taste—she couldn't get enough of it. There were so many flavors, each one more unique, more secret, more dangerous than the last. She dragged her mouth from his and sank her teeth into his shoulder. His moan sent little explosions of pleasure through her. She was torn between twin desires—she wanted to devour him whole and she wanted to savor one delicious body part at a time.

His hands. Everywhere they pressed and molded, her skin burned, then itched to be burned again. She felt the pressure of each finger and that hard, wide palm as he ran his hands down her sides and slipped his fingers beneath the lacy band at her waist. Then he was gripping her buttocks with both hands, kneading her flesh and pressing her closer until the hard length of him was pushed flush against her. She arched her body, straining against him as everything tightened inside of her. She arched again, but it wasn't enough. She had to—

"I want you." His voice was a rough whisper in her ear.

"Yes." She wasn't sure she could survive without him.

"Right now. I want to be inside of you. Are you protected?"

"Hmm?" She tried to shake her head to clear it.

"Are you on the pill?"

"Yes," she said as the words finally penetrated. "Yes. Hurry."

Listening to the three words, Hunter felt something inside of him snap. He let her down so that he could free himself from his jeans. Then he pushed aside the lacy triangle of the thong and pulled her close again as he guided himself into her. But it wasn't enough. Gripping her hips, he drew her even closer, and then with a hard thrust of his hips, he sank deeper. He could feel her stretch, as he made a place for himself in her slick, hot core. His climax immediately began to build inside of him.

Drawing in a quick breath, he tried to maintain some control, but it was no use once she began to move. Digging his fingers into her hips, he thrust into her, harder and faster, driving her, driving himself until he surrendered to the hot, dark pleasure.

When he could think again and breathe again, he was lying beside her on the floor of the dressing room. He wasn't quite sure how they'd gotten there, nor was he sure how long they might have been lying there when his cell phone rang.

Swearing, he unfastened her arms from around his neck and levered himself up so that he could take the call. "What is it?"

"There's been…sir…"

"What is it, Michael?" Hunter frowned. Michael Banks was usually cool and unflappable, but he barely recognized his executive assistant's voice.

"A bomb."

"What?"

"A bomb was delivered to your suite."

RORY STILL WASN'T SURE she could move. Her body had never felt so free, so relaxed, so pleasured. But the Terminator was already getting to his feet and moving away from her. She wanted him back down beside her. Without him, she suddenly felt cold. The chill grew worse when he scowled at whatever news he was getting. She couldn't yet separate what he was saying into words, but when she sat up, she could feel the hard floor of the dressing room under her bottom. She figured her brain cells were beginning to function again because the analytical side of her mind was beginning to realize what had just happened.

She'd just made love with a complete stranger in a dressing room of a ritzy lingerie shop. Well, maybe he wasn't a complete stranger. But when she'd made up her fantasy man, she certainly hadn't expected him to walk right into her life.

It was the kind of thing that happened in movies—or in hot, steamy romance novels. In real life, people didn't really make love to strangers in the dressing rooms of fancy lingerie shops.

But she had. And she wanted to do it again. Astonishment warred with the hot lick of desire that was fanning itself to life again. She had dared to do something she'd never done before.

And she'd liked it very much.

"Are you and Alex and Ms. Malinowitz all right?"

Rory felt a little ribbon of relief roll through her system.

She could make out what he was saying now. And she knew who Ms. Malinowitz was. In another minute she'd be back to her old self. And then she'd figure out what to do next.

Chemistry, a little voice at the back of her mind told her. Hadn't she read that the chemistry between two people could be very powerful. Irresistible. As the Terminator paced back and forth in the small space, Rory caught a glimpse of herself in the mirror. She was still wearing the red bra and thong. She recalled Irene's prediction that the thong would make her feel different about herself.

Oh, yeah. She'd definitely felt different ever since she'd put it on. She narrowed her eyes. Was the red thong the cause of what had happened? Or was it Harry's advice?

"A note?" he asked.

Rory tore her gaze away from the mirror and shoved the thoughts out of her mind. The here and now were what she had to concentrate on. The complete stranger was standing just outside the dressing room door, and he wasn't happy.

"What did the note say?" he asked. "I'll be right there."

Rory used all of her concentration to gather her thoughts as he shifted his gaze to her again.

"Are you all right?" he asked.

"Yes," she said, crossing her fingers to protect her nose from growing at the lie. She was certain she would be all right…soon.

"I have to go."

She nodded. Obviously, the red thong hadn't changed her that much after all. He'd bounced back from the chemistry overload a lot faster than she had. Her knees were still weak. But her brain cells were definitely perking up. "About the interview…?"

There was a brief flash of puzzlement in his eyes before they narrowed and turned into lasers. "Interview."

If she could have scooted any farther away, she might have, but she was sitting with her back against the mirrors. "With Jared Slade," she said. "That was the deal."

"So it was." He inclined his head slightly and patted his pocket. "Just as soon as I get these developed, I'll be in touch."

Rory watched as he turned and moved away from the dressing room. He'd be in *touch*. He'd only had to *say* the word to melt her insides. Pressing her hand to her heart, she began to rise awkwardly to her feet. When she heard the bell ring over the door of the shop, she remembered— she'd given him the wrong film. "Wait!" she yelled. "Just a minute!"

She crawled to the bench and tore the container of film off the bottom of it, leaving the gum behind. Then she managed to stand and race out of the dressing room. He was still there in the doorway, and with the sunlight behind him, he looked more formidable than ever.

"Here!" She held the film out. "These are the real pictures that I took. Take them."

He plucked the film from her hand and slipped it into his pocket. "You could have let me walk away without these."

Rory drew in a deep breath. "Yes, but my whole future at *Celebs* depends on my getting that interview with your boss. I want you to know that he can trust me to paint an honest and fair picture."

He nodded at her. "I'll tell him."

Rory watched him walk out and close the door behind him. Only then did she sink to her knees. It had to be the red thong. She'd just made a deal with the Terminator to get the interview of a lifetime.

Maybe she truly was a daredevil.

LEA WAS GOING through the drawers of Rory's temporary desk again when her cell phone rang. She willed it to be Rory, but this time she read the caller ID before she answered.

Private.

Ignoring the little sliver of fear that slid up her spine, she said, "Yes?"

"Do you have the film yet?"

"No. It's only been an hour since you called the last time."

"I want the name of the person you sent in your place."

Lea hesitated for a moment, hating that this disembodied voice could frighten her.

"The name."

What did it matter? she thought. "Rory Gibbs. I'm expecting her at any moment."

"You'd better get those pictures."

4

HUNTER STOOD in the French doors that opened onto a patio and offered a view of rolling lawns and tennis courts. He spotted a pool beyond a low row of hedges. A woman sat in a lounge chair, sipping something from a tall glass. He assumed she was Lucas Wainwright's wife since he recalled that his old friend had married a little over a year ago.

Looking at the scene, he couldn't help but think that Lucas was a very lucky man—he had a home and someone to share it with. Long ago, he'd accepted that he would never have either of those. It was too much of a risk for someone who had to hide his true identity. Pushing the thought aside, he turned to face Lucas. "Nice spot."

"Thanks." Lucas removed three bottles of beer from a small refrigerator. "It's private, and Tracker here can attest to the security."

Hunter took the bottle when Lucas handed it to him. Though he hadn't seen his old friend face-to-face since they'd been in college together, they'd kept in contact. When Lucas had taken his phone call today, he'd agreed to meet with Hunter immediately once he'd explained that a bomb had been delivered to his suite at Les Printemps.

A bomb.

Hunter had been trying to get his mind around that reality ever since Michael Banks had told him about it on the phone. Thank heavens Michael and Alex had been meeting with Irene Malinowitz in a different suite.

While he took a long swallow of his beer, Hunter studied the tall, quiet man Lucas had introduced as Tracker McBride. He felt perfectly comfortable with Lucas. He felt less comfortable with the man who handled Lucas's security arrangements.

As if sensing his reservations, Lucas said, "Tracker and I served in a special-forces unit together seven years ago shortly after I left college. He handles all my security, and he's the best. You can trust him."

Hunter wasn't so sure he could trust anyone anymore, but he was willing to take Lucas at his word. Moving to the desk, he extended his hand to Tracker. "Okay."

"I thought it would save time if you explained to both of us what happened," Lucas said.

"First, I need to know how confident you are that you weren't followed," Tracker said.

Hunter had to give the man points for asking. "I wasn't followed." He'd made damn sure of that once he'd had his meeting with Michael and Alex. The small bomb had been delivered to the suite assigned to Jared Slade, a suite he would have been working in if he hadn't followed Rory Gibbs into Silken Fantasies. And then there was the note. He'd still been rattled about what had happened in that dressing room when Michael Banks had given it to him.

Hell, he was still rattled now. He'd taken a woman he didn't know—a reporter—in the dressing room of a lingerie shop. Acting on impulse was a luxury he hadn't allowed himself in years—not since he'd transformed himself into Jared Slade.

And then he'd just left her there. Not that he'd had a choice. Hell, someone had delivered a bomb to his suite. And she'd said that she was all right, though he knew he couldn't be sure about that.

"Are you sure?" Tracker asked.

Hunter dragged his thoughts back to the question. McBride obviously wanted details. Lucas had picked a good man to head up his security. "Once I read the note, I decided to make myself scarce by escorting Irene Malinowitz back to her shop." He'd insisted on escorting her back so that he could make sure that Rory really was okay. But she hadn't been there.

"Then I went back to Les Printemps, left the lobby by the side door and hailed my own taxi. I had the driver drop me off at the Four Seasons where I called Lucas from a pay phone. Then I walked through the lobby, exited by another side door and hailed another cab. This time I went to the airport, rented a car, and followed your directions out here. Not even my two assistants know where I am."

"Good." Tracker gestured to one of the chairs in front of Lucas's desk. "We can talk now."

Almost amused, Hunter sat down in the chair. "Glad I passed the test. What would you have done if I'd been stupid enough to bring a tail with me?"

Tracker smiled. "We'd have gone somewhere else for our meeting. I don't like to lose clients."

"Fair enough," Hunter said as he reached into his pocket and pulled out the note. "My assistant Michael Banks found the package with the bomb and the note when he went to my suite to get some papers. It was on a table in the sitting room."

"What do the police think?" Tracker asked.

Hunter's brows shot up. "I didn't ask them. And I didn't show them the note. When I left, I heard that they had disassembled the bomb, and they were waiting to question Jared Slade."

Tracker took the note from Hunter and read it out loud.

"Slade
Ticktock. Ticktock. The bomb is ticking. No matter what you do, soon the world will know who you are and what you did ten years ago. Then you'll die."

Tracker met Hunter's eyes. "Succinct. Lucas mentioned this wasn't the first note."

"There've been three in all. The other two said the same thing—*No matter what you do, soon the world will know who you are and what you did ten years ago.* They're in my safe in my office in Dallas. The first one came right after there was an incident of food poisoning at my hotel in Atlanta. I flew there personally, and even though I'm always careful to keep my whereabouts a secret, the note was delivered to my hotel room. The next note was delivered to my private plane after another incident—a fire in a factory I own in upstate New York. I'm very careful about protecting my privacy, my anonymity. Someone at the very top levels of my organization has to be either behind this or at the very least feeding information to the person or persons who are behind this."

"Any ideas about who's after you?" Tracker asked.

Hunter shook his head. "I'm traveling with my chief accountant and my executive assistant, Alex Santos and Michael Banks. I made the reservations at Les Printemps myself, but I informed them where we were staying yesterday. My chief administrative assistant in Dallas, Denise Martin, also knew. There was a woman in the lobby of Les Printemps when we arrived this morning—from *Celebs* magazine. She took some pictures, and I chased her from the lobby. She says that she got the information from an anonymous tip that was delivered by special messenger to her boss yesterday."

"Her name?" Tracker asked.

"The name she gave the bellman was Rory Gibbs, and she told me she works for *Celebs* magazine."

Tracker and Lucas exchanged glances.

"You know her?" Hunter asked.

"Yeah, we've met," Tracker said. "One of her sisters is a good friend of mine. She's a detective in the D.C. Police Department. Her other sister works with Lucas's wife at Georgetown. They're triplets."

Without warning, Hunter found his mind wandering back to those few moments when Rory's legs had been wrapped around him and he'd been deep inside of her.

"Hunter?"

It was Lucas's voice that drew him back. "Sorry."

"I was just saying that I can talk to her and see if she'll give me more information," Tracker said. "I'll also see what I can find out about the magazine. It's interesting that the informant chose *Celebs*. Why not the *Post* or something?" Tracker wondered.

"Ms. Gibbs may have been in contact with my office. She's done research on Jared Slade, and she's very intent on getting an interview. Denise or Michael may have spoken with her."

Tracker glanced at Lucas. "If she's anything like her cop

sister, odds are she'll keep after you." He looked back at Hunter. "Did she get your picture?"

Hunter shook his head. "No. The pictures she snapped were of Alex and Michael. I took them with me."

Tracker grinned at him. "Good work. If you ever get tired of running Slade Enterprises, I can offer you a job working security for Wainwright Enterprises."

Hunter's answering smile was grim. "If we don't get to the bottom of this, I might have to take you up on your offer."

Tracker's grin faded. "We'll get to the bottom of it."

Lucas circled around his desk and sat on one of the corners. "You've already narrowed the suspects down to Denise Martin, Alex Santos or Michael Banks. That's why you let only those three know where you were staying here in D.C. Have you picked a favorite?"

Hunter took a swallow of his beer. Lucas had always been smart. That was what had drawn them together in college. That and the fact that they had family problems in common. Before the notes had started coming, Hunter would have sworn that Lucas was the only person in the world who knew he'd changed himself into Jared Slade.

Now he was afraid that someone else knew, too. But who?

"Denise has worked with me from the beginning of Slade Enterprises. Over the years—six now—she's become vital to me. I'd have to hire three or four people to replace her. Alex has been with me for four years and Michael for three. They each came to Slade Enterprises right out of business school. For the past year, I've worked closely with both of them. Alex is thorough, but not that great with people. But he's the best number cruncher I've got in the company. Michael is a quick study and his instincts are excellent. And he's good with people. Today, I felt perfectly comfortable letting them handle the final paperwork with Irene Malinowitz."

Pausing, he sighed. "I don't want to pick a favorite. "But if I had to narrow the list, I would lean toward Alex or Michael. Either of them would have had easy access to the suite where the bomb was left. However, I'm not sure I see any of them objectively. They're like family."

But he'd been betrayed by family before.

"Where were you when you learned about the bomb?" Tracker asked.

"I was in Silken Fantasies. I'd offered to stay there while Michael and Alex had Ms. Malinowitz sign the papers. They used Michael's suite, thank heavens."

"When you went back to the hotel, tell me exactly what happened," Tracker said.

Hunter replayed the scene in his mind, trying to capture every detail. "Michael answered the door when I knocked. The police and hotel security were closeted in my suite. Michael's hand shook when he handed me the note. I only caught a brief glimpse of Alex over Michael's shoulder, but he seemed to be calmer. Irene was smiling at something he'd just said when I asked Michael to step into the hall so that he could report."

"What did he say?"

"He told me that he'd had to go to my suite to get a copy of something that Irene had requested. When he saw the note and the package, he was immediately suspicious because of the other two incidents, so he read it. He left the suite immediately and called me. Then he called hotel security and the police. He kept the note out of sight until I got there."

"So Michael had ample opportunity to plant the bomb," Lucas said.

"Yes. But he and Alex hadn't been together the whole time. So Alex also could have left it there. Denise could have hired someone to plant it. All of which leaves me with no clear suspect. That's why I need your help."

"You've come to the right place," Lucas said with a smile. "Tracker's the best. He's managed to save my sister's life twice, so you're in good hands." He turned to Tracker then. "Any preliminary thoughts?"

Tracker looked at Hunter. "I'd say someone knows your past—who you really are—and they have an old score to settle. Any idea who that might be?"

Hunter shook his head. "I've been racking my brain since I received the first note."

"Could it be someone in your family?" When Hunter said nothing, Tracker continued, "You know, in a homicide, the prime suspects are either lovers or close relatives."

"No one in my family cares whether I'm dead or alive."

"Any other enemies from that time?" Tracker pressed.

Hunter thought briefly about the woman who'd been his lover and who'd betrayed him. He doubted that she ever gave him a thought. "No. I've been through it over and over."

Tracker glanced at Lucas. "I'm going to have to pay a visit to your hometown and dig around a little bit there."

Hunter opened his mouth, but Lucas spoke first. "Tracker can be very discreet. He's also good. No one will know that he's even interested in you."

Hunter didn't like it, but he couldn't see any way around it. "Okay. But I don't think the death threat is imminent. I think whoever this is—he or she—wants to expose me first, perhaps do more damage to Slade Enterprises. The important thing is to prevent my past from coming out. It's very important that Slade Enterprises never be connected to my family."

"Yeah, I figured that," Tracker said. "That's why I'm recommending that we try to flush this person out before he or she is ready. Is that okay with you?"

Hunter nodded. "The sooner the better."

Tracker paused to grin at Lucas. "He's a lot like you." Then he turned back to Hunter. "Here's the plan. Lucas has a place down in the Keys, an island where his grandfather built a fishing shack. You're going to let Denise, Alex and Michael know that you're going down there for a few days for a little R & R. I'll put tails on them, taps on their phones, the whole deal."

"And I'll wait for them down in the Keys," Hunter said.

"Oh, no. One of my men will wait down in the Keys. You'll be right here where I know I can keep you safe."

Hunter frowned, but it didn't keep Tracker from continuing.

"I told you before. I don't like to lose clients. Maybe this person wants to make you suffer by exposing you first. But maybe not. There was a bomb delivered to your suite. And it was discovered and disassembled. But who's to say it wouldn't have killed you if you'd been close enough to it when it went off? I'd rather err on the side of caution. Plus, we'll be working at the problem from both ends. I'll be trying to find out who from your past has a connection with one of the three top people in your organization, and we'll see if the trap set down in the Keys nails our suspect down. That should mean faster results."

Hunter turned the plan over in his mind. It made sense. "The only thing I don't like is not being personally involved."

"The farther away I keep you, the less chance there is of any of this leaking to the press," Tracker pointed out. "And Lucas's estate has a lot to keep you occupied. Tennis courts, horses, sauna, pool. To my way of thinking it beats the hell out of that old fishing cabin in the Keys for a little R & R."

Hunter turned to face his friend. "I don't want to intrude on you and your wife."

"Not at all," Lucas assured him. "Mac has an apartment in Georgetown and we'll be driving back there tonight because she starts the second summer session at the college tomorrow."

"There's just one thing I ought to mention," Hunter said, glancing from one man to the other. "I promised the Gibbs woman I would get back to her about the interview."

"Why don't I take care of that?" Tracker said. "When I talk to her, I'll tell her that Jared Slade was called out of town suddenly and you'll be in touch about the interview as soon as possible."

"Good," Hunter said. That was the best plan. Hadn't he already decided that it wouldn't be wise to see Rory Gibbs again?

"If we're done with business, I think we ought to go out to the pool so that Hunter can meet Mac," Lucas said.

"It's not necessary," Hunter said. "It's probably better that I keep a low profile until you leave."

"I insist," Lucas said, exchanging a look with Tracker. "See, my wife has just published a book on male sexual fantasies—part of a research project she did." He cleared his throat. "She's presently on her cell phone sharing the best parts with my sister, Sophie—Tracker's significant other. If we don't interrupt them soon, Tracker and I are going to have a very strenuous night ahead of us."

Tracker laughed then. "I'm not complaining."

As he followed the two men out to the pool, Hunter found himself envying them. His mind once more slipped back to those few moments that he'd shared in the dressing room with Rory Gibbs.

It was on impulse that he'd escorted Irene Malinowitz back to the shop, and he hadn't been able to stop himself from going into the dressing room again. He could still smell Rory. And she'd left the red bra and thong. He'd acted on impulse again when he'd bought them and had Irene send them to her at the magazine.

He wouldn't see Rory Gibbs again, and there was no way he could give her that interview. It was too risky. Acting on impulse wasn't something that he could afford to do again.

RORY SPOTTED NATALIE at the bar the moment she walked into the Blue Pepper. At five-thirty, the dinner crush hadn't started yet, but there was a good crowd enjoying the cocktail hour. Tightening her grip on the bag she was carrying, Rory pushed and nudged her way to the upper level to join her sister. Natalie's message on her voice mail had been cryptic. "Meet me at the Blue Pepper at five-thirty. I have some info on your mystery man."

She was sure that Natalie was referring to Jared Slade, but Rory had begun to think of Slade's bodyguard as her current mystery man. Even now when she thought about what had happened in that dressing room, she had to pinch herself to make sure the whole thing hadn't been a dream. Of course, the red thong she was carrying in the pink Silken Fantasies bag was proof positive of that.

No man had ever made her feel so wanted, so needy, so

sexy, so…everything. The Terminator, as she called him, was her fantasy man made flesh, right down to the dimple. But even in her fantasies, she hadn't imagined that clever mouth and those incredible hands. And she didn't even know his name. He hadn't signed it to the message he'd sent with the red thong and bra.

I've never enjoyed a kiss so much. That's what the message had said. The one sentence had been playing itself over and over in her mind since the pink bag bearing the logo of Silken Fantasies had been delivered an hour ago to her temporary desk at *Celebs.*

The message had set off a string of questions. Did it mean he wanted to see her again? Did it mean he was going to get the interview for her? When she'd stopped by Les Printemps, all she'd been able to discover was that Jared Slade had checked out.

But the question foremost in her mind was would she feel the same way if he kissed her again? In her fantasies, Rory had explored that particular scenario several times. But the more logical side of her mind understood that fantasies and reality were worlds apart. And the logical side of her mind suspected the lingerie was a "dumping gift." Paul had bequeathed her his toaster when he'd moved out of her apartment. His note had said, *No hard feelings.*

How many such gifts could she accumulate over a lifetime?

As Rory crossed the floor to the bar, she rubbed her left temple where a little headache was beginning to throb. Well, a red thong was a much classier "dumping gift" than a used toaster. And she hadn't given up yet on tracking down the Terminator.

It was only when she reached Natalie that she recognized the man on the stool next to her sister.

"Hi, Chance," she said and tried not to giggle when he took her free hand and kissed it. "I didn't know you were back from London."

"Always a pleasure, Rory," Chance said. "I can't stay away from your sister for very long."

Rory wrinkled her nose. "You make it tough on a plain Jane like me. She's even prettier when you're around."

Surprise flashed into Chance's eyes. "Where'd you get the idea that you were a plain Jane?"

"Her ex planted that in her mind," Natalie said. "He was a class-A jerk."

"Want me to beat him up for you?" Chance offered.

"He's history," Rory assured him.

"Sierra and I have it covered," Natalie said. "We have a voodoo doll in his image, and we take turns sticking pins into it."

He pretended to look alarmed. "Remind me not to cross you." As Chance slipped off the stool, he turned to Rory and winked. "Let me know if you change your mind. Right now, I have orders to disappear for a few minutes so that I won't intrude on the girl talk."

Rory climbed onto the stool and set her bag on the bar. "You know, I like him more each time I see him. You really hit the jackpot, Nat."

Nat's eyes were glowing as she watched Chance walk away. "Yeah, I did."

"What'll it be, Rory?"

"Hi, George." Rory shot the tall, bronze-skinned man a smile. "A glass of white wine would be nice."

"You got it," he said as he pulled a glass from an overhead rack. When he set it down in front of her, his gaze fell on the pink bag, and his brows lifted. "What's in the Silken Fantasies bag? Inquiring minds want to know."

Natalie stared at the bag. "I thought only the rich and the famous could afford to shop there."

Rory could feel the heat rise in her cheeks. "I didn't shop there. Not exactly. I just ran in to try some things on, and—it's a gift. Not for someone else. For me." She was stuttering. "Someone gave it to me. I'm deciding if I should give it back."

George winked at her. "Never give back expensive lingerie. But you'll have to model it before I can give you an informed opinion."

"Not a chance," Rory said.

"Who gave you something from Silken Fantasies?" Natalie asked when George had moved down to the far end of the bar. "Did you get that from Jared Slade?"

"No." Then she sighed. "It's a long story."

Natalie's brows shot up. "Can I at least have the *Reader's Digest* version?"

Rory took a sip of her wine and then gave her sister a modified version of her morning's adventure. Since Natalie was a natural-born worrier, she left out the part about actually making love to a complete stranger and played up the kiss part.

"You didn't get your interview, but you kissed Jared Slade's bodyguard. And now you have a five-hundred-dollar red thong and matching bra and a note that says *I never enjoyed a kiss so much*," Natalie summarized.

"In a nutshell."

Natalie's eyes narrowed. "And I thought Harry's letter had changed *me*. How was the kiss?"

Rory ran her finger down the condensation on her wineglass. "On a scale of one to ten, it was about a thirty."

Natalie grinned at her. "Good."

Rory shook her head. "It was the kind of kiss that makes you want it to happen again. And that's not good. I'll probably never see him again. I probably won't get that interview, either. I gave up any leverage I had when I gave him the pictures. Not that I could tell which one of the two men was the real Jared Slade anyway."

"Hey, where's that devil-may-care attitude? You're sounding far too negative."

Rory stared at her sister. She was right. "Negative's the old Rory. The new Rory doesn't want to be like that."

Natalie smiled. "Sierra and I liked you just fine. But I think that you're having more fun as the new Rory. And I have some news that may help you to nurture your inner daredevil."

"What?"

Natalie leaned closer. "This is all off the record."

"Of course."

"I told you my partner and I were trying to keep tabs on Jared Slade. Right around noon, there was a call put in to the police. Someone delivered a bomb to his suite at Les Printemps. No one was hurt, but Matt and I were called to the scene."

"Did you see Jared Slade?"

Natalie shook her head. "He wasn't in the suite when it happened, and he took off before the uniforms arrived. But I do have a lead for you. Chance and I stopped by Sophie Wainwright's shop this afternoon, and from something she said, I think this Jared Slade might be staying out at the Wainwright estate in Virginia."

"What did she say?"

"Rory. Rory Gibbs, is that you?"

Recognizing the voice of her boss at *Celebs,* Rory placed a hand on Natalie's arm and turned to smile at Lea Roberts who was striding toward them. Lea was looking very put together in a beige linen suit, and wore her dark hair long and straight in an attempt to carry off a maturing Demi Moore look.

"Lea," Rory said, "this is my sister, Detective Natalie Gibbs."

As the two women nodded at each other, Rory continued, "Lea has been my boss and mentor at *Celebs.* She's done a lot to help me there."

"I pick my protégées very carefully," Lea said to Natalie. Then she turned to Rory. The smile on her face didn't reach her eyes. "I've been trying to reach you all day. When I missed you at the office, I went over to the hotel, but I was told that Jared Slade had already checked out. Tell me you got the picture."

"Yes, but—" Rory began.

"Wonderful. Let me see." Lea held out her hand, her fingers wiggling.

Rory felt the heat rise in her cheeks. "I don't have them with me. I—"

"You left them on my desk then." Lea glanced at her watch. "I have time to—"

"No." Rory swallowed. "By the time I got them developed, I knew it would be too late to give them to you at the office, so I left them at home. I'm sorry. I had no idea I would be running into you."

Lea's smile didn't waver, but her eyes heated several degrees and her foot started to tap. "You're sure you got a picture of Slade?"

"Absolutely."

Lea hesitated, and Rory was sure she would have said more if Natalie hadn't been present.

"I was counting on having them today. Please have them on my desk at eight-thirty tomorrow morning."

"Sure."

Lea gave a brief nod to Natalie. "Detective." Then she whirled and strode away.

"She's not a happy camper," Natalie said.

"She's been very good to me."

"She reminds me of the villain in those *101 Dalmatians* movies. All she'd need is a white streak in her hair."

Rory grinned. "Cruella DeVil. They are a bit alike, I guess. Lea's always on goal. She doesn't let much stand in her way. I've learned a lot from her."

Natalie studied her sister. "And you just lied through your teeth to her."

Rory shrugged. "I couldn't very well tell her that I'd given the pictures back. If I can still get that interview, she'll be happy."

"And if you don't?"

Rory beamed a smile at her. "I have a sister with connections who's about to tell me where I can find Jared Slade. How can I fail?"

Natalie was still studying her. "This is really important to you."

"Yes," Rory said. But even as she said it, she realized that her quest to interview Jared Slade wasn't the only reason she wanted to track him down. Jared Slade was her ticket to seeing the Terminator again.

"Tracker McBride—that's Sophie's significant other— is spending the entire day on the Wainwright estate because some rich businessman who keeps a low profile with the press had an attempt made on his life today."

"Interesting coincidence," Rory commented.

"Tracker heads up security for Wainwright Enterprises. Chance and he go back to the days when they worked in a special-forces unit. I asked Sophie if she was talking about Jared Slade, the rich mystery tycoon, and she couldn't confirm that because Tracker didn't mention a name. He just said that this mystery man and Lucas had gone to college together. But how many rich, media-shy businessmen could there be visiting D.C. this week? I figured you might want to check it out."

Rory's mind was racing. A bomb had been delivered to Jared Slade's suite. Why? By whom?

"I have to admit that I feel a lot better about you going after this interview now that I know Slade's connection to the Wainwrights. They're solid people."

"If this person *is* Jared Slade. Did Sophie say how long this mystery man would be staying at the Wainwright estate?"

Natalie nodded. "At least until tomorrow. She doesn't expect Tracker back until late tonight."

"You don't by any chance have directions to the estate?"

Nat grinned at her as she took a folded paper out of her purse. "Yeah. I figured you might want them. I went to a party there last winter. Good luck."

Rory pressed a hand against the nerves jumping in her stomach. "Thanks."

She had a hunch that she was really going to need her inner daredevil to come out now.

IT WAS MIDNIGHT when Lea's cell phone woke her out of a half sleep.

"Well, is Jared Slade the man you knew as Hunter Marks?"

Lea resented the way the voice on the other end of the line could chill her. "I haven't seen the photo yet. But I'll have the pictures first thing in the morning. She definitely got one of Slade, but we kept missing each other all day long."

"This is not going well."

Tell me about it, Lea said to herself. She'd come within an inch of firing Rory in that bar. But that wouldn't have gotten her what she wanted. She needed those photos first. What she said out loud was, "I talked to her and she definitely got the picture. We'll both have what we want in the morning."

"Where are the pictures right now?"

"She said she left them in her apartment. I'll have them at eight-thirty."

"I'll be in touch."

I sincerely hope not, Lea thought as she ended the call. Once she had the pictures, she wouldn't have to have anything more to do with her anonymous informant.

RORY STIRRED, WHACKED HER ELBOW hard against something, and came abruptly awake. Before the bubble of panic could even fully form in her stomach at the bewildering surroundings, she remembered where she was—in her car a short distance from the Wainwright estate.

The streaks of pink in the east told her that it was close to sunrise. The moon had shone full and bright in the pitch-black sky when she'd parked her car at the side of the road shortly after one o'clock, and now, finally, she was going to make her move.

Leaning back in the seat, she crossed her fingers and prayed for all of her luck to be up and running. No more backsliding. She was not going to slip into the pattern of

self-doubt the way she had when she'd been talking to
Natalie in the Blue Pepper. Just as a little extra precaution,
she'd put on the red bra and thong. Irene had told her that
it would make her feel more confident about herself—and
she was going to need every shred of confidence she had—
or could borrow—to get the interview with Jared Slade.

She wasn't even going to think about what she would
do if she met the Terminator again, let alone what would
happen if he kissed her again.

After stepping out of the car, she hurried across the road
and used the grasses growing in the ditch for cover as she
approached the drive that led to the Wainwright mansion.

As far as she could see there wasn't a guard. Just a wide
wrought-iron gate between two twelve-foot brick walls.
Thanks to a full moon, she'd gotten a good view of the
main house and grounds when she'd crested the last hill,
and she'd noted that a brick wall bordered the rambling estate on all four sides. She'd counted two other buildings
besides the house—a pool house and what she guessed to
be a stable. Lucas Wainwright had some pretty nice digs.

Pushing her way through the grass, she climbed out of
the ditch and crossed the road. The gate held when she
pushed against it. Moving to the right, the direction she'd
come from, she studied the wall. The bricks looked fairly
new—the mortar that held them was smooth. Not a chink
in sight. But she'd passed a tree. Breaking into a jog, she
headed toward it.

The limb was just out of her reach, so she jumped for
it. When her hands slipped the first time, she landed on her
butt. Making a mental note that she had to start going to
her gym on a more regular basis, she scrambled to her feet
and leapt for the lowest branch.

This time her grip held, but it took her three tries before she managed to swing her legs up and hook them around the branch. For a moment, she hung there and just concentrated on breathing. Upper-body strength was what she needed. Along with that fanny lift. She'd start first thing tomorrow.

For now, she wiggled, swore, wiggled and swore again until she sat upright on the branch. The ground looked far away and, up close and personal, the branch looked a lot less sturdy. It bobbed and swayed in perfect rhythm with the way her stomach was pitching around as she inched her way along its length. Once she reached the wall, she crawled carefully onto it, then made herself take slow, calming breaths.

A quick assessing look around didn't make her stomach feel any better. There was no tree in sight on this side, and the ground still looked far away. All she had to do was dare herself, then wiggle to the edge and drop. Twelve feet wasn't that far. She'd just count to three and take the plunge. Eyes closed, she'd counted to two when she heard the dogs barking. She opened her eyes and spotted two large black Labs barreling toward her. Any thought of sweet-talking them evaporated when she saw the man following them. Her Terminator.

She felt that same punch to her system she'd felt the first time she'd spotted him in the lobby. He was walking toward her with that same ground-eating stride, that same focused purpose. Each step he took increased the sensations racing through her—the tingling in her palms, the race of her heart. And she was suddenly very aware of the way her nipples had hardened against the sheer fabric of her bra.

This time, he was wearing gray sweats and a sleeveless gray tank top. As he drew closer, Rory could see the muscles that she'd only felt in the dressing room. She'd also become very aware of the way the red thong circled her hips and dipped low at the small of her back and she could feel the thin piece of lace that lay dampening at the center of her heat.

Questions tumbled through her mind. Why was she reacting this way to this man? And why couldn't she seem to control it?

She still had time to climb back down the tree and run. The moment the idea slipped into her mind, she shoved it out. This man was her best chance of getting an interview with Jared Slade.

The dogs reached the wall and were barking and leaping as high as they could. But Rory couldn't take her eyes off the Terminator. Fear, anticipation and excitement tumbled through her, nearly making her dizzy. She pressed her hands hard into the top of the brick wall to steady herself.

When he reached her, he settled the dogs with one quick gesture. Then he met her eyes and said, "What the hell are you doing here?"

5

"YOU DON'T LOOK HAPPY to see me," Rory said.

He wasn't. He'd been just about to take a run when a security guard had pointed her out on one of the monitors, and Hunter hadn't been able to prevent the quick flash of pleasure that had shot through him.

As she'd tested the front gate, he'd made a list of the reasons he shouldn't be happy to see her. For starters, her presence meant someone knew where he was, and the trap Tracker was setting might be totally useless.

Secondly, he didn't need the distraction. Just in the short time that it had taken him to reach her, his body had hardened painfully, and he was very much aware of his arousal pressing tight against his sweatpants. His reaction to this woman seemed to be completely out of his control.

There had to be a reason for that. Studying her, he took in the black T-shirt she was wearing and the faded jeans that had worn thin at the knees. The red boots had been replaced by serviceable-looking sneakers. There was nothing at all about the outfit that should be remotely sexy. Nothing that should make him wonder how fast he could get her out of it and what she was wearing beneath it.

She wasn't his type. How many times had he reminded himself of that in the past twenty-four hours? He preferred women who were sophisticated, who knew the score, who were beautiful.

Rory Gibbs wasn't beautiful. He raked his glance over the pixie features, the slim, strong-looking body. Cute was the most he could grant her. She looked small, defenseless and strangely defiant sitting there looking down at him. That shouldn't appeal to him, either—but it did.

When she licked her lips, he fisted his hands at his sides and stifled the urge to reach up, grab her ankles and pull her off that wall. He wanted her thousands of miles away from him. But even more than that, he wanted that small, compact body bucking beneath his as he thrust into her.

Tightening his grip on the control that had never deserted him before, Hunter said, "I asked you what in hell you're doing here."

When she lifted her chin and met his eyes squarely, he couldn't help but admire her.

"You've had time to develop the pictures I gave you. So I've come for the interview you promised."

His eyes narrowed. "I didn't promise you an interview."

"Close enough. You promised to talk to Jared Slade, and you look like a pretty persuasive man to me. Did you talk to him?" Her tone was quiet and her gaze never wavered.

"He left before we could discuss it."

"He left? I missed him?"

There was such shock, such disappointment on her face that Hunter wondered how there could be a dishonest bone in her body. If she tried to lie, surely her face, her body language would give her away. "How did you know he was here?"

She raised a hand. "No. Wait a minute. You're here. He wouldn't go away without his bodyguard."

Hunter's brows shot up. "Bodyguard?"

Rory pointed a finger at him. "Don't try to deny it. You chased me out of Les Printemps to get the film. You're obviously Mr. Slade's bodyguard. And you're still here, so I don't believe he's gone."

"I'm not Jared Slade's bodyguard. I'm his executive vice president in charge of retail acquisitions. He left me behind to finish up a deal we're working on."

"With Irene Malinowitz at Silken Fantasies?"

"No comment." She *was* sharp. Either that or someone in his organization was keeping her well-informed. His eyes narrowed as her face suddenly flushed.

"I—I want to thank you for the…red…under things. You really shouldn't have, but…I mean…"

A very vivid image slipped into Hunter's mind of that moment when he'd first seen her wearing the red thong and bra—the way she'd looked wearing nothing but those thin wisps of lace and those red boots. Whatever cooling off his body had done stopped and went into an abrupt reverse. Shoving the image out of his mind, he said, "You haven't answered my question. Who told you my boss was here?"

She hesitated and he could almost hear the wheels inside her head start to turn.

"You can't lie to me. So don't even try."

RORY GRIPPED THE EDGE of the wall and wished that she hadn't left her bubble gum in the car. He had the Terminator look back on his face, and there was a part of her that wanted to do a Humpty Dumpty into his arms and just see where she would fall.

But she'd come here to get an interview. "If I tell you, will you call Mr. Slade and set up the interview?"

"I'll call him and ask him about it. That's all I can promise."

She nodded. "Okay. It's a little complicated. My sister Natalie is a friend of Sophie Wainwright and Sophie told Natalie that a reclusive tycoon who was worried about his safety was consulting with her brother's chief of security." She paused to take a breath. "And Lucas Wainwright's chief of security happens to be Sophie's main squeeze. No names were mentioned—but Natalie works for a special D.C. police task force, and her office was called about the bomb scare in Mr. Slade's suite. She told me about that—strictly off the record. But how many media-shy tycoons with security problems could be in Washington at one time?"

Hunter wasn't sure whether he wanted to laugh or to swear. The story was way too convoluted and way too plausible for him to doubt it. Unless Rory Gibbs was a very talented liar.

"Did you let anyone at your magazine know that you were coming out here?" he asked.

"No. If it didn't pan out, I'd look like a fool, wouldn't I?"

Another convincing answer. Whether she was lying or not, he'd have to let Tracker know she was here—and he'd have to at least pretend to make a phone call to Jared Slade.

"Come with me. We'll talk inside," he said.

"What about the dogs?"

"They're friendly." He moved closer to the wall. "Jump and I'll catch you."

Rory saw those hands reaching for her and her whole system began to have a meltdown again. Images slipped into her mind of what she'd seen them do to her in the mirror in that dressing room. Whatever else happened, she wanted those hands on her again.

Scooting to the edge of the wall, she didn't even count to three before she took the plunge. And then he was holding her tightly against that body again. For one scorching moment, she was aware of nothing but hard angles and rock-hard muscles pressing into her. An instant later, he set her on her feet with an abruptness that had her taking a quick step back to the wall for support. Before she could even be sure of her balance, he turned away and started toward the drive with the dogs loping along happily at his side.

Rory frowned at him. Then she took several quick steps to catch up. She'd come here to get an interview with Jared Slade. The one she'd been promised. And she wasn't going to give up.

But as she followed him up the curved driveway, she found her focus slipping again. Even from the back, he radiated a kind of raw energy that was both primitive and sexual. If she'd inherited just a portion of her sisters' planning genes, perhaps she could have stopped staring at the damp hair that curled low at the back of his neck. Or she might have kept her gaze from drifting down the length of his back and lower.

His sweats were made of some thin material that fit snugly over his backside. Her eyes lingered there as her stomach clenched and she started to lose the feeling in her legs. She knew what it would feel like to slip her hands beneath the waistband and explore that taut, smooth skin. Would it be as hot as it had been the last time—as hot as hers was beginning to feel? Rory's eyes widened as she watched her hands reach out of their own accord. Snatching them back, she stumbled.

In a move so quick, it sent whatever breath she had left backing up into her lungs, he turned and grabbed both of her arms to steady her. "You all right?"

No, she was anything but all right. She was turning into one big puddle of lust. And it was clear that he wasn't. At least not anymore. His eyes were almost clinical as they searched her face. "I'll get you something to drink when we get to the house."

She didn't need anything to drink—except perhaps a long swallow of him, but he didn't seem to be on the same wavelength anymore.

Wasn't that just the story of her life when it came to men? Try as she might, she just didn't have the equipment to turn men into lust puddles. At least not for very long. Otherwise, he would have pulled her to him and that gorgeous mouth would be feasting on hers again.

But it wasn't. And she was *not* going to think about what that mouth had felt like on hers. She couldn't afford to go there. One thing at a time, she told herself. Getting the interview required all of her concentration. Drawing in a deep breath, she met his eyes and said, "I'm…fine."

His gaze remained locked on hers for one more moment, and Rory held her breath, hoping that nothing he saw would betray her.

Finally, he nodded. "Watch your step on the gravel." Then dropping his hands, he turned and led the way along a path to a patio. Just as they passed through open French doors into what looked like a study, the phone rang. She lingered in the doorway as he strode to the desk and picked it up. Grateful for a slight reprieve, she pulled her eyes away from him and looked around the room. Three of the walls were lined with books that looked like they'd been read.

"Yes?" He spoke the word into the phone as if he'd been expecting the call. "We need to talk. Just hang on a minute, will you?" He set the phone down, then moved toward her. "I have some business to discuss. Would you mind waiting out on the patio for a bit?"

"No." She stepped back through the French doors.

"There's a housekeeper—a man named McGee. The Wainwrights left him in charge when they went back to D.C. I'll have him bring you something to drink. Would you prefer coffee? Iced tea? A soft drink?"

"There's no need. Really."

His brows lifted. "I'm going to tell him to bring you something, so you might as well take your choice."

She raised her hands, palms out. "Okay. Coffee would be fine."

"Good. Why don't you go over and sit by the pool? It's cooler there. I'll join you as soon as I'm finished on the phone."

When he stepped back into the study and closed the French doors in her face, Rory had the distinct feeling she'd been handled and dismissed. Through the glass, she watched as he circled the desk, then met her eyes again and waited. For five long beats, she stayed right where she was. But it was the wrong battle to draw a line in the sand for. Turning away, she started toward the pool. As Jared Slade's vice president in charge of retail acquisitions, he was probably used to giving orders and having them obeyed.

She'd never been good at taking orders or following someone else's agenda, but she'd do what he wanted for now. She had a feeling she'd need all the energy she could muster up to get that interview.

FOR A LONG MINUTE, Hunter didn't pick up the phone. Instead he let himself recall just what she'd felt like pressed against him for that moment after she'd jumped off the wall. He hadn't wanted to let her go. For an instant, every bit of the desire he'd felt for her in that dressing room had returned. And it wasn't going to go away.

Not seeing her again might have solved the problem. But avoiding her wasn't going to be possible now. Frowning, he picked up the phone and said, "Tracker?"

"I'm still here. I take it you have a visitor?"

"Yeah. Rory Gibbs. Seems she got wind of the possibility that Jared Slade was here to consult Lucas Wainwright's chief of security. She knew about the bomb scare, too, but she assured me that part was off the record."

Tracker swore, then said, "Do you know her source?"

"Sources. And you're not going to like it," Hunter said. Then he repeated Rory's explanation.

"Damn," Tracker said. "Sophie is usually more discreet than that."

"Don't blame her," Hunter said. "She was talking to friends. One of them just happened to be the sister of a woman who's determined to interview Jared Slade. My bad luck and Rory Gibbs's good fortune."

"Look, I just put my man on Lucas's private plane. I'll come out to the estate and have a talk with her."

"I don't think that's a good idea," Hunter said.

There was a beat of silence on the other end of the line. "I'm listening."

"She seems to always be at the right place at the right time, but I don't think she's being fed information. She's just got brains and good luck. And a reporter's curiosity—which could mean trouble."

"What are you going to do?"

"I wish the hell I knew." But talking to Tracker was helping him work through it. And it wasn't hurting that Rory Gibbs wasn't in the same room. His brain cells were beginning to function again. Through the window, he could see her reaching the gate of the pool. The dogs were romping around her, but they didn't seem to scare her. She stooped down, picked up a stick and shot it away. The dogs tore after it. "She's…"

"Yes?" Tracker asked.

A constant surprise, Hunter thought. But what he said was, "She's a loose cannon."

"Meaning?"

"I'm afraid if you talk to her, warn her off, it's only going to make her more curious. She'll start digging, probing." He started to pace back and forth in the space behind the desk. "It's like she's got a sixth sense or something. I'm afraid that she may even come up with the theory that *I'm* Jared Slade."

"And if she does?" Tracker asked.

"I'm trying to prevent that. I told her that Slade's gone, that I'm his vice president in charge of retail acquisitions. That's when she guessed I was acquiring Silken Fantasies."

Tracker couldn't prevent a laugh. "She's as smart as her sisters."

"I wonder if she knows that," Hunter mused.

"How's that?"

"Nothing." He watched the huge black Labs race toward her, topple her over on the grass. When she sat up and looped her arms around their necks and let them lick her face, he was abruptly and totally charmed.

"I'm going to keep her here until we sort this out," Hunter said.

"And just how do you plan to do that?"

The plan was beginning to take shape in his mind. "Jared Slade doesn't give interviews. I'll offer her the next best thing—an interview with his vice president in charge of retail acquisitions, Mark Hunter. I use that name when I travel," he explained. "There's even a personnel file on Mark Hunter in the Dallas office." Then he thought to ask, "I assume there won't be any problem with her staying here on the estate?"

For five beats there was dead silence on the other end of the line. "She's the sister of a friend of mine. I don't want to see her hurt. Her sister wouldn't want to see her hurt. Neither would Lucas."

Hunter's brows rose. There was a clear warning in Tracker's voice. "Let's look at it this way. The interview will be legit, and it will be the next best thing to interviewing Jared Slade. She'll have the scoop she needs to get her a full-time staff position at *Celebs*. And I'll have the certainty that she's here where I can keep an eye on her while you're springing the trap we've set."

"I don't know," Tracker said.

"There's something else to consider. What if she's not just lucky and smart? Someone sent an anonymous tip about my hotel to *Celebs* and not to the *Post*, as you mentioned earlier today. What if the bastard who set the bomb is using her as a pawn in the game he's playing? Until we know what's going on and who the players are, she'll be safer here with me than she'd be trying to get a lead on Jared Slade's whereabouts."

As he watched Rory throw a stick for the dogs, he waited out the silence again.

"Why do I think that there's a more personal side to this than you're telling me?" Tracker finally asked.

"Because your nature is to be suspicious. But neither one of us wants her stumbling onto something that will lead her down to the Keys," Hunter said.

"Yeah." He sighed. "You're right. I'll be in touch when I have something."

After hanging up the phone, Hunter walked to the French doors. Whatever he'd said to Tracker, he wouldn't lie to himself. He wanted Rory Gibbs with him for very personal reasons that had nothing to do with her safety or protecting his anonymity.

He didn't kid himself, either. Keeping her here was every bit as risky as letting her go. But he hadn't built Slade Enterprises by running away from risks. He would just have to be careful. He watched her race across the lawn with the dogs chasing her and felt his body begin to harden again. Would she be that reckless, that abandoned when they made love again? He wanted to find out. He would find out, Hunter decided. Soon. That decision made, he began to plot a strategy for handling Rory Gibbs.

6

RORY WAS OUT OF BREATH by the time she reached to open the gate to the pool. The dogs pushed through it, jumped at her, licked her face, and finally sent her tumbling into one of the lounge chairs. Laughing, she patted one head then the other. "Down," she ordered, then watched in amazement as they settled, tongues hanging out, one on each side of her chair.

"How do you like your coffee, miss?"

She glanced up from the dogs to see an older, distinguished-looking man in navy blue shorts and a crisp white short-sleeved shirt set a tray on the table next to her chair.

"Black, thank you," she said. "I'm sorry for the trouble. I told him that I really didn't need anything. Oh, my… cookies." She beamed a smile at him as she reached for one and took a bite. "You've saved my life. Food always settles my nerves. Plus, chewing makes me think, and I left my bubble gum in the car." She took another cookie. "These are delicious, Mr.…"

"You can call me McGee. And the cookies are no trouble. Mr. Lucas likes to know that his guests are well cared for."

"You shouldn't have brought so many. I'll probably eat them all."

When he handed her a mug of coffee, Rory took a sip

and then closed her eyes and sighed. "Perfect. This is French-pressed, isn't it?"

"Indeed." McGee smiled at her. "You have a discerning taste. Mr. Lucas prefers French-pressed coffee."

Rory smiled at the man over the rim of her mug. "I do, too. Could you pour yourself a mug and join me? Is that allowed?"

The corners of his mouth twitched. "Strictly speaking, no. But it's kind of you to ask."

"What about the coffee beans? You must grind them yourself?"

"Yes, miss. The beans are grown in Kenya. Mr. Lucas has them flown in."

She nodded. "Heavenly. And please call me Rory. Can you at least sit?"

When he did, she took another cookie. "You've been with Mr. Wainwright for a time?"

"Ever since he came back to take over the company. My son, Tim, works in the stables. If you want to ride, let him pick your mount. He's a good judge."

"Thanks. I won't be staying long." She took another sip of the coffee. "Mr. Lucas's guest—do you happen to know his name?"

"Mark Hunter," said a voice that she recognized. Turning, she watched him enter through the gate and approach her in that long-legged Terminator stride.

"Will that be all, miss?" McGee asked as he rose.

"Yes. Thank you," she replied as nerves sprung to life again and twisted into a knot in her stomach. Mark Hunter. The last name suited him, she thought. Hadn't she seen the hunter in him from the first? He had that look about him now as he sat down on the foot of the lounge adjacent to hers.

He was prepared, his quarry in sight. And she'd spent the time playing with the dogs and talking to Lucas Wainwright's butler. She could have kicked herself. As usual, she was going to have to develop a plan by the seat of her pants. Once McGee had let himself out the gate, she reached for another cookie. "These are delicious."

Mark Hunter filled a mug from the carafe. "You eat when you're nervous, don't you?"

"What makes you think I'm nervous?" she asked around a mouthful of chocolate crumbs.

He took her hand as she reached for another cookie. "Because your hand is trembling."

"Did you talk to Jared Slade?" she said quickly, changing the subject.

He met her eyes. "Yes. He won't agree to an interview."

She straightened, swinging her legs off the side of the lounge so that her knees brushed briefly against his. "Mr. Hunter, there's got to be some arrangement we can make."

"You can call me Hunter. That's what my associates call me."

"Hunter, then. Mr. Slade doesn't have to see me or even talk to me. I could give you some questions to ask him. You could tell me the answers."

Hunter shook his head. "He hates the press. He's not going to change his mind."

Her eyes narrowed suddenly. "You knew that from the beginning. You conned me out of those pictures, knowing that I'd never get an interview. I could have published them. I should have turned them over to my boss. But I stalled her."

He studied her as she spoke, watching temper darken her eyes and emanate from her in little sparks he could almost feel on his skin. Here was the passion that he'd only begun to explore in that dressing room. He wanted to taste it again. He wanted to push it, push her until she exploded in his arms.

Rising, she paced away toward the pool. He rose and moved toward her.

"I never should have given you those pictures." When she whirled back to face him, she walked smack into him, then took a quick step back. He grabbed her arms to keep her from falling into the water. It might have worked if those excitable dogs hadn't gotten involved. Two strong paws hit him right in the small of his back. He stumbled forward, then twisted and took her with him as he fell back-first into the pool.

When they came up for air, she was sputtering and coughing. Then to his surprise and delight she began to laugh.

Treading water, he stared at her. Any other woman would have been angry. Her eyes were light now, liquid gold with darker flecks. And with her hair plastered to her head, she looked like some kind of water sprite. And that mouth. He had to taste it again. Soon.

But first they had business to settle between them. He moved toward her and urged her to the side of the pool where the dogs were barking and hoping for more horseplay.

"Down," he said, and they moved back to settle themselves on either side of a lounge chair.

He returned his gaze to Rory. The depth was shallow enough that he could stand, but he noted that she secured herself by placing a hand on the ledge that ran around the side of the pool. Her legs tangled with his before she pulled hers back.

"I'm still angry with you," she said.

"But not for pushing you into the pool."

Her brows shot up. "You didn't. The dogs did." She leveled her gaze on him. "I try to be a fair person. But you weren't fair with me."

"Strong words," he murmured.

"If the shoe fits…"

He raised a hand, palm out. "Okay. You're right. I did know from the beginning that Jared Slade was not going to give you that interview."

"So, you negotiated a kiss on a lie."

"Okay. But maybe you dazzled me so much that I shouldn't be held responsible for that."

She snorted. "Yeah. Right. I go through life dazzling men. Wherever I go, they fall at my feet."

He studied her for a moment. Was it possible that she didn't know how attractive she was? That might explain the innocence he kept sensing in her. Hunter ran a finger down her cheek to her throat and felt her pulse scramble. "Before I become dazzled again, I have a compromise I want to offer you." He traced his finger along her collarbone, and then he saw it—the thin red strap. His mouth went dry, and the water surrounding them in the pool suddenly seemed warmer.

"Compromise?" she asked.

He dragged his thoughts back from the red bra and the red… "Yes." He swallowed hard as he forced himself to meet her eyes. Every time he got this close to her, she sent every rational thought he had flying away.

Yet she didn't think that she had any power over men.

He'd come out here with a plan, a strategy all worked out. And he simply didn't care about it anymore. Hunter held her gaze. "Are you wearing the thong?"

Her eyes darkened from amber to dark, rich cognac in a heartbeat. "Yes."

"Show me," he said as he backed a few steps away. Then he watched as she dropped her hand from the edge of the pool and tugged the snap of her jeans open. Impeded by the wetness of the fabric and the water, she had to tug and wiggle, then tug and wiggle some more as she slid the jeans down those slender, strong legs and kicked them off. It seemed to take forever, and the water surrounding them grew steadily hotter and hotter until the sun beating down on his shoulders felt cool in comparison.

Still, he didn't rush as he moved his gaze slowly up her legs to where the little triangle of red lace beckoned to him. His hand felt heavy as he moved it to her and traced the lace edge with one finger. She was wearing a silver bar in her navel, and when he touched it, desire curled within him, tangling with an ache that was unexpected and raw.

More than anything, he wanted to push that sheer red fabric aside and watch what happened to her eyes when he slid into her heat. He let his gaze move higher up that slim waist to linger on her breasts. The nipples were hard and he could see them through the wet fabric. He was going to touch them, too.

His original plan had been to wait—to give her part of the interview, wine and dine her…then succumb to his need for her. But he'd never been pulled so strongly by a woman before. And he'd waited long enough.

Meeting her eyes, he said, "I want to kiss you again. And I want to make love to you. If you have a problem with that, now would be a good time to say so."

She met his gaze steadily, keeping her head above water by merely kicking her feet. It was happening again—just as it had in the dressing room. He wanted her. She could read the desire in his eyes, feel it in the heat of his body.

She'd come here for this as much as for the interview, and there wasn't a chance for her to fall back into the old indecisive Rory when he looked at her the way he was right now. But there was one thing she had to clear up first.

"I'm not going to kiss you again for an interview or a compromise. Let's just get that straight. This time I'm going to kiss you because I want to."

Hunter nodded. "Agreed. Now, take off your shirt."

The ache inside of her only twisted tighter as she did what he asked, bobbing gently in the water as she struggled to get the damp T-shirt over her head. Then she was naked except for the red lace.

"We shouldn't do this here." His voice was hoarse as he closed the small distance between them.

"No. I should be asking you about the compromise. But I can't seem to keep my mind on task when I'm with you." She looped her arms around his neck and brushed her legs up against his.

With a groan, Hunter trapped one of her legs between his. "We'll get to the compromise. Later." He wasn't sure whether it was her words or the way she looked in the water—part sex goddess, part mermaid, but he felt the same urgency that he'd felt in the lingerie shop. All that mattered was having her. Now.

"Hurry."

Hearing her say that one breathless word had an arrow of heat shooting through him. His head was spinning. The restless, wanton movements of her body against his had him swaying. To steady himself, to steady both of them, he pushed forward until her back was against the side of the pool.

"Kiss me."

He wasn't sure who'd spoken the words or if he'd just thought them, but he took her mouth with his.

OH, YES, RORY THOUGHT as his flavor exploded on her tongue and poured into her. Yes, yes, yes, yes. Her mind took up the chant as his tongue moved in a slow, steady rhythm over hers, and his hand stroked down her body possessively. His flavor was just as she remembered—dark and rich like some exotic kind of chocolate. Forbidden and addictive.

Her breath caught in her throat and her body arched toward his as his fingers began to toy with the waistband of her thong. Her skin trembled and arrows of heat shot through her as they moved along her waist to her back. But he didn't linger. Instead, he moved his hands, those long fingers, those wide palms, to caress her buttocks. She felt each individual finger burn into her skin like a brand before the pressure increased and they drew her cheeks apart.

Pleasure and anticipation streaked through her, and heat built in her center. Then he began to trace the thong along her bottom, spreading her cheeks even farther to give his fingers more access until he was pressing them just where she wanted.

"Harder," she whimpered as she arched and wiggled herself against them. "Please."

He lifted her then and she wrapped her legs around him, pressing herself against the hard length of him.

She moaned when he slowly retraced the path his fingers had just taken along the lace strap of the thong between her cheeks.

Tightening her legs around him, she said, "I want you inside of me, now."

He had no choice. After shoving his sweats down, Hunter found her opening and pressed himself against it. Then he pushed himself into her and felt her heat grip him tightly. After withdrawing a little, he drove in even farther.

"Yes," she whimpered against his ear.

He withdrew and thrust in even deeper. Just this one more time. Hadn't he told himself that if he could have her this way again, that would be enough? But as her heat burned him, and her muscles fastened around him like a clamp, he wasn't sure that his hunger for her would ever be sated.

He withdrew and thrust in again, this time to the hilt.

"More."

Every muscle in his body sang with the need to obey her command, but he was aware that the lawn mower that he'd heard earlier had moved closer. Above the hedge that bordered the pool, he could see the straw hat of the driver. This time when he withdrew, she clamped her legs around him tightly.

"Don't you dare stop."

He leaned closer and whispered, "Shh. We're not alone." Though he was confident that the man on the mower wouldn't be able to hear them, he couldn't be sure that the man wouldn't glance over the hedge and see them.

"I can't wait."

Even though he was gripping her hips firmly, she managed to thrust herself against him. Suddenly, he couldn't wait, either. Very slowly, he withdrew and then pushed into her again. When she stiffened and murmured his name, he heard something inside of him snap just as clearly as he heard the sound of the lawn mower fade.

He slapped his hands against the tiles and then thrust

into her again—faster, harder, again and again. Each time he pushed into her, she seemed to grow hotter, and her grip on him—inside and out—tightened.

No, this was not going to be enough. He would need this again and again. Even as the realization poured through him, he felt the water around him churning, heard little waves slapping against the sides of the pool. She was moving with him, thrust for thrust. Just as the heat became searing, unbearable, he felt her stiffen. Then he surrendered to her climax and to his.

RORY WAS AWARE that on some level, her body had gone as limp as her mind. If Hunter's body hadn't been pressing hers so firmly against the wall of the pool, she would have slid right down to the bottom and drowned. She could still feel him embedded inside of her, and though she wouldn't have thought it possible, the knowledge, the pressure had something inside of her warming again. She drew in a breath, and when her lungs burned, she wondered just how long her body had been without oxygen.

"Are you okay?"

She managed a weak nod. "But I can't move yet."

She felt his lips curve against her shoulder. "I'm having a bit of a problem with that myself."

When she felt him pull out of her, she nearly cried out in protest. She might have tightened her legs to keep him there, but they still felt like soft, runny butter. A minute later, she found herself sitting beside him on the steps leading out of the pool.

"Wow," she said, snuggling her head against his shoulder because she simply didn't have the strength to hold it upright.

"Ditto."

"Next time, I vote we do this on dry land."

"I can vote for that, too," he said. "And to hurry that process along, why don't I get you a towel?"

For a moment after he pulled away, Rory felt cold and a bit bereft. The ringing of a phone caught him halfway to the pool house, and he strode quickly back to the table near the lounge chairs to pick up the extension.

"Yeah?"

She saw the frown come to his face a second before she swept her gaze down the length of him. The wet sweats were clinging to his body, revealing every hard angle and plane. And he was still wearing his running shoes. A short distance away, her sneakers lay on the bottom of the pool, peeking out from beneath her jeans. He was still fully clothed and she was wearing only a red bra and thong.

And she'd just been ravished at the side of a pool. Well, not ravished really. Technically, to be truly ravished, she suspected that the ravishee had to put up at least a token resistance.

She hadn't. The only thing she'd done was make it very clear that making love with him was not going to be some quid pro quo thing. What they'd just done had nothing to do with the interview. Leaning back against her hands, she extended her legs and examined her body. Was it the red thong that was giving her the confidence to do things she'd never done before?

Her gaze returned to Hunter. Or was it the man who'd made her feel so daring? Slowly a smile curved her lips as she thought of the way Sierra would answer that question. The only way to find out would be to do some further research.

"LOOKS LIKE YOU WERE right," Tracker said on the other end of the line.

"About what?" Hunter asked.

"About Rory Gibbs. I stopped by her apartment on a hunch."

"A hunch?" Hunter shifted his gaze to Rory.

"I've been known to have them. Perhaps it was your characterization of her as a pawn. But it occurred to me that if she was stumbling into information that you didn't particularly want her to have, someone else might not want her to have it, either. Anyway, her place just happened to be on my route from the airport to the Wainwright offices."

"And you knew the address because…?"

"Hey, I'm a top-notch security expert. We know these things—or can find out."

As Tracker continued to talk, Hunter's eyes narrowed. Rory shivered a little as she drew up her knees and wrapped her arms around them. She was cold, and he'd promised her a towel.

"Hunter, are you still there?"

He dragged his thoughts back. "What?"

"The door of her apartment had been forced, and the place had been trashed. I suppose it could be a random break-in."

"I don't think so."

"Neither do I. That means that someone was probably watching her place. And they were looking for something."

"What?"

"Answer that and you, too, can become a security specialist. You can pass along any theories you have when I get there in an hour or so."

Hunter lowered his voice. "I think we should keep this

under wraps for now. She might want to leave—and for the time being she's safer here."

"I can't argue with the logic of that."

Hunter kept his eyes on Rory as he hung up the phone. How much danger was she in?

7

"SO YOU DROVE OUT HERE last night and slept in your car?" Hunter sat at the head of the table in a dining room that was as large as her whole apartment.

"More chicken salad, Miss Rory?" McGee asked, offering her the bowl.

"Yes…I mean no, thanks." She glanced down at her plate to find that it was empty. She'd had two helpings already in hopes that the nerves in her stomach would settle. "Well, maybe," she said, sending McGee a smile. "It's delicious." She piled another spoonful onto her plate. "And the answer to your question is yes, too," she added as she met Hunter's eyes.

She tore off a piece of croissant and popped it into her mouth. Perhaps the nerves were due to the fact that Hunter had slipped back into Terminator mode from the moment he'd hung up the phone at the pool. Oh, he'd been perfectly polite. He'd found her some dry clothes in the pool house, and he'd even had McGee show her to a guest room where she could shower. But since they'd sat down to lunch, he'd been treating her like a perfect stranger.

Exactly the way he'd treated her after the phone call that he'd taken in the dressing room at Silken Fantasies.

"Did you have any reason to suspect that you were followed out here?" he asked.

"Followed?" The thought had her frowning. "Why would anyone follow me?"

"Mr. Wainwright's security team would like to know if they should expect any more visitors to climb over the wall."

"Ah." She busied herself, scooping up another forkful of chicken salad as she thought about it. Could she have been followed? She hadn't even gone home after she'd spoken to Natalie at the Blue Pepper. Instead, she'd had something to eat, talked with Rad and George and then decided on the spur of the moment to drive out to the estate that night.

It had been late when she'd crossed the bridge into Virginia. Glancing up, she met Hunter's eyes. "I wasn't followed. Once I got off the main highway, I didn't notice any headlights behind me. And out here in the country, I think I would have." She gestured with her fork. "I read a lot of Nancy Drew mystery stories when I was growing up."

"Nancy Drew mysteries?" he asked.

"Yeah. Nancy Drew, girl detective. You probably read the Hardy Boys. But I liked Nancy. She had great girlfriends, drove a great car, had a steady, faithful boyfriend, and she had a great father."

He was looking at her curiously. "You read stories as a child and so you're sure you would have noticed headlights following you on a country road."

She nodded. "You try reading thirty or so books where a girl detective is looking for clues and being chased by bad guys. You'll notice all kinds of odd things. Didn't you ever read the Hardy Boys?"

He shook his head. "Can't say that I did. Should I consider my education lacking?"

She tilted her head to one side. "Only if you wanted to

grow up to be a supersleuth. You probably had other goals in mind." After setting down her fork, she pushed her plate aside and crossed her arms on the table. "Why are you asking me all these questions? Does this have something to do with the bomb scare at Les Printemps?"

Hunter had known that the question would come sooner or later, and he thought he had a plausible strategy for handling it. "I mentioned at the pool that Mr. Slade is prepared to offer you something in lieu of an interview with him. Part of the compromise I'm prepared to offer you requires your assurance that there will be no mention of the bomb scare in any article you might write. Mr. Slade is disturbed enough that you're here. However, he's aware that you gave back the pictures you snapped in the lobby. So he's willing to offer you something in place of an interview with him."

Her eyes narrowed. "What?"

Hunter wiped his mouth with his napkin and set it at the side of his plate. "If you're finished, why don't we take a walk while I explain?"

Without a word, she rose and followed him down the hall to the study and then through the French doors. He didn't cross the lawn to the pool, but instead guided her down a path that wound its way past the tennis courts toward the stables.

They walked in silence for a few minutes while Hunter reviewed his plan. It should provide both of them with what they wanted, and that was the key to any successful negotiation. In his mind, he pictured the plus columns on each side. An interview with "Mark Hunter," someone high up in Slade Enterprises, should be enough to get Rory Gibbs the staff job she wanted at *Celebs* magazine. And keeping her occupied on the estate while Tracker sprang a trap on whomever was behind the threats would ensure her safety.

Of course, there was the possibility that she would figure out that he was "Jared Slade." But he'd decided to risk that.

Hunter glanced down at the top of her head as she walked by his side. Who was he kidding? He wasn't really offering her the interview because of the advantages to either one of them. He was going to offer her the interview with "Mark Hunter" because he wanted to make love to her again. Dammit. He wanted her right now.

Desire had always been something he could handle, something he understood. But he had a hunch that desire was only a part of what he was feeling for this curious woman. He wanted to get to know her. He wanted to figure out how that agile mind of hers worked.

He hadn't allowed himself to really get to know a woman in years. He'd never intended to. It wasn't fair to them or to him. But he wanted to be as fair as possible to Rory. So he would clarify the parameters of their relationship. He would let her know exactly what to expect and what not to—

She stopped suddenly and pointed up into a tree. "Look. A tree house."

He glanced up and spotted the wooden floor wedged in a circle around the tree trunk and the small roofed structure that sat on two sturdy limbs.

"I always wanted one as a kid." Rory grabbed the rope ladder and began to climb, talking as she went. "My dad was going to build me one, too. He would have if he hadn't left. Of course, it probably would have freaked my mother out. She was always so afraid we would get hurt, break an arm or a leg. I take after her in height and coloring, but I'm glad I didn't inherit all of her fraidy-cat genes."

When she scrambled onto the ledge, the branch swayed, and the tree house tilted.

"Grab the railing," Hunter said as he climbed up the rope ladder to join her. Together, they gingerly settled themselves on the wooden platform outside the little house itself. Below them the lawns rolled away on all sides. To the left there were tennis courts, and beyond the pool, he could see the white fences that surrounded the stables.

"Do you ride?" he asked.

She wrapped her arms around her knees the way she had on the steps of the pool. "Yes, but I haven't had the opportunity in years." She angled her head to face him. "Do you ride?"

"I used to play polo," he said. Then he could have kicked himself. Where in the world had that come from? His polo days had ended when he'd stopped being Hunter Marks.

"Very cool. The closest I've come to a polo match is watching clips in a movie or on TV. I just love it, though. It's the same feeling I get when I watch the Kentucky Derby on TV. For the five or six minutes while the horses are being led to the starting gate and the race is run, I always feel like I'm one of the rich and the famous. Then it's over, and I'm back to being plain Rory Gibbs again."

"Why do you think of yourself as plain?" he asked.

"Because I am. No." She raised a hand to stop him. "You're a nice man. But I'm twenty-six, I'm short, and I'm sandwiched between two sisters who are truly beautiful. You should see them. Sierra's a blonde—not the dumb kind. She's the smartest one in the family, with two Ph.D.s. You know what they say about blondes having more fun? In Sierra's case, her work is what she considers 'fun.' Natalie's a redhead, and she's a cop. They say redheads get into more trouble, and she does. But she loves it. I'm a brunette. You never hear anything about brunettes. We're just ordinary."

He tamped down his anger as he studied her. Going with an impulse that he didn't quite understand, he put his arm around her. When she snuggled her head into his shoulder just as she'd done in the pool, he had an odd feeling, as if his heart had turned a little somersault. "Someone did a job on you."

"Ancient history. I have a talent for attracting men who are eventually going to dump me, starting with my father who walked out when I was ten."

"Your father must have been a fool."

She sighed. "You *are* a nice man. But there were extenuating circumstances—he was an international jewel thief and my mother wanted to raise us in a stable home."

"Your father was a jewel thief?" he asked incredulously.

Rory nodded. "A very good one. He couldn't seem to give up his profession and my mother didn't want us following in his footsteps. So they made this deal that he had to leave. Now that I'm older I can see it from their perspective. They did it because they loved us."

He ran a hand over her hair. It couldn't have been easy to understand it at ten. He'd had to separate himself from his family when he was nineteen—and he hadn't fully understood it even at that age.

"So?" She lifted her head and met his eyes. "We could spend the whole day sitting in a tree house. Or you could tell me about the compromise."

Hunter turned to study her. She looked strangely at

home in a tree house with dappled sunlight highlighting her features.

With some effort, he pulled his mind back to business. "First off, you should know that I'm not a nice man."

To his surprise, she grinned at him. "Of course, you're probably not nice when it comes to Slade Enterprises. The first time I looked at you, all I could think of was the Terminator."

Baffled, he stared at her. "The Terminator?"

She waved a hand. "Only in the first movie—you know, Arnold Schwarzenegger, when he was the bad guy, before he transformed himself into a superhero and eventually ran for governor."

"Oh." Mentally, Hunter dragged up an image of the mechanical robot fixated on destroying the woman and her future son in the first *Terminator* movie.

Rory laid a hand on his cheek. "I know that you can be a ruthless negotiator. Jared Slade would never have hired you otherwise, and you did talk me out of those pictures. But you can't expect me to forget how sweet you are."

"Sweet?"

"You sent me that lingerie. And now you're letting me ramble on and on about my family."

Hunter's mind was swimming. How in the world was he supposed to deal with a woman like this? "Do you always say what you're thinking?"

"Yeah. Mostly. I know it's not a good thing. My most recent ex-boyfriend found it quite annoying."

He gripped her chin in his hand. "It's fine. You're fine, and you should stop beating up on yourself."

"Okay." She smiled at him. "Didn't I tell you that you were sweet?"

Hunter gave up. There wasn't anyone who'd ever dealt with him who would have called him that. Ruthless, yes. And usually fair. But never *sweet*. Maybe it was time that he proved that to her. He dropped his hand from her face. "This is the compromise, Rory. You get to interview me instead of Jared Slade. I'll be here for a day or two until I finish my business, and I'll give you what time I can— under certain conditions."

RORY'S HEART BEGAN TO SKIP and race. She was almost used to the feelings that he could stir in her when he looked at her in that intent way—as if he could see right into her soul. First there was a pulse of fear, then a sliver of anticipation, followed by a hot clutching sensation in her stomach—the lust. She licked her lips. "What conditions?"

"First, you have to stay here a day or two. I'll sandwich the interview in between the work I have to do."

"And?"

His eyes narrowed. "You can't imagine that we can stay in close proximity and not have a repeat of what happened in the dressing room and the pool."

Somewhere in the vicinity of her heart, she felt a stutter of relief. But her throat had become so dry that she had to swallow. "No. I mean…you mean…?"

"I can't be around you and not want to have you again."

"Oh."

He studied her for a moment and said, "One doesn't have anything to do with the other. Mr. Slade was agreeable to having you interview me. My wanting to make love to you again is an entirely separate matter."

"Okay. I couldn't agree more. I wouldn't sleep with you to get an interview. The two matters are completely separate." She was rambling, mostly because of the melting sensation that seemed to be turning her insides into liquid.

"And this day or two. It's all we'll have. I want you to understand that. As soon as my business is finished, I'll go back to Dallas."

Rory studied him. It was the first time that she'd ever had a man set up the dumping ahead of time. And he didn't look anything like the Terminator right now. No, the man facing her now was cool and collected, his mind focused on business.

Perhaps that's why the idea popped into her mind. Or maybe it was her father's advice. She drew in a deep breath. "Okay. But I might have some conditions of my own."

She saw the surprise glimmer for a moment in his eyes, but it was masked as quickly as it appeared.

"State your terms," he said.

"It's…" Secretly, she wished for her bubble gum. Anything that would settle her nerves and give her courage. But the idea had sprung full-blown into her mind. Well, maybe not full-blown. Perhaps the seed had been planted that very first time she'd seen him in the lobby of Les Printemps, and it had certainly been nurtured by their encounter in the dressing room at Silken Fantasies. The whole thing about taking risks and trusting in your luck was that you weren't sure exactly how you came to decisions—they just happened.

"Yes?" he prompted.

"I'll accept your terms for the interview. Thanks. I mean, interviewing you will be the next best thing to interviewing Jared Slade. I guess."

"But…"

She shook her head. "No *buts*. My terms have to do with

the sex part. And the whole thing is a little delicate. I'm not sure…exactly how to put this."

"When in doubt, just say it."

Rory let out a sigh of relief. "Okay. Here's the deal. You say you want to continue our…relationship."

He met her eyes steadily. "I do."

She tried to ignore the heat that shot through her again. "It's not that I didn't like what happened in the pool—or in the dressing room."

His eyes narrowed. *"But…?"*

She drew in a deep breath. "It was all a little fast."

"Fast."

She reached over to put her hand on his. "It was incredible. Really. The best sex I've ever had. Only…"

"Yes?"

She met his eyes then. "It's hard to say this."

"Shoot from the hip, Rory."

She drew in a breath and let it out. "I haven't had much experience…sexually, I mean. I've had three lovers—four if you count the frat boy in my freshman year in college. He was the first boy to really pay any attention to me, but we only had one date and we did it in the back of his car. I've tried very hard to have amnesia when it comes to him and the whole experience."

"Good plan," he murmured as he turned her hand over and linked his fingers with hers.

"You're a good listener. But I won't bore you with all the details of lovers two, three and four. Not that they're worth describing. In summary, most of the men that I've had sex with have the wham-bam-thank-you-ma'am technique down pat."

"And you'd like more variety this time," he said.

"Partly." She squeezed his hand. "And I want you to know that the wham-bam in the pool was the best that I've ever had."

He cleared his throat. "Thank you."

She sighed. "I'm not doing this right. I tend to speak first and think things through later."

He squeezed her fingers. "You're doing fine."

"It's not just variety that I want. I'm sure that you could be very good at…making love to a woman in a number of ways. But what I'd like is for you to let me experiment a bit and take control. I'd like to try some things I've only fantasized about. I've never been able to do that before. Would that be all right?"

HUNTER STARED AT HER. She was every man's fantasy come to life and she didn't have a clue. "I can handle that."

She beamed a smile at him that had his heart stuttering again. "You really are sweet."

He met her gaze squarely. "I'm not sweet. I want you to remember that."

"Okay. When do you want to get started?"

Right now, he thought. But if he touched her, he was sure that what would happen would be of the wham-bam variety. So he said, "You'll need to tell your sisters where you are, but I'd appreciate it if you'd swear them to secrecy. Tracker will talk to them, assure them that you're safe."

"Sure. And I'll need some clothes."

"I'll arrange for that." The sweats she was wearing were too big. She'd had to roll up the legs and sleeves, and the end result was that she looked a little like one of the seven dwarfs. Not that the outfit had dampened his desire or his intentions. In his personal opinion, she would have looked sexy in anything, but she didn't believe that. Not yet. He was going to change that.

"And I'll need a place to work—a computer. I left my notebook and pen in the car."

"I'll have McGee handle that."

"Then we have a deal." She held out her hand.

He looked at her hand, then at her. "One question."

"What?"

"You don't have to always be in control, right?"

"No. Just sometimes."

"Good." He took her hand. "Because I want to make love to you right now."

Her eyes widened. "But I haven't even thought about what I want to do."

"I like spontaneous, don't you?"

"Sure, I—" She broke off when he lifted her onto his lap.

"You don't mean right here. In a tree house?"

"Afraid so." He moved a finger along her collarbone and watched the little pulse at her throat scramble.

"We could fall."

He dipped his head and brushed his lips over hers. "Funny. I didn't peg you for someone who was afraid of taking risks."

"Really?"

"Really." He nipped her lower lip and then soothed the small hurt with his tongue. "And I'm a man who can never resist a challenge."

And she had challenged him, whether she knew it or not. This time he'd go slowly, make sure they took their time. His mouth made a lazy journey to her ear and then back again to her mouth. But he didn't kiss her, not yet.

"I wasn't gentle with you before?"

"I liked it."

He smiled against her lips. "So did I. But let's try this." He kissed her then and kissed her again. And again.

Rory felt as if she were falling under a spell. He'd never kissed her this way before, as if he had all the time in the world and intended to take it. His mouth was so soft, so warm. And so skilled. She'd never been kissed like this before by anyone. Each time he withdrew, it was only to change the way his mouth fit against hers, and then he would take her deeper. Even his flavor was different, richer, sweeter.

She wanted more, but she couldn't seem to move. Her arms felt so heavy, and her head was spinning. When he moved his hand beneath her sweatshirt and skimmed those clever fingers up her ribs to her breast, she trembled.

She…should…do something. Pull back to clear her head—or draw him closer. Something. She'd had a plan. She wanted to seduce him. But her mind began to float and then her body. Oh, she knew that she was still sitting on his lap. She could feel the hardness of his erection pressing against her thigh, but it felt like floating.

When he moved his mouth to her throat, those teeth nipping, that tongue soothing, her skin began to burn. He was running the pad of his thumb over her nipple, and suddenly the need inside of her grew edgy. "Hunter, I—"

"Mmm?" His voice was just a vibration on her skin, but it sent twin sensations of fire and ice dancing along her nerve endings. "If you don't like what I'm doing, I could stop."

"No." She raised her hand then to grip his shoulder and arched against him. "I want—"

The branch of the tree dipped slightly, and they both suddenly slid toward the edge of the platform they were on.

"Whoa…" Hunter gripped her tight as he grabbed onto the railing and shifted back toward the door of the tree house.

"Maybe we should postpone this," she said. But she didn't pull away.

"Is that what you'd like to do?"

She shook her head.

He smiled at her. "Then I think we can rise to the challenge." He moved some more until they were inside the tree house.

"There's not a lot of room in here," he commented but he didn't hesitate to draw her shirt off and toss it aside. When he reached for the waistband to her sweats, she batted his hands away and grabbed the bottom of his T-shirt instead.

"I haven't seen you naked yet."

Together, they got him out of the shirt and his sweatpants and then she wiggled out of her own, a bit awkwardly considering the place was not more than five by six feet.

"This is going to be some challenge to rise to," she said. "I think I already have a sliver in my knee."

"I don't even want to think where I might get one," Hunter said.

She gestured with a hand. "There's a fifty-room mansion right over there and we're naked in a tree house."

When her laugh bubbled up and filled the tree house, Hunter found himself joining her. He felt like a teenager. Surely he'd been an adolescent the last time he'd done something this foolish. But somehow he wanted her even more—and he didn't want to wait.

Just as he reached for her, she said, "I have an idea."

"Me, too." He eased her down onto some of their discarded clothes, then positioned her so that he was kneeling between her legs.

"Whatever happened to ladies first?"

"I'll let you go first down the rope ladder," he said as he lowered his mouth until it hovered over her breast. "I'm a man who likes to finish what I start, and I started this. First, I'm going to taste you all over. And I'm going to take my time."

And he did—starting with her breasts. It was as if she were a meal that he'd been starving for. Using teeth and tongue, he circled the top and underside of her breast before he closed his teeth on the nipple and then took it into his mouth to suck. Arrows of heat shot through her, and she was sure that she felt the pull of his mouth right down to her toes. When he turned his attention to the other breast, she threaded her fingers through his hair and simply held on as the air around her seemed to grow hotter, thicker.

He moved his mouth lower, whispering kisses down the valley between her breasts, and then down her stomach. He lingered at her waist as if there were some taste there that he favored and then he went lower.

He drew her legs farther apart and held them down. And then she could feel his breath right there where she burned for him.

"I'm going to kiss you here—in a moment. But first…" He trailed kisses up and down one thigh and then the other, at times coming close to where she wanted him…but not close enough.

Sensations swamped her, each one growing more intense than the last—the scrape of his teeth at the back of her knee, the texture of his tongue on her thigh and the terrible aching emptiness that seemed to fill her. When she thought she couldn't stand it one more minute, he was there close to where she wanted him again.

"Now, Rory. I'm going to taste you now."

Then his mouth was exactly where she wanted it, his lips brushing little kisses—not nearly hard enough. But when she tried to arch closer, he tightened his grip on her legs.

Finally, he pressed his mouth fully against her and used his teeth and his tongue. Heat shot through her, scorching her. She tried to move, but he wouldn't allow it. She was trapped—she could barely breathe as he used his tongue to penetrate her again and again. She couldn't lift her hips.

"Hunter!"

As if he had been waiting for her to say his name, he used one thumb to rub her hard and plunged the other one into her. She erupted, pleasure careening through her in one wave after another.

He gathered her to him, holding her tightly against him until the last echo of her climax died away.

"A little improvement on the 'wham-bam' in the pool?" he finally asked.

Although she wouldn't have thought it possible in her present state, she laughed. "It was wonderful. But I would never complain about the pool. You may be turning me into a sex maniac."

"My good luck."

She lifted her head and met his eyes. "No, it's my good luck. And I think it's my turn now."

Using both hands and all of her strength, she rolled him on his back and straddled him. Then she took his erection into her hands. "Another time, I'll return the favor, but right now I want you inside me."

As if her wish were his command, he gripped her hips, lifted her and penetrated her. She wanted to laugh with the joy of it, but the hunger was building too quickly. His first two thrusts sent her spinning back to the world of sensations he'd trapped her in only minutes ago. Her skin burned where those long fingers pressed into her hips. And those eyes—they were focused on her with that intentness that heightened the pleasure of each thrust. Grasping his shoulders so that she wouldn't fall, she kept her gaze steady on his. The instant his features tightened, her own pleasure exploded again. "Come with me, Hunter. Come with me now."

Then she began to move faster and faster until she heard his cry of satisfaction.

8

"LEA ROBERTS IS RORY'S EDITOR at *Celebs?*" Hunter turned from the French doors in Lucas Wainwright's office to face Tracker.

Tracker's gaze narrowed. "Sounds like you know her."

Hunter's mind was racing. "I know the name. If it's the same Lea Roberts I used to know, we go back a long way." He stopped then, wondering how much he would have to tell Tracker.

"You'd better tell me everything," Tracker said after a beat. "I'll find most of it out anyway, and it might speed up the solution to your problem."

Though his respect for the man seated behind the desk was growing each time they met or talked, there were some things that Tracker would not discover. Hunter intended to keep it that way.

He walked forward and took one of the two chairs in front of the desk. "I haven't seen the Lea Roberts I used to know in ten years. She worked for the local newspaper in the town where I grew up, the *Oakwood Sentinel*. She was twenty-eight, bright, beautiful and skilled in many ways that would appeal to a nineteen-year-old boy."

Tracker's gaze narrowed. "You were lovers?"

Hunter nodded. "For about six months. It started out as

a summer romance during my last summer before college, and then it continued when I came home on breaks that first semester. She even visited me on campus once. My family owned the paper as well as the bank. She was beautiful, smart, and though I didn't see it at the time, she was ambitious. She probably figured that having an affair with one of the Marks sons would eventually pay off career wise. And it did."

"How did you feel about her at the time?"

Hunter met Tracker's eyes. "I thought I was in love with her."

"Did your family know about the affair?" Tracker asked.

Hunter thought for a minute. "I never considered that before—but they might have."

"And they didn't object?"

Hunter paused again to consider the question. This was a period of his life that he rarely reflected on. "They might have even approved. I was pretty wild my last year in high school. Driving under the influence, minor vandalism. Classic behavior for a kid in rebellion. That changed some when I went off to college. Meeting Lucas was good for me. My family problems at the time seemed to fade when he talked about his. But I had the well-established reputation in Oakwood of being the black sheep of the Marks family. My older brother was the model child, groomed to take over the company, and perhaps even to go into politics. Looking back, I can see that my parents might have thought Lea was a good influence on me."

Tracker leaned back in his chair. "I'm planning on making a trip to Oakwood this afternoon to see what I can dig up on whatever your anonymous enemy is going to reveal about you. You could save me some time."

Hunter spread his palms wide. "My life is an open book in Oakwood. I was still seeing Lea when I came home from college over Christmas break. And that's when the scandal broke."

"The scandal?"

"You can access the whole story in the *Sentinel*. It spread to other major newspapers, too. In a nutshell, while I was away at college, my family, namely my brother and my father and mother, discovered that there were millions missing from investment accounts that they'd been managing at the bank, and that was due to the fact that I'd been doing a little embezzling. Of course, I'd intended to pay it back, but my gambling habits made that impossible. If the news had leaked out, there would have been a run on the bank. Luckily, my family discovered it in time and forced me to liquidate my trust fund to cover the amount. I left town in disgrace. The bank, the townspeople and my family lived happily ever after."

Tracker studied him for a moment. "No one pressed charges?"

"I didn't stick around. And my father and mother got off easy. They had a lot of friends. Plus, the way the story was handled played up the fact that the Marks family saved the bank in spite of my unfortunate gambling and embezzling habits. The day that I left town was the last day that Hunter Marks existed."

Tracker studied him for a moment. "How much would it hurt Slade Enterprises if your past came out?"

"Enough. I've built a good reputation, but some people would hesitate to do business with an embezzler."

"You're not telling me everything."

Hunter merely held the other man's gaze.

"Okay. We'll leave it at that for now. But I still have a couple of questions. Does this Lea Roberts know what you're still keeping from me? And does she know that Jared Slade and Hunter Marks are one and the same?"

"Good questions," Hunter said. He couldn't have phrased them any better himself. "There are several possibilities. I can't believe she's behind the threats. And she doesn't necessarily know who I used to be. So she could just be after an exclusive with Jared Slade. Or she could be working with whomever is making the threats. Or she could be a pawn, someone that's being fed information."

"You think it's just a coincidence that *Celebs* got the anonymous message?" Tracker asked.

"No. But it could be that whoever is behind this has an ironic turn of mind. Writing about the downfall of Hunter Marks was Lea Roberts's ticket out of Oakwood. Exposing the true identity of Jared Slade could give another big boost to her career."

"But she didn't come in person to the hotel. She sent Rory Gibbs," Tracker mused.

"Lucky for me."

"Maybe she didn't want to be anywhere near the hotel in case the bomb went off. I'll find out where Lea Roberts was when the incidents in New York and Atlanta occurred. I'm also still checking the whereabouts and phone records of Denise Martin, Michael Banks and Alex Santos for those dates." Tracker paused and leaned back in his chair. "One more question—though I hate to ask. Could someone in your family be behind this?"

Hunter shook his head. "No. They don't know who I've become. Hunter Marks has been dead to them for a long time."

Tracker sighed. "This would be a lot easier if you told me everything."

Hunter avoided that topic and instead said, "There's another question—one you haven't asked," Hunter said. "Is Rory Gibbs a pawn or is she involved right up to her pretty little neck?"

Tracker met his eyes. "I figure that's an answer you've decided to get for yourself."

RORY STARED DOWN at the array of clothes that McGee had delivered to her room.

"Just a few things Mr. Hunter wanted you to have since you didn't have time to pack," McGee had said.

Hunter had said that he'd get her some clothes, but…she hadn't expected him to send McGee shopping at a nearby mall. She'd seen the names of the stores on the boxes— high-end places that she wouldn't have the courage even to walk into.

No, scratch that, she thought as she reached out to finger the lace on an oyster-white camisole. This had come from Silken Fantasies, and she'd been in that shop—at least in the flagship store. A smile curved the corners of her mouth. That had been her lucky day. Would any of this have happened if she hadn't ducked into that store to escape the Terminator? Or if she hadn't tried on that red bra and thong?

Rory pressed a hand to her stomach, then lowered it to where the red triangle fit snugly beneath her jeans. When she'd returned to her room to shower, she'd put it on again for luck.

She let her gaze sweep the room. During the course of the afternoon, McGee had delivered more than clothes. A laptop computer sat on an antique mahogany desk. She also had Internet access and a printer. Plus, McGee had informed her she had an appointment to meet with Mr. Hunter at five o'clock for the first part of the interview. Hunter had even sent up a little schedule of the evening's events: *Interview—5–6; Dinner—7–8; Interview Cont'd—8–10.*

She had to hand it to him. Hunter was a ruthlessly organized man. A quick glance at her watch told her that she still had half an hour to prepare for the interview. And that was what she should be doing rather than gazing at a wardrobe fit for royalty.

With a sigh, she ran a hand down a silky red sundress. Next to it was a pair of matching sandals. The ivory-colored suit was pretty, too—slim-legged pants with a short double-breasted jacket and tank top. There were strappy sandals to match that outfit, too. There was even a strand of pearls with matching earrings. Unable to help herself, she picked up the earrings and put them in her ears. She moved to the mirror and smiled at the way the small pearls dangled from thin gold chains. Then she walked back to the bed. Looking at the clothes, she felt a little like Julia Roberts in *Pretty Woman*—way out of her league.

Then her gaze fell on the last thing that McGee had unpacked and set on the bed—a small brown bag filled with bubble gum. Her heart did a slow tumble in her chest just as it had when she'd first peeked inside.

Hunter had asked McGee to bring her bubble gum. She picked up the bag and held it close.

HUNTER LOST TRACK of the time as he stood there in the open doorway watching her. But when she lifted the bag of bubble gum and clutched it to her chest, the doubts seemed to slip away again. True, he'd been led down the garden path by a woman reporter when he was nineteen. But he wasn't a naive nineteen-year-old anymore, and Rory wasn't Lea Roberts.

Still, he wasn't so sure that he fully trusted his instincts where she was concerned. From the first moment he'd seen her in that lobby, she'd clouded both his senses and his mind.

But she wasn't sleeping with him to get a story. Hadn't she made that clear? And he noted with a slight frown that she was wearing the faded jeans and T-shirt she'd arrived in that morning. Plus, she was barefoot.

"You don't like the clothes?" he asked.

She whirled to face him and he watched the heat rise in her cheeks.

"I didn't hear you come in."

"You're not wearing any of them."

"They're beautiful. They're just not me."

No, she wouldn't think they were right for her. Hunter tamped down on a quick spurt of anger. It wasn't the first time that he would have liked to get his hands on her four ex-boyfriends.

"What kind of clothes *are* you?" he asked.

She glanced down at what she was wearing. "Blue jeans, T-shirts. When I get dressed up, I usually go for modern and funky things that make a statement—rather than classic and elegant."

He moved closer to the bed. "You don't see yourself as elegant?"

"I'm barely five foot two. Elegant is more like my sisters."

He frowned. "Why are you always comparing yourself to them?"

She raised her eyebrows. "Do you have any siblings?"

He thought of his brother. "Point taken."

"Did your parents favor your sisters?" he asked. Then he wondered how in the world the question had popped out. Until his recent conversation with Tracker McBride, he hadn't let himself think about his family in years.

"No. They were great. My dad especially was always pointing out my talents to me and encouraging me to nurture them." She shrugged. "He did that with all of us. Natalie inherited my father's knack for cracking safes and his gift for disguise. Sierra got his brains."

"What did you inherit?"

"I just got his luck."

"Don't knock luck. I'll take it any day in a pinch." He reached out and brushed a finger against her earring. "Some people see pearls as elegant. I'm glad that you're wearing them."

"I couldn't resist. But I'm going to give them back. And you should be able to get your money back for the dresses. We're hardly going to need them. I'm going to be interviewing you here. It's not like we're dating or anything."

He regarded her steadily. "We're not dating?"

"No…we're…that is, I'm…I'm interviewing you, and that's business. And in an entirely separate arrangement, we're also enjoying a temporary, mutually enjoyable… adult relationship." She paused to frown a bit. "Not that I'm trying to put words in your mouth when I say it's mutually enjoyable."

"Not at all. In fact, you took the words right out of my mouth." The nerves and concern in her eyes had him reaching out to place a hand on her cheek. "Did you think I had the clothes delivered as a sort of payment for sexual favors?"

"No. That's not…I really didn't." She paused to gather her thoughts. "I didn't mean to imply that at all. It's just that they're clearly expensive and unnecessary. And if I don't wear them, you can get your money back."

He'd never met a woman quite like her, Hunter decided. Studying her for a moment, he wondered what tack to take. Finally, he said, "Why don't you think of them as costumes?"

"Costumes?"

"You did say that you wanted to experiment a bit at being in control? Dresses, jewelry, shoes—aren't they just part of the arsenal a woman uses to seduce a man?"

Rory glanced down at the clothes. "I suppose."

"I've always found that elegant can be quite sexy."

She met his eyes then. "Really?"

"Uh-huh. Right now, I'm picturing you sitting across the table from me in the main dining room wearing that red dress. McGee is serving us, and all I'm thinking of is how quickly I can get you out of it."

She glanced at the dress and back at him. "I don't think it would pose much of a problem."

"And I'll be wondering if you're wearing the red thong underneath it. Or nothing at all."

He could see her bite back a grin, but all she said was, "For a man so successful in business, all you think about is sex."

He flicked the pearl dangling from her ear again. "In the right company, it's pretty much all I can manage. Right now, I'm imagining you wearing nothing but pearls."

She took a step back from him, but she was smiling now, and he sensed that the battle had been won.

"All right, I'll wear them."

"Good." He gave her a satisfied nod.

She cocked her head at him. "You're one smooth negotiator, aren't you?"

"I do my best."

"Well…" She glanced at the bed. "Before I fulfill any of your adolescent fantasies, we're going to start that interview—and we're going to do it in the downstairs office."

"Damn," he said amiably as he led the way out of the room. "If I were really a smooth negotiator, I would have convinced you to postpone the interview, and we'd be doing something much more interesting on that bed."

Her laughter filled the air as they walked companionably down the stairs together.

RORY BLEW A BUBBLE as she studied the sheets of paper—three in all—that Hunter had handed her the moment that they'd entered the office. They reminded her of Sierra's note cards. Everything was perfectly clear, concise and prioritized with numbers. Nerves had knotted in her stomach the moment she'd seen them. She should have anticipated that he'd be fully prepared for the interview. For a moment, she allowed herself to feel a pang of envy. He was as organized as her sisters, maybe more so. Then she remembered what he'd said about not comparing herself to others, and she blew another bubble.

She could handle this interview. So what if she didn't have three pages of questions or a clue as to what angle to take yet? She'd find it.

"You should find everything you need right there," Hunter said.

The papers she held contained a brief profile of Mark Hunter, along with a résumé. Donald Trump would probably find the information impressive. But as she skimmed through it, Rory discovered that it gave very little away about the man she'd talked to at the pool or in the tree house.

Finally, on the third page, something caught her eye. He'd lost his entire family—his parents and a brother—when he was barely nineteen. A tight band settled around her heart as she glanced up at him. "I'm so sorry. That must have been horrible—to lose your whole family when you were so young. My sisters and I were orphaned when we were twenty, but we still had each other. Did you have any other relatives?"

"No," Hunter said.

When he didn't elaborate, she asked, "How on earth did you manage?"

"I don't see how that's pertinent."

"It's part of what made you who you are."

"I'd rather stick to what's on those papers."

Rory didn't doubt for a moment that he'd have preferred to control the interview just as much as he wanted to manage what she wore and what they did when they made love. She was going to have to find a way to change that, so she took a moment to study him.

He looked confident and thoroughly at ease, his hands folded in front of him on the desk. This was a man who'd be perfectly at home in a boardroom. But behind that facade was someone who'd also be perfectly at home in a street fight. Hunter was both those men. Even now, there was a leashed energy radiating from him that hadn't been acquired in an Ivy League school. And there was no explanation for that on the three sheets he'd given her.

What was it going to take to get him to open up to her? And what was it going to take to get him to hand over control later tonight when they made love again?

She skimmed through the information again. He'd attended Harvard and he'd played polo—so there must have been money or connections. Looking up at the wall behind his head, she spotted something she'd noticed when he'd first ushered her into the room. "Harvard. Lucas Wainwright graduated from Harvard, too. Is that where you met him?"

There was just the slightest hesitation before he said, "Yes. We were classmates."

She rose and moved closer to the photo. "Which one are you?"

"I'm not in it. I dropped out right after my parents died. You're very observant."

Her brows shot up. "I wouldn't make a very good reporter if I weren't. Why did you drop out?"

"Financial reasons."

A partial truth, she decided as she studied him. "I wanted so much to drop out of college after my parents passed away, but my sisters wouldn't hear of it. I started to call them the school police."

"What would you have done if your sisters hadn't pressured you to stay in school?"

Rory moved to perch on the edge of the chair again. "I would have traveled. Is that what you did?"

"A bit."

"Where?"

"Here and there. Everything that's pertinent to my work at Slade Enterprises is right there on those papers."

And everything else is a big secret, Rory thought. Well, she'd always been fascinated by secrets. But the man sitting in front of her didn't look to be someone who would part with them easily. She skimmed down his work history and blew another bubble. What she needed was a question that would take him off guard and make him open up.

"You're nervous," he said as she licked the bubble gum back into her mouth.

"A little," she said. "I want to do this right, and you're not cooperating."

He gestured to the papers. "I've laid everything out for you. You should be able to write a good article from that."

She set the sheets on the desk. "It's not that this won't be helpful, but the problem is this tells me only about your success in business."

He raised his eyebrows. "I'm a businessman. I thought that would be the angle you'd take."

She smiled at him. "Have you ever read *Celebs?*"

He shook his head. "No, I can't say that I have. But I've seen it on the newsstands."

"You should be able to tell by the headlines and the cover pictures that it's not the *New York Times* or the *Wall Street Journal.* The people who read it are looking for the story behind the story."

"Gossip?"

She laughed. "It's number two on the list right after love for making the world go round. But we're a cut above the tabloids. And we prefer to say that we take a more personal slant on a celebrity's life."

Hunter frowned a little. "What if I told you that my work is the whole story?"

She shook her head as she moved forward to sit on the very edge of her chair. "It's not. Oh, it explains part of who you are—the person who went to Harvard for a year and got snapped up by Jared Slade when he was just building his business. But that's just the tip of the iceberg. When I look at you right now, that's what I see, just the surface stuff—a very self-contained man who prefers to be in control, someone who weighs every decision he makes very carefully." She lifted the papers and set them on the edge of his desk. "I'm really not going to be able to use much of what you've given me here."

Hunter studied her for a moment. "Just what is it that you're after?"

She met his eyes steadily. "The secrets. What lies below the surface. I want to know why you dropped out of Harvard, what you did after that. I want to know what kind of books you read, what kind of sports you play besides polo, what it's like to work for a man like Jared Slade." Acting on instinct, she decided that she might as well go for broke. "I want to know if Jared Slade really exists and why someone set a bomb off in his suite at Les Printemps."

9

CAREFULLY MASKING HIS SURPRISE, Hunter studied Rory. He hadn't expected either question, and she'd fired them off like a pro. That should have bothered him. Instead, he couldn't help but admire her technique. Clearly, this wasn't going the way he'd planned, but that seemed to be par for the course with Rory Gibbs. Was her unpredictability why she fascinated him so?

She'd been in almost constant motion from the moment that he'd led her into the room. She'd fidgeted her way through the papers he'd prepared for her, blowing bubbles and tapping her feet. Even now, she was perched on the edge of her chair like a butterfly that might take flight at any moment. Was that why he was constantly tempted to reach out and grab her? For a moment, he let himself imagine what it might be like to do just that—to pull her across the desk and onto his lap.

"Well?" she asked. "Who wants to hurt Jared Slade?" Then she frowned. "Or is it you they want to hurt?"

"Me?" Startled by the question, he narrowed his eyes. But it wasn't just curiosity he saw in hers. No, it was a flood of concern, and he couldn't help but be moved by it. "Why would you think someone would want to hurt me?"

She waved a hand. "Because you're here, isolated."

"I'm enjoying Lucas Wainwright's hospitality while I finish up the business that brought Jared Slade to D.C. That's all. Why do you think that my boss doesn't exist?"

Leaning back in the chair, she rested her elbows on the arms and steepled her fingers. "I have this theory that he's just a figurehead like Betty Crocker, and that people like you really run his businesses."

Hunter smiled and hoped that it reached his eyes. "Jared Slade is every bit as real as I am." Her mind was as sharp as a razor, and if he wasn't careful…

"Why all the secrecy then?" she asked.

Hunter met her eyes very steadily. He couldn't recall the last time anyone had made him feel as if he were walking along the edge of a cliff. "Mr. Slade prefers his privacy."

She tapped her fingers on one arm of the chair. "He's hiding something, isn't he? And it must have something to do with the person who planted the bomb."

Hunter raised both hands and made a T. "Time out. I agreed to give you an interview, but I'm not at liberty to discuss Mr. Slade, and there won't be any mention of the bomb in your article."

"Okay." Rory moved to the edge of her chair again. "Why don't we just get back to those questions that I originally asked? Why did you drop out of Harvard and what did you do in those five years before you joined Slade Enterprises?"

Hunter couldn't help but admire the way she'd manipulated him. She wouldn't press on the bomb issue if he answered the more personal questions. She was good. He should have foreseen that and prepared for it. The information on the three sheets he'd given her would check out, but if she wanted personal information on Mark Hunter, he would have to create it out of whole cloth. It wouldn't be the first time that he'd created a personal background story for himself. But he'd never before done it off the cuff and for a reporter.

Was it the fact that she posed a risk for him that intrigued him? If he could figure out exactly why she appealed to him so, he could control it.

"I won't promise to answer every question you ask," he said finally.

"Fair enough."

"And I want to read the story before you send it to your boss."

"You want to censor it?"

He shrugged. "Take it or leave it."

"Are you going to answer the questions that I've posed so far?"

"I think I can agree to that."

"Then you've got a deal." Rory plucked a pen out of a container on the desk and turned over the three sheets of paper. Then she edged her chair closer to the desk.

"One other stipulation," Hunter said. "For every question you ask, I get to ask you one."

Surprise flooded into her eyes. "Why?"

"I'm curious about Rory Gibbs."

She shrugged. "Okay. Sure." Then she shot him a quick grin. "But if you write it up and decide to sell it, I get to okay it first."

He couldn't help smiling back. "You've got a deal."

"Okay. Tell me about Mark Hunter."

"That's not a question."

"Okay. First, what made you drop out of Harvard?"

"I already told you that I dropped out of Harvard for financial reasons."

"You couldn't afford to go there after your parents died?"

"That was part of it."

She waited, tapping her pen on the desk.

Hunter thought of several stories he could make up, but he'd learned a long time ago that when you were lying through your teeth, it was better to stick as closely as possible to the truth. "I wanted a change, a new start." That was partially true. By the time his family had laid out the little scenario they'd wanted him to play a part in, he'd very much wanted a whole new life as far away from the Marks family as he could get.

"So you were running away from your old life?" Rory asked.

"I'd rather look at it as running toward a new one."

"Why did you need a new life?"

"Isn't it my turn for a question?" Hunter asked.

Rory shook her head. "You have to finish answering this one first. Why did you need a new start?"

Persistence was something else about her he had to admire. Because he hadn't prepared the answer, Hunter chose his words carefully. "My family always thought of me as a black sheep. My older brother was one of those people who did everything right. Since in my parents' eyes, I never quite measured up to him, I fell into a habit of proving to everyone that I never would." He paused with a frown. "I'm not sure I'm explaining it right."

"You're explaining it perfectly. I had the same problem with my sisters. After my father left, I even went through a period when I thought it was my fault that our father had left us. So I started—I think the term the school psychologist used was *acting out*. Basically, I skipped classes at school and got into fights."

Hunter studied her. She spoke so matter-of-factly about her insecurities. He wanted to change that. "So you thought of yourself as a black sheep, too?"

She shot him a smile. "I thought of myself more as an ugly duckling."

"You're not ugly at all," he said impatiently. "The first time I saw you, I thought you were incredibly cute."

Rory snorted. "Cute? You mean like a puppy?"

This time Hunter pushed down the impatience. "A cute lady wearing sexy red boots and a cap. The contrast intrigued me. And when I saw you again in Silken Fantasies, I thought you were some kind of sex goddess."

"Really?"

Hunter raised a brow. "I've never followed another woman into a dressing room and made love to her. I had no business doing that with you. I don't have any business wanting you right now. But I can't seem to stop myself. Every time I look at you, there seems to be a total disparity between what I know I should do and what I want to do."

She was listening to him now, really listening. He could tell by the way her eyes had become totally focused on his.

"A few minutes ago, I wanted to reach across this desk and drag you onto my lap. Then I would have kissed you and touched you until you could think of nothing but how it feels when I make you come."

Her pulse was fluttering at her throat. Hunter wanted to taste her right there, but he wanted something else even more. "Promise me something."

"What?" Rory asked.

"When you dress for dinner tonight, put on that red

dress and the pearls. Then you take a good look at your-self in the mirror and think *princess*."

She snorted. "Princess?"

"No. I mean it. And see if I'm not right."

Rory's eyes narrowed. "You're trying to build up my self-confidence."

"You don't do enough of that for yourself. So what if you're different from your sisters? You have your own unique qualities. You need to believe in them more and push them to work to your advantage."

Rory blinked. "That's what my father advised me to do. Is that what you did to compete with your brother?"

Hunter frowned as she scribbled something on a sheet of paper. "No."

Rory glanced up, then reached out to lay a hand over his. "I'm sorry. Of course, you couldn't do that. There wouldn't have been time, not when he was snatched away so suddenly."

Hunter saw the quick rush of sympathy in her eyes and felt it in her touch. Once again, he was moved by her concern. They'd both lost family, he realized. He wasn't even fully aware that he'd turned over his hand and linked his fingers with hers, but suddenly, he was tempted to tell her what had really happened that summer when he was nineteen. Not the edited version he'd given Tracker, but the real story.

He couldn't afford to do that, he reminded himself. Rory Gibbs was a reporter. If he told her the real story, she would be that much more likely to connect the dots between Mark Hunter and Hunter Marks.

Still, it bothered him that she felt bad about something he'd fabricated.

"I never should have asked that question," Rory said. "It

was clumsy of me. I'm sorry. I'm a beginner at this interviewing thing."

"For a beginner, you're very good at it," Hunter said. She'd only begun and she'd already steered him in directions he'd didn't want to go.

"Thanks. I've never done anything this important before."

"And your question was a good one. I was too hasty in saying no." Releasing her hand, he leaned back in his chair. "Before the…accident, I was acting out, too—drinking, coming home late, letting my grades slip. After I reached a certain age, I gave up on competing with my older brother." It hadn't done any good. Sports had been an area where he could outshine Carter, but his parents had always gone to Carter's games and not his. Carter Marks III had been born with a silver spoon in his mouth, and he'd been raised to take over the family business. Hunter's mother had made it clear to him that the only reason he'd been conceived was that she was hoping for a daughter.

"What happened after the accident?" Rory asked.

Hunter gathered his thoughts. It had been years since he'd allowed himself to remember this part of his life. "I wanted to create a new life and prove to myself that I could be better than anyone could have dreamed." Even as he spoke the words, Hunter realized that there was a lot of truth in them. Beneath the anger and disillusionment, he'd been driven by a desire to prove something to himself. And to his family.

"How did you go about doing that?"

Hunter narrowed his eyes. "Oh, no, you don't. It's definitely my turn for a question…or two or three."

Rory wrinkled her nose. "You can't blame a girl for trying." Then she leaned back in her chair. "What do you want to know?"

Are you wearing the red thong? That was the question that popped into Hunter's mind and he barely kept it from popping out of his mouth. He had an agenda here, too, he reminded himself—and he'd better stick to it. "Tell me about your boss at *Celebs* and what it's like to work for him or her."

Rory grinned. "That's not a question."

He nodded. "Okay. Who is your boss, and what is it like to work for him or her?"

"It's a her. Lea Roberts." Rory's fingers tightened on the pen she was holding and she chewed on her bubble gum.

"She makes you nervous."

"A little. She's very good at what she does. I was lucky to be assigned to her. She's demanding. But she's been very encouraging. Most of the time."

"She can't be happy that you gave me the pictures."

Heat stained her cheeks. "Well, I didn't tell her about that. When I ran into her at the Blue Pepper yesterday, I lied and told her they were in my apartment and I'd get them to her today. I'm hoping that when I turn in this interview, she'll overlook the fact that I had to buy it with the pictures."

For a moment, Hunter said nothing. His mind was too busy sorting through possibilities. Lea Roberts had thought that the pictures were in Rory's apartment. Was she behind the break-in? And why was she using Rory? Had she known about the bomb ahead of time? Was Tracker right about that being the reason why she hadn't come herself to Les Printemps?

"My turn again," Rory said. "I want to know how you spent the five years between leaving Harvard and taking a job with Slade Enterprises."

Hunter dragged his thoughts back to the question. For this part he was on much safer ground. He could stick close to the truth because he'd used several different names, and none of them could be connected with Hunter Marks or Mark Hunter. Leaning back in his chair, he said, "The first job I took was with a cruise line. I started out in the kitchen and ended up dealing blackjack in the casino."

"Really? I'm so jealous. How did you get the job? What was it like?" Rory rattled off the questions as she reached for the sheets of paper. "Tell me everything."

For the next two hours, Hunter found himself doing just that.

RORY CHECKED THE BEDROOM one last time. McGee had provided the candles, and they flickered on the nightstand and dresser. But it had been Hunter who'd sent up the champagne. That probably meant that he had a plan, too.

Well, she'd just have to figure out a way to handle him. She had during the interview.

The whole dinner was a blur. McGee had served it on the patio, and she'd worn the red dress and the pearls. Hunter hadn't taken his eyes off her once. She couldn't even remember what she'd eaten or what they'd talked about.

Rory stopped at the window and looked at the last streaks of color in the western sky. She was waiting for her lover to come to her. Two phone calls. That's what he'd said he had to make before he joined her.

Turning, she glanced around the room again. Everything was in place—the red thong was on the nightstand next to the champagne. Moving to the full-length mirror on the closet door, she checked herself one more time. She was wearing the lace chemise that McGee had brought to the room that afternoon. The thin creamy color was a perfect match for the pearls. Raising a hand, she fingered the double strand of small, perfectly shaped beads at her throat.

She'd done just as Hunter had suggested before she'd gone down to the dining room. She'd stood here looking at her image and thinking *princess*. Cool, confident. Grace Kelly. Diana. But as she studied herself in the mirror now, she felt more like the princess Audrey Hepburn had played in *Roman Holiday*—not quite sure of herself, still sort of experimenting with life and prone to making mistakes.

Lifting her chin, she straightened her shoulders and reminded herself that Audrey Hepburn managed to carry everything off at the end of the movie. Rory Gibbs would, too. Tonight might be her last night with Hunter.

So she was just going to push her luck to the limit. And if she didn't quite pull it off? Well, there just wasn't a downside to making love with the Terminator.

Now, where was he?

THROUGH THE FRENCH DOORS in Lucas Wainwright's office, Hunter looked at the darkening sky. Night was falling and he was here waiting for Tracker's call when he wanted to be upstairs with Rory. This might be the only night that he could spend with her.

He'd had McGee take up the champagne. And he'd planned all during dinner exactly how he was going to seduce her. Once Tracker had a line on who was behind the threats, he would return to Dallas and he wouldn't see Rory again, so he wanted to make the most of what could be their only night together. Something tightened around his heart.

Recognizing the feeling, Hunter lifted his hand to rub his

chest and frowned. Loss. He hadn't allowed himself to feel that in years. If you didn't allow yourself to get too attached to something or someone, loss was never an issue. Hell, he'd only known her—what? Less than forty-eight hours. And he was going to miss her. He missed her right now.

When the phone rang, Hunter picked it up. "Yeah?"

"We picked someone up in the Keys," Tracker said.

"Who?"

"A guy by the name of Robert Saldano. He has a fairly extensive rap sheet with the Miami police, mostly assault. He was indicted once for murder, but it didn't stick. He claims he doesn't know who hired him."

"Any chance he's telling the truth?" Hunter asked.

"Sure, if you believe pigs fly. But he's a pro and he's not likely to give away a name."

"Lea Roberts may have broken in to Rory's apartment," Hunter said and then filled Tracker in on what Rory had told him. "If she did break in, she's not going to be happy that she didn't find the film."

"Somebody's not going to be happy that Robert Saldano didn't finish his job in the Keys. We make enough people unhappy and someone might get careless."

"Have you turned up anything on Denise, Alex or Michael?" Hunter asked.

"Not yet. Tomorrow, I'm going to fly into Oakwood and see if I can find some kind of connection between one of them and your hometown."

"I'd like to come with you," Hunter said. Then he was stunned that he'd not only said the words, but that he'd meant them. When he'd left Oakwood, he'd vowed to himself that he'd never return.

"No. You stay right where you are. That was our deal."

"Yeah." That *was* the deal. What had come over him that he would even think of going back there?

"And keep Rory with you. I don't like the idea that Lea Roberts might have broken in to her apartment."

"I don't like it much myself."

"I'll check in as soon as I have news," Tracker said and ended the call.

Hunter hung up his receiver slowly. He hadn't been back to Oakwood since he'd left on that Christmas eve ten years ago. Not once had he ever thought of seeing his family again. He hadn't wanted to. Had revisiting his past with Rory today changed all that?

Hunter gazed out the window again. The sky was dark gray now, and he could see several stars and a thin sliver of moon. The problem with digging up the past and looking at it was that at twenty-nine you were bound to have a slightly different perspective than you did at nineteen.

Objectively speaking, his mother and the other board members had come up with a solution to the embezzlement problem that had minimized the effect on Marks Banking and Investments and the town. His services as a scapegoat had saved the company. From a business standpoint, he could even admire the scenario that his mother had created. But none of that changed the way he felt about what they'd done to him.

And he was wasting time thinking about the past when Rory was waiting for him. There were so many things he wanted to show her, and this might be his only chance. Turning, he strode from the room and climbed the stairs.

10

THE DOOR TO HER ROOM was closed, so Hunter knocked.

"Come in."

The room was dark except for the candles that burned on every surface and the moonlight that flowed into the room through the open balcony doors. But the moment he looked at her, his senses were swamped. Music—something soft and bluesy—thrummed, and he smelled the citrus scent of the candles, but those sensations were muted. What overwhelmed him was her.

She stood halfway between the balcony and the bed wearing nothing but pearls and a swatch of creamy-colored lace. He felt his breath back up in his lungs and begin to burn. Bathed in moonlight, she made him think of a porcelain statue. Fragile and untouchable. But she was very much alive. Even now, he could tell that every muscle in her body was tensed for movement. And the fear shot through him that if he moved toward her she might take flight like some will-o'-the-wisp, and he would never find her again.

Nonsense, he told himself as he drew close. He knew she was real, and he knew how her flesh would heat when he touched her and tasted her. He knew how that body would come to life beneath his. Even as the thoughts swirled through his mind, desire sharpened inside of him until it turned into a deep, aching need.

He took one step, and she raised a hand. "I have a plan."

He didn't stop moving toward her. He wasn't sure he could. "A plan?" His had nearly evaporated the moment he'd seen her. The long, slow seduction he'd mapped out during dinner was threatening to disappear somewhere in the mist that was now fogging his brain.

"Well, maybe not a plan." She clasped her hands together and twisted her fingers. "Exactly. I didn't write it out. It's more some things that I'd like to try out."

He freed one of her hands and raised it to his lips. "So it's flexible?" With his other hand, he traced his finger along the edge of the silk that rode over her breasts.

"I guess you could say that. But we did agree that you would give up control."

He trailed a finger down to where her nipples had hardened into dark berries beneath the thin lace of the chemise. "We did. But we didn't say when. And I have a plan, too. Don't you want to know what it is?"

She grabbed his wrist with her free hand. "No. I mean, yes. Eventually. It's not that I think it wouldn't be enjoyable. Because I do. You're the most incredible lover I've ever had."

He leaned down and brushed his lips over hers. "A point in my favor. My plan starts with champagne."

"So does mine." Rory concentrated very hard. His mouth was so close, so tempting. Already her bones were melting.

"Plus, I think I still need some more practice on slowing down my wham-bam technique. Why don't I show you?"

"I—umm." She broke off when his lips brushed against

hers again. It took all her concentration to focus on her plan and to take two steps back from him. "I know that you want to make love to me, and I want you to. But…" She paused for a moment to search for the right words. They never came easily to her when he was this close. "I know that you like to be in control. But I just want to return the favor."

He held out a hand. "It isn't necessary. Do you have any idea of how much pleasure you give me each time you come in my arms?"

"No," she replied, shaking her head. "That's just it. I don't. And I want to. I've never had a lover like you. I don't think I ever will again. I'd also like to know what you're feeling when you make me come. I want to experience that kind of power. Just once. Is that so hard to understand?"

"No."

Rory drew in a breath and let it out. "Then you'll let me do whatever I want to you?"

The corners of his mouth twitched. "You want me to agree to that without any more information?"

"Yes."

"If you worked for Slade Enterprises, you'd have to submit a three-page proposal."

She felt some of her tension ease. He was going to go along with her. "But I don't work for Slade Enterprises."

Hunter's eyes narrowed. "Maybe you should. You're a pretty good negotiator."

She smiled then as a little thrill moved through her. "Thanks. Shall we get started?"

"It's a shame to waste that champagne."

She led the way to the bed and climbed onto it. "Who says we're going to waste it? But first, you have to take off your clothes."

HUNTER STUDIED HER as he began to unbutton his shirt. The idea of being seduced by her was appealing. But even if it hadn't been, he wouldn't have been able to resist her argument. She wanted to experience a feeling of power, and what better way could he help her gain more self-confidence than to let her experience that? At least for a short amount of time. Years in business had taught him that there was more than one way to negotiate a deal. So he'd merely take another tack.

Keeping his eyes on hers, he shrugged out of the shirt and dropped it to the floor. Then he tackled his belt. Her eyes shifted to watch just what his hands were doing as he unfastened the button of his slacks. "What if I can convince you to let me take over?"

"Take over?" She was still watching as he slowly pulled down his zipper. Then he eased his slacks down over his hips and let them drop to the floor.

"Okay?" he asked.

"No. You're not going to convince me. And you still have too many clothes on."

"Why don't you help me get them off?"

She shook her head, but her eyes never left the spot where his penis was pressing against his briefs. "You do it."

Obligingly, he slipped his fingers beneath the waistband, pushed his briefs to the floor and then he clasped his shaft in his hand. "You can have this right now, if you want."

"I'm going to touch it in a minute." Her voice was husky, but she didn't move. "First, lie down on the bed."

"You'd like what I have in mind," he said as he moved toward the bed, then climbed onto the mattress. He still held his erection in his hand, and he was so close that she could reach out and touch it.

She didn't. But he saw the effort it took for her to tear

her gaze away from it, and this close, he could see the rapid rise and fall of her chest. "You want to touch it," he said.

"Oh, yeah." The words were expelled on a breath. But she merely clasped her hands more tightly together.

Suddenly, he wanted those hands on him. He wanted to feel her fingers gripping him, pumping him. "Touch me."

She met his eyes and he could feel himself sinking into those deep, warm golden pools. "You have to lie down first."

He did because the teasing he was doing was backfiring. He wanted her hands on him. Now. Then he'd convince her to let him take over.

"Give me your hands," she said.

He saw that she was holding the red thong.

"If you want me to touch you, you have to give me your hands."

The moment he did, she captured both of his wrists in the lacy straps and then drew them over his head and tied them to the headboard.

"What are you doing?"

"Something I wanted to try." She shrugged. "You could get yourself loose, but I want you to pretend that you can't, that you're my captive."

Hunter frowned. "Why would I do that?"

"For several reasons," she said as she threw one leg over him to straddle him at his waist. "First, because you've agreed to let me be in control—at least until you convince me otherwise. Second, because you're going to like what I'm going to do to you. If you don't, you can just suggest an alternative. Third, because if you touch me while I'm touching you, we'll both be distracted, and I want you to just feel. Fourth, because if you lose control, you can get yourself free. Fifth, because—"

"I don't lose control," Hunter said.

"Shh," she said, leaning down to brush her lips over his. "I know. It's going to be all right." She ran her hands experimentally down his chest. "Just relax."

Relax? It was hardly an option when her fingers were running so softly over his skin, leaving little ripples of static electricity in their wake. "You're not touching me where I want you to."

"Soon." She wiggled up his body to brush her lips against his again. He tried to capture them. If he could kiss her, really kiss her, he could convince her to put an end to this game. But she wiggled out of reach of his mouth.

This time, as she slid down his body, the shock wave of heat nearly melted his bones. He could feel exactly how hot and wet she was. When he caught his breath, he said, "You're not wearing any panties."

"No. I needed my thong for something else tonight."

She moved again to reach for the bottle of champagne, and the dampness of her heat sent another shot of fire through him. His hips rose off the bed of their own accord. "Move lower. I want to be inside of you."

Rory tipped champagne into a glass. "I thought you wanted me to touch you first."

"I did, but—" His thought was cut off when he felt the icy drops of champagne on his face, his lips, his neck. "What are you doing?"

"I'm going to find out what you taste like mixed with champagne."

"That was my plan."

"Too bad." She used her tongue on his forehead, his eyelids and cheeks, then lingered at his lips to trace the fullness from one corner of his mouth to the other. The little

tremors that rippled over his skin sent explosions of pleasure rocketing through him.

"Rory—" When she used her teeth on his shoulder and
shifted lower on his body, he lost the rest of the sentence.
Each lick of her tongue, each scrape of her teeth created
sensations so sharp, so intense that they left no room for
thought.

And the heat. It wasn't just the fiery dampness of her
tongue—it was that hot, moist heat at her center, pressing,
and then sliding over his skin as she shimmied lower. It
seared him until he was sure his body would melt and
merge into hers.

He sucked in a breath when she sprinkled icy pellets of
champagne over his chest, and the throaty sound of her
laugh made his blood begin to pound.

He could stop her. He could easily twist his hands free.
Then he could grab her, lift her and pierce her. She would
take him in and tighten around him like a tight wet fist. But
he couldn't seem to move.

"I want—"

"I know what you want." Her hand closed around him
for one second. "But I'm not through tasting you yet.
Mmm. Your flavor is even better here," she murmured as
she closed her teeth around one nipple.

"Rory—" He moaned her name as she flicked her
tongue hard into his navel.

"Delicious. But I'm not sure which flavor I like best. Let
me see…" She moved up to brush her lips over his. "There
are so many flavors in your mouth—dark and forbidden—
better than the best chocolate I've ever had." She slid her
tongue along his. "When you kiss me, I can never seem to
get enough."

He couldn't, either. He'd felt hunger for a woman before, but not like this. And he wasn't sure how much longer he could wait for more. Her mouth was only inches from his. He could free his hands now and put an end to the torture. But his arms felt weak. No woman had ever made him feel weak before.

She tangled her tongue with his again, then said, "Before I decide if I like your mouth best, there's a part of you that I haven't sampled yet. I wouldn't want to rush to judgment."

Her breath against his lips along with the image that was forming in his mind set his body aflame.

"First, I'm going to sample some of this champagne."

He watched her sip from the bottle, replace it on the table. Then as if she were moving in slow motion, she shifted so that she was straddling his legs.

He waited, watching her through narrowed eyes as she closed her hands around him and lowered her head. The first lick of her tongue on the tip of his shaft had him moaning her name. It was cold from the champagne and the shock sent a shudder moving through him. Then she licked him again…and again.

"Rory—" He barely recognized the raspy sound of his own voice. He couldn't for the life of him figure out what he wanted to say. Did he want her to stop? To go on? Each lick of her tongue as she moved her mouth lower and lower on his shaft sent a knife-sharp arrow of pleasure shooting through his system. She was devouring him as if he were some treat she'd been starving for. The sensations were agonizing. Incredible. He closed his fingers around the posts of the bed and held on tightly. Then when he was sure he couldn't take it anymore, she took him into her mouth.

"Mmm."

The soft murmurs of pleasure she made vibrated

through him and drummed their way into his brain. His heart was beating so fast that he was sure it would burst through his chest.

Her mouth was hot now, almost as hot as the fire raging inside of him. Each time she moved those lips down and then up, she pulled one emotion after another from him—things that he'd buried deep. And he was powerless to stop her.

His climax was building. He could feel it the same way he could feel a storm building when thunder rumbled and lightning flashed. No one had ever made him feel helpless like this. The sensation shuddered through his stomach and burned through his brain. He shouldn't, he couldn't let her do this to him.

Twisting his hands free, he reached for her and pulled her on top of him. The moment he entered her, it was too late to regain control. The storm that she'd been building inside of him from the moment that he'd walked into the room suddenly broke free, and he began to move inside her, matching her rhythm until with one last thrust, he gave himself to her.

RORY COULDN'T HAVE NAMED the feelings swirling through her when Hunter finally drew her to him. Should she have known that making love to a man like that would bring such a variety of pleasures? Should she not have been amazed that a sigh could make her burn or that the raspy sound of her name on Hunter's lips could make her almost forget what she was doing?

Each time she'd touched him, each time she'd tasted him, the thrill of his response had only increased her hunger for him. Even now, his scent tantalized her, and the damp heat of his flesh beckoned to her. There were flavors that she hadn't discovered yet. She was sure of it.

When she angled her head and licked his neck, he tightened his hold on her. "Give me…a moment."

She could do that. His heart still thundered under hers, and he was holding her as if he never intended to let her go. That brought its own very separate kind of feeling. Because he would go. They'd laid the ground rules.

Even as a little pang of loss stung her heart, she pushed the thought out of her mind. She wasn't going to think of what it would be like not to have him like this. Not to be able to touch him or taste him again.

"That was…incredible."

He was still short of breath. How amazing to learn that making a man breathless, making him shudder, could bring such a pleasure-filled power. She couldn't wait to experience it again.

She nipped his shoulder. "I'm up for seconds. How about you?"

The next thing she knew, she was beneath him on the bed. And he was amazingly ready. She could feel the hard length of him probing her. Wrapping her arms and legs around him, she said, "I guess all you really needed was a moment."

"I want you again right now."

She thought she heard a hint of anger in his tone, but what she saw in his eyes was vulnerability. Whatever power she'd felt before changed to wonder. She wanted him even more than she had a second ago. Tightening her hold on him, she struggled to pull him in even deeper. But it was like trying to move a rock. "You can have me. What's the problem?"

He framed her face with his hands. "I'll tell you what the problem is. I want to do to you what you just did to me. I want to touch you and taste you and torture you until you can't think of anything but wanting me inside of you."

"That's all I can think of right now." That was nothing less than the truth. She wiggled, tried to thrust against him, but he stayed right where he was. Her insides were melting, but he wasn't where she needed him to be. "Please."

He withdrew and then pushed himself a little farther into her. Still not far enough.

"Every time I'm near you, the same feeling comes over me that came over me in that damn dressing room," he said. "I have to be inside of you."

She arched against him, trying again to take all of him. "You know, if torture was what you had in mind, you're on the right track."

She felt him smile as he pressed his lips against hers. But when he lifted his head and met her gaze again, his eyes were serious. "It's never been this way for me before. I've never wanted anyone this much."

"Same goes for me," she said.

"That's a problem."

There was that hint of vulnerability in his eyes again, and she wanted to soothe it away. "Can we solve it tomorrow? I have a much bigger problem for you to take care of right now. I'm think I'm going to explode if you don't make me come."

"I can take care of that," Hunter said as he pushed himself a little deeper.

Her breath caught in her throat, but she managed to say, "More. Kiss me and come all the way inside. Now."

THE MOMENT THAT HIS MOUTH took hers, Hunter felt himself sinking into her. Would it always be like this? He'd never had this temptation—no, this *need*—to lose himself in a woman before. On one level it terrified him, but on another, it drew him like a magnet. He caught her bottom lip between his teeth and pushed into her all the way.

She tightened around him, trapping him with arms, legs and with that slick, hot core. He lifted his mouth from hers, then held himself perfectly still as he met her eyes. He could see himself trapped there, too—by everything that was Rory. Slowly, trembling with the effort, he withdrew and pushed into her again, withdrew…and pushed in.

"Please—" She arched against him.

He wanted to keep the pace slow—to spin out the pleasure for both of them. But he was losing that battle, too. Each time he withdrew from her, he left parts of himself behind. Each time he pushed in, he felt as if he were coming home. Needs, emotions and pleasure entwined to drag at his control.

"Faster. I need you."

Hunter wasn't sure if she'd said the words or if it was his own inner voice speaking. Suddenly all he knew was that he had to bring her to that peak again where she would shatter around him. He thrust into her faster now, and she matched him move for move. She was his now. He wanted to keep her this way, remember her always with her cheeks flushed, her eyes clouded but fastened on him. Then she stiffened, her fingers dug into his hips and he was helpless to do anything but pour himself into her.

RORY WASN'T SURE HOW LONG she let herself drift, savoring the pleasure of lying beside her Terminator. She wasn't even sure when he'd shifted her so that they were lying side by side on the bed. But her head was resting on his arm and the fingers of her left hand still clasped his. Finally opening her eyes, she saw that he was studying her, his gaze dark and intent.

"No one has ever looked at me that way," she said.

"What way?"

"As if you could see all my secrets. And I feel as if I don't know *you* at all."

He lifted their joined hands and pressed a kiss on her knuckles. "You know me."

"I know parts of you. But there's so much I don't know."

"Like?"

"Your favorite food, your favorite color, what you like to do when you're not working for Jared Slade." She felt his fingers tighten slightly on hers when she spoke the name, and instantly she regretted it. "This isn't the reporter talking. It's me."

He said nothing for a moment. "It's important that you know those things?"

She nodded her head. "I want to know everything."

"I don't think I have a favorite food, but I'm partial to anything Italian. And my favorite restaurants are all in New Orleans."

"I've never been there."

"I'd like to show it to you."

For a moment, there was silence in the room. Then he said, "As for my favorite color, I don't think I ever had one. But recently I've developed a fondness for red, as long as you're wearing it."

Pleasure streamed through her, not so much triggered by the comment as by the intimacy of the moment. She felt so comfortable lying here like this, talking to him. "What about your favorite thing to do?"

"That's easy. This." He ran a hand up her inner thigh.

"Besides that," she said. But her heart was already beginning to beat faster.

"Well, let me see." He opened her cleft and ran his finger slowly down it. "There's this."

Her hips shifted involuntarily. "I'm serious. What do you do when you're not working—besides have sex?"

For a moment, he didn't say anything. But he didn't remove his hand, and she didn't ask him to. She was so aware that his fingers were right there, almost entering her.

"I like to ride," he said finally.

"Me, too. My father used to take my sisters and me for riding lessons every Saturday when we were little. Nat never took to it, and Sierra was always afraid. It was the one thing that I could do better than either of my sisters. My dad was really proud of me."

"We'll go for a ride tomorrow morning."

"Really? You'll have the time?"

"I'll make the time. But, right now I have a different kind of ride in mind." He levered himself up and positioned himself between her legs.

"Yes," she murmured as she arched up to take him in.

They began to move together, but it wasn't long before Rory said, "Faster."

"You're so demanding," Hunter teased, keeping the rhythm slow and steady. "As a rider, you must know that it's never good to rush your fences."

"Please." Her breath was coming in the short pants that always made him burn. It took all his control not to rush.

"Why don't I tell you what I eventually intend to do with that red thong and the champagne?"

Leaning down, he began to whisper his plans in her ear. And it wasn't long until they were rushing the fence together.

LEA ROBERTS BARELY MANAGED a smile for the guard as she pulled up to the booth and flashed her parking permit.

"Working late, weren't you, Ms. Roberts?" he asked as he gave the permit a cursory glance.

"Yes." She was careful not to let her frustration show in her voice. Long ago, she'd found that being nice to security guards, secretaries and receptionists made her life run more smoothly. But she couldn't prevent her fingers from tapping on the steering wheel as she waited for the guard to open the gate.

It was nearly four in the morning, and she'd spent the entire day and most of the night trying to locate Rory Gibbs. Not even her sisters had been able to help. But they knew where she was all right. The cop had been cool and polite, but she'd been lying through her teeth when she'd claimed not to know where Rory was.

Lea hadn't had any better luck with the academic. Dr. Sierra Gibbs had peered at her through glasses that made her eyes look owlish and acted as though she could barely remember she had a sister named Rory. But the twit had known where Rory was. Lea would have bet her next paycheck on it.

But she didn't need them. It had taken her a while, but she was pretty sure she knew exactly where Rory was. And she owed it all to a hunch. A good, old-fashioned reporter's hunch. How long had it been since she'd had one?

Years. Ironically enough, the last time she'd had a good one had been back in Oakwood, Connecticut, when she'd broken the embezzlement story at Marks Banking and Investments.

She'd known from the moment that she'd started a relationship with Hunter Marks that the family was her ticket out of Oakwood. And she'd been right.

She hoped to hell she was right this time, too. After pulling out of the garage, she headed up Fourteenth Street. When the light at the corner turned red, Lea swore under her breath, then began to tap her fingers on the steering wheel again. If her hunch was right and Rory was where she suspected, she needed to hurry.

She felt the press of cold metal at the back of her ear at the same time that she heard the voice.

"Don't move."

Lea didn't think she could, not with the blood freezing in her veins. The voice was even more frightening in person than it was over the phone.

"You're not answering your phone. Why not?"

Keep calm, she told herself as she cleared her throat. "I've been busy."

"The pictures weren't in Rory Gibbs's apartment."

Lea moistened her lips. "I don't have them. I've been working all day trying to locate her. I'll have them for you soon."

"I don't like people who fail. Those pictures should have been on the front page of the *Washington Post* by now."

Lea shuddered when she felt the cold metal trace a path to the back of her neck. "I think I know where Rory Gibbs is."

"Why should I believe you?" The metal pressed harder into her neck.

Despite that she was cold to the core, Lea felt beads of sweat form on her forehead. "Look, we want the same thing. We both want a story that exposes the true identity of Jared Slade. If I'm right, Rory Gibbs is with Jared Slade right now, and I can tell you exactly how to get there."

There was a pause. It couldn't have been long because the traffic light hadn't yet changed. But to Lea, the stretch of silence in her car felt like an eternity.

"Tell me."

Fingers gripping the steering wheel and sweat dripping down her face, Lea said, "They're on the Lucas Wainwright estate in Virginia."

11

As they rode across the first field, Rory couldn't prevent an envious glance at Hunter's horse. It was large and black, a real beauty named Lucky, and she was sure it could outrun the lady's mount that McGee's son and Hunter had chosen for her. Not that she was unhappy with the pretty filly she was riding. She leaned forward and patted Priscilla's neck and then glanced at Lucky again. She was developing a definite preference for dark, slightly dangerous males.

Hunter hadn't been in her bed when she'd awakened that morning. But McGee had brought a note with her coffee and told her that Hunter was in the stables, seeing to the horses. There'd been a flower, too—a red rose from the gardens. The note had read simply, *Wear the red thong.* She had.

"Why don't we head up that hill over there and get the lay of the land?" he asked.

"Sure." Eager to see what Priscilla could do, Rory urged her into a trot, then a canter. Hunter rode at her side as they crossed the field and crested the hill. Though it hadn't looked to be steep, Rory discovered that it offered a breathtaking view. Ahead were rolling fields and a stream that snaked its way through them and into woods. Over her shoulder she could see the entire Wainwright estate—the pool, the tennis courts and the stables.

There was a security guard at the gate watching them now through binoculars. He hadn't been happy when they'd announced their intention to go for a ride, but he hadn't argued with Hunter. Suddenly, Rory recalled the bomb scare at Les Printemps. How could she have forgotten that? She'd agreed not to ask questions about it, but how could it have completely slipped her mind?

"A penny for your thoughts," Hunter said.

Turning, she met his eyes. "Have they found out any more about the bomb scare in Mr. Slade's suite?"

When he hesitated, she held up a hand. "Off the record."

"What makes you ask?"

"The security guard down there wasn't happy." She studied him as a sudden thought occurred to her. "They're guarding you, too, aren't they? You're in danger." She reined in her horse. "We should go back. I mean, this is wonderful, but you have to put your safety first."

He reached out a hand to cover hers before she could turn the horse. "They're just being careful. Mr. Slade was concerned. That's why Lucas Wainwright offered to let me stay here. We're perfectly safe, and I didn't suggest you go for a ride with me to make you worry."

She glanced around at the empty fields. "You're sure you'll be safe?"

"I'm positive, and so will you. You see that stream down there?" he asked. "Are you up to a race?"

He saw the excitement leap into her eyes, and for a moment he was so distracted that he simply sat there as she shot past him. She was halfway down the hill before he dug his heels into Lucky. She was good. More than good, he amended after a few moments. The only reason he was gaining on her was that he had the faster mount.

It wasn't until they were halfway across the next field that Hunter drew even with her, and for several moments, they galloped side by side. There was nothing but the sun beating down, the scent of the fields, the wind rushing past, and the feel and the sound of the powerful horses beneath them. This was how he'd always centered himself and found his strength. And he'd never shared the experience with another person before.

Except for his brother.

The hedge came up fast. He barely had time to worry if she could make it when they were sailing over it. Then heads down, knees hugging their horses, they raced neck and neck toward the stream. Lucky surged ahead. Seconds later, Hunter reined the horse in at the stream. Then she pulled up beside him.

"You're very good," he said.

Laughing, she said, "Did I mention that the equestrian club at my college made it to the state finals in steeple chasing?"

He shot her a grin. "No, but I can believe it. How did you do?"

"Second place. I took a personal blue ribbon."

He studied her for a moment. Her face was flushed, her eyes laughing. Why hadn't he noticed before that she made his world a brighter place? That he was… He felt his heart stumble.

"Rory, I—" He caught himself, a sliver of panic moving through him. What words would he have blurted out if he hadn't stopped? Would he have told her what he was feeling—that he might be falling in love with her?

"What?"

No. Another needle of panic raced up his spine. Love?

That couldn't be true. It was ridiculous. He'd known her for two days. Still, the urge to reach out to her was so strong that he tightened his grip on the reins. Lucky began to dance. He had to think, make a plan. One thing he did know—once words were spoken, they couldn't be taken back.

"Let's ride along the stream for a while," he said.

"Sure." She eased her mount to his side as he steered Lucky along the water's edge.

Hunter searched for a topic of conversation, something, anything, that would stop the words that he couldn't seem to get out of his head.

But it was Rory who asked the first question. "Why did you decide to go into business?"

"It was a family tradition."

"What kind of business was your family in?"

"Banking and investments. I'd always thought I'd become part of it." Even when he'd been heavily into rebellion. At nineteen, he'd thought he had a knack for investing. At the end of that first semester of college when he'd come home, he'd intended to sit down and talk to his father about working in the investment section of the bank.

"I'm so sorry. Forget I asked that. I mean…you lost so much when you lost your family."

When he looked at her, he saw nothing but pure distress on her face. Impatience and guilt streamed through him. "You don't have to be sorry. It was a long time ago." He hesitated for a moment, then said, "There's a story I'd like to tell you. I'd like your take on it." The words had poured out, surprising him.

"Sure. Go ahead," she said.

"I told you part of it yesterday. There was a young man—he had parents, a brother, and a family business that he figured he'd go into eventually, although it had always been made clear to him that his older brother was slated to step into his father's and grandfather's shoes and run the business. He felt resentful and since he wasn't destined for the role of crown prince, he decided to assume the role of black sheep."

"Understandable."

Hunter wondered why it was so important that he tell her the whole story. Perhaps he needed to lay it all out for himself again. Perhaps he needed an objective opinion. Whatever the reason, he couldn't seem to prevent himself from continuing. "The last summer before he went away to college, he didn't stifle any of his rebellious urges. He had an affair with an older woman, he partied, he drove fast. He reported in late to work at the family bank and he left early. No one was happy with him, except for the woman he was having an affair with. She seemed to be highly amused by his behavior."

When he paused this time, she said nothing, but as the horses continued to walk, she reached out a hand and covered one of his.

"Then he went away to college and began to see things a little differently. He could continue to play the role of black sheep, or he could find a way to carve out a niche for himself in the family business and prove everyone wrong. Then something happened when he went home for the holidays."

Rory tightened her grip on his hand. "He lost the family that he wanted to make amends to."

"Yes," Hunter said. The horses stopped, and they loosened the reins. "He lost them—but not in an accident. On the night he came home, the family was having a meeting. They were all seated at the dining room table."

As he spoke, Hunter could picture it in his mind as if it had only just happened. "One of the bank's attorneys was there, too. It seems that his father and brother had piled up some gambling debts at a nearby casino, and they'd 'borrowed' quite heavily from the investment accounts at the bank."

"They'd embezzled investors' money?" Rory asked.

"In plain terms, yes. Of course, they'd expected to be able to pay it all back before the quarterly audit, but they never quite managed to win that jackpot in the sky at the casino. The news of the embezzlement was going to hit the papers within the week. They'd called in some favors and had managed to delay the story, but they couldn't bury it forever."

"And once the story hit the newspapers, there would be a run on the bank's funds, and thousands of people could be hurt."

He turned his hand and linked his fingers with hers. "Exactly. But the attorney and the family had a solution. All they needed to pull it off was a scapegoat. The key element of the plan was to make sure that investors didn't lose their faith in the bank or in the people running it."

"So the black sheep became the scapegoat?"

The anger in her voice softened something deep inside of him. "Yes. Since he'd never been associated with the running of the bank, he was the perfect choice. All he had to do was confess, sign over a trust fund he'd inherited from his grandmother to cover the losses, and promise that he would never work for the family business."

"What about the crown prince? Did he have to sign over a trust fund, too?"

Hunter nodded, almost amused by the fury in her voice.

"Oh, yes. There was a lot of money to replace. But the attorney had the papers all drawn up. The trust-fund money would eventually be replaced with legitimate bank profits. And there would be an advisory board appointed by the board of directors to see that no one was able to do any more 'borrowing.' The solution had been carefully thought out."

"Except that no one was thinking about the scapegoat."

"No. Everyone at the table seemed to think that he'd be perfectly willing to go along with it."

"What about the older woman he was having the affair with? Didn't she stick by him?" Rory asked.

Hunter shook his head. "She was a reporter and the family gave her an exclusive on the story."

"She couldn't have believed it."

The conviction in her voice had him staring at her. "Why do you say that?"

"She should have known him better than that."

Hunter wondered for a moment what difference that simple kind of faith might have made in his life ten years ago.

"Did you...did the scapegoat go to jail?"

"No. The family and the bank's attorney had connections that extended to the prosecutor's office."

"What happened to him?" Rory asked.

"The day that the story broke, he made all the required public apologies. Then he left town and never went back."

She threw her arms around him then and held tight.

Hunter couldn't have described the emotions swirling around inside of him. First faith and now understanding. He'd lived without them for so long. If someone, any member of his family, had shown him either ten years ago, everything might have been different.

When she finally lifted her head, he saw that her lashes

were wet, but her eyes were still angry. This time he felt his heart take a long, slow tumble.

"Why did you tell me this?" she asked.

Using his thumb, he wiped away one of her tears. "I'm not sure. I guess I've been thinking about going back there."

Priscilla raised her head and gave it a shake. Taking it as a signal, Lucky took a step forward, and Rory tightened her grip on the reins as her horse followed. "I think they want to get going."

For a few moments they rode in silence. Then Hunter asked, "What would you do?"

She glanced at him in surprise. "I'm not sure that I can advise you. I can only tell you that family stuff can really haunt you. I was so angry with my father for years. I thought he'd abandoned us. Then out of the blue, my sisters and I got a letter for our birthdays a few weeks ago. From him. He'd left them with his attorney. For the first time, I saw things from his point of view."

"Did it help?"

She smiled at him. "Some. It didn't change the fact that he left us. But I learned that he loved us and he regretted leaving. I think if he'd had it to do over again, he would have stayed."

Hunter wasn't so sure that if he went back to his hometown, he'd find such a happy ending. "I swore I'd never go back."

"Maybe that was the best decision back then. But I think that being older and looking back can sometimes shift your perspective. You can change your mind about going back."

Yes, he could, Hunter thought, and he wondered if he'd been moving toward the decision ever since the first threatening note had been delivered to his hotel room. When he glanced at Rory, their eyes met and held for a moment. "Rory, I—"

Whatever else he might have said was interrupted by the ringing of his cell phone. After lifting it to his ear, he said, "Yeah?"

"You weren't supposed to go off of the estate," Tracker said.

"Good morning to you, too," Hunter said.

"You're not going to think it's so good when you get back here. I just arrived a few minutes ago and I ran into Lea Roberts at the front gate."

Hunter swore under his breath, then said to Rory, "Lea Roberts is at the front gate."

"There's no telling who she might have told or who might have followed her. Where exactly are you?" Tracker asked.

"We're on the other side of the hill across from the estate. We've been following the stream toward the woods." On the other end of the line, he could hear Tracker talking to someone. Then he came back on the line. "Follow the stream through the woods. McGee's son and I will bring the horse trailer, but it's going to take us a half hour or so. We'll take the long route to avoid being followed."

"Got it," Hunter said.

"Do me a favor and get into those woods. I don't like the idea of you riding around out there in the open."

"Yeah." Tucking his phone back into his pocket, Hunter said, "Tracker wants us to get into the woods ASAP. They'll be picking us up on the other side in half an hour."

Rory nodded and then urged her horse into a canter. Hunter followed suit, but he was on the alert now, scanning the surrounding fields and the hills. It wasn't until they entered the woods and slowed the horses that Rory turned and spoke. "I know Lea wants those pictures, but how could she know about this place? I didn't tell her."

"Good question." He'd been thinking about the same question, and the most probable answer didn't make him happy. Lea had remembered that Hunter Marks had gone to college with Lucas Wainwright. That meant that she suspected his true identity.

They rode in silence until Rory said, "I can see the road ahead."

Through the trees, Hunter saw an SUV drive past. A glance at his watch told him that they still had another twenty-five minutes before Tracker would pick them up. "We might as well circle back and rest the horses in that clearing back there."

Once they'd dismounted and tethered the horses, Hunter began to pace. There was only one solution. He was going to have to go back to Oakwood and find a connection between one of his employees and what had happened ten years ago. As good as Tracker McBride was, the man hadn't been there. He didn't know the players.

"I know it's hard to wait," Rory said. "According to my sister, Tracker McBride's about the best there is when it comes to security."

"Yes," he said, stopping to turn to her. She was leaning against a tree, and in the dappled sunlight, she reminded him of a wood sprite. Feelings moved through him again, and each time they did, they grew stronger.

She extended a hand to him, and he found himself moving toward her before the thought had even entered his mind. Would she always have this kind of pull on him?

"I have an idea of how we could pass the time," she said as she grasped his hand.

"By blowing bubbles?" He dug into his pocket and pulled out two pieces.

Laughing, she said, "Not exactly. I have a better idea."

"Me, too." He shoved the gum back into his pocket.

"Tell me your idea. You know how I hate waiting."

He brushed her lips with his. "I noticed that last night." Then he was delighted when heat flooded her cheeks.

"Thank you for last night, by the way," she said. "For letting me try all those…things. And the stuff you tried, that was good, too."

He raised her fingers to his lips. "My pleasure."

"I want you to know I'll remember last night forever. I'll remember you forever."

Hunter felt his heart turn over again as a new realization streamed through him. He wanted more than memories of Rory. Barely understanding his feelings, he couldn't tell her yet what he was thinking, but he could show her. "Why don't we create some new memories for both of us?"

"You're reading my mind."

He leaned down and nipped her earlobe, then whispered, "Are you wearing the thong?"

"Maybe." She pressed two hands against his chest and looked up at him. "Since we're creating another memory, there's something that I didn't get to try last night."

His eyes narrowed. "Does it involve tying me up again?"

"No, unless you'd prefer that."

"I'd like to keep my hands free."

She touched the pearls she was wearing around her neck. "It involves this necklace you gave me. I read about it once, and I'd like to try it."

Hunter wondered if he could have refused her anything. "We've only got about twenty-five minutes."

She smiled at him. "I'll have to make you come very fast, won't I?" Then she reached down and touched the swollen length of him.

He sucked in his breath, and Rory felt that same ripple of power that she'd felt last night when she'd been in control. Moving her fingers up and down his length, she said, "I don't think there'll be a problem. Just put your back against this tree."

While they were shifting positions, she said, "Since we're pressed for time, I won't ask you to strip, although I enjoyed watching you do that last night." Talking helped her keep her mind on her plan, she discovered. While she opened his belt and pulled down the zipper, she continued, "Sierra, that's my academic sister, says that power is a potent aphrodisiac, and…" Once she had him free of his briefs, her breath backed up and she lost her train of thought for a moment. But her body seemed to know what it was doing. Her hand enclosed him and she felt his erection hard yet velvet smooth against the palm of her hand.

"You better get on with whatever you're going to do, or this will be very fast indeed," Hunter rasped.

"Yes." Rory licked her lips and nearly bent down to taste him, but then she remembered. "The pearls." After releasing him, she fumbled with the clasp, then freed the necklace. Fighting against the trembling in her hands, she finally managed to get the strand of pearls wrapped three times around the base of his shaft.

At his raspy groan, Rory glanced up at him. His eyes were dark, Terminator eyes, her fantasy man's eyes. But now she knew the real man—and he was kinder, gentler, and much better than anything she could have imagined. Keeping her eyes fixed on his, she closed both hands over the "bracelet" of pearls and slowly drew them up the length of his aroused penis.

"Rory—" His voice was raw, and she was sure she could feel the heat in his eyes sear her skin.

"You like that," she murmured as she managed to reposition the pearls.

"Like? I—" He broke off as she drew the pearls up his length again.

"I like it, too," she said. "I like to hold you like this. I like knowing that I can give you pleasure." His breath was coming in pants now, and the power she felt brought a fresh wave of pleasure. "You asked me earlier if I was wearing the thong. I am."

"That's it." He gripped her hips and shifted her so that her back was against the tree. Then he all but tore her jeans and boots off.

She heard a low moan when he fingered the waistband of the thong, and then his hands were pressed like a brand against her naked buttocks, and he was lifting her.

"Wrap your legs around me," he ordered.

And then at last he was inside of her. When he withdrew and thrust in again, she felt the scrape of the bark against her back and the hard length of him filling her completely. She was tender down there from the ride, but that only seemed to add to the pleasure.

"Hold tight. This is going to be a very rough ride." Then he began to move and each thrust brought a sharper wave of sensations.

"It's just like it was the first time," she said.

"It's nothing like it was the first time."

He was right. That first time, he'd been a stranger. The Terminator. Her fantasy man. But Hunter was real. And for the moment, he was hers.

"Say my name. Tell me you want me," he said.

"I want you, Hunter."

He increased the pace. "Say it again."

"Hunter," she said as she felt her climax begin. Even as the waves of it began to roll over her, catching her up in its power, the realization moved through her again—this was nothing like the first time. Because she'd fallen in love with Hunter.

"Mine."

She was barely aware of him crying out the word. All she could see was his face, all she could feel was him as he drove her, drove them both, over an airless peak.

12

"ARE YOU ALL RIGHT?" Hunter asked.

"Mmm. Perfect." She sat on his lap, her head resting against his shoulder. She loved this man. She felt as though she'd been sitting, letting him hold her, for a very long time. "I don't ever want to move."

"Tracker will be here soon," he said.

Maybe not so perfect. The moments were ticking away, and the time that they had together was fading fast. As long as they were here in the woods, he was hers. Deep inside she knew that when they got back to the house, everything would change. Lifting her head, she met his eyes. "I wish there was a way to stop time."

"Me, too."

Was she imagining it or did she see in his eyes some of the confusion and the wonder that she was feeling? "Hunter, I—"

Behind them, Lucky snorted impatiently, and Priscilla gave a ladylike whinny. A cell phone rang.

"This will be Tracker," he said as he shifted her off his lap and tugged out his cell phone out. "You'd better get your clothes on."

Rory grabbed her jeans and pulled them on. If the phone hadn't rung just then, would she have blurted out to him that she loved him? She jammed her foot into a boot and steeled herself to look at him again. He was totally focused on the call, frowning at something Tracker was saying. She had to get a grip. His boss was being threatened. He might be in danger. He certainly wouldn't want to hear some babbled profession of love. She didn't want to hear it herself. Great sex, fun and a story. That's what they'd agreed to, hadn't they?

"Right," he said.

Right, she told herself as she jammed her foot into her other boot. When she glanced down, she saw that they were on the wrong feet and she tugged them off again. Life was just never perfect. She was standing ready, her boots on the right feet, by the time he finished his call.

"Tracker's waiting for us at the bridge where the stream intersects the road."

With a brief nod, Rory walked over to mount Priscilla. When he was seated on Lucky, he reached over to put a hand on hers. "You were about to say something when the phone rang."

Rory managed a smile. "It was nothing." She placed a hand on his cheek. "Just thank you. I enjoyed the ride. Both rides."

His grip on her hand tightened. "Rory, I—"

Lucky took two steps back, forcing him to let her go.

"We'll talk when we get back to the house." He tightened his grip on the reins and urged Lucky forward. Neither of them spoke again as they followed the stream out of the woods.

Tracker and McGee's son, Tim, were leaning up against the side of a large SUV that was pulling a horse trailer. Neither one looked very happy.

The moment she dismounted, Tim McGee took Priscilla's reins. "Ladies first. Lucky has an aversion to trailers. It'll be better if she's on board before he puts up a fuss."

As if on cue, Lucky whinnied and rose on his back legs.

"Easy, boy." Tim and Hunter spoke the words in unison, and Tracker moved to help Hunter handle the black stallion. Rory stepped out of the way and waited on the grass verge as Priscilla walked like an angel into the trailer, and then all three men turned their attention to Lucky.

They had him halfway up the ramp when a tractor trailer whipped by, sending enough wind and vibrations to have Lucky backing quickly down the ramp and rearing again.

"Sure. You had to ride the stubborn one," Tracker complained to Hunter, but Rory noted that his hands were gentle on the horse.

Hunter patted the horse's neck and crooned softly, "Don't listen to him, boy. You're a beauty."

"Ms. Gibbs," Tim called from the mouth of the trailer, "if you see another truck, let us know."

"Sure." She moved out far enough into the road behind the trailer that she could see approaching vehicles from either direction. "Everything's clear right now."

The moment they had Lucky settled down, the three men started urging him up the ramp again. It was slow going. Tim was at the front, keeping the reins taut while Hunter walked beside Lucky, his hand spread on the horse's neck, talking to him softly the whole while. Tracker joined her as he waited for the horse to get all four feet on the ramp.

Rory glanced at him and saw that his eyes were scanning the road and the fields. "You're really worried about Hunter, aren't you?"

"I don't like to lose a client," Tracker said.

Rory frowned. "I thought your client was Jared Slade."

Tracker glanced down at her. "Mr. Slade and his associates. Right now that includes both Hunter and you."

Lucky chose that moment to stall halfway up the ramp.

Tracker grinned and called, "Maybe you'd like a pro to show you how it's done."

"The more the merrier," Hunter said.

As the three men continued to chide one another and coax the horse, Rory glanced between the road and Hunter while her mind raced. If Tracker McBride had been hired to protect Jared Slade, why wasn't he with Jared Slade right now? He had security people stationed at the Wainwright estate who could guard Mark Hunter. Yet he'd been here yesterday and today in person. Why? And why would he go to all this trouble to make sure they got back onto the estate safely unless…?

Could Hunter be Jared Slade? The moment the question completed itself in her mind, it began to make sense. Hadn't she had a hunch all along that Jared Slade was merely a figurehead? What better way to keep Jared Slade's identity a secret than to travel under a different name like Mark Hunter?

The scene in the lobby of Les Printemps replayed itself in her mind. Two men had gone to the registration desk, one had stayed with the luggage. No one—not even the bell captain in the lobby, would be able to say they'd seen or met Jared Slade for sure. The reception clerk would have been as confused as she'd been. And in the meantime, Hunter would simply slip into the elevator with the luggage and go up to the suite. Anyone would assume what she had—that the Terminator was some kind of manservant/bodyguard.

And if Jared Slade hadn't chased her out of the lobby and tracked her down in Silken Fantasies, would he have been injured by that bomb?

The chilling thought was still spinning around in her mind when Rory heard the car approaching. Shading her eyes, she tried to gauge the distance. "There's a car coming," she called out. "But you should still have time to get Lucky in."

As if he'd understood what she'd said and wanted to protest, Lucky whinnied and pawed the end of the ramp where it intersected with the trailer bed.

Hunter laughed softly. "Easy, boy. It's going to be all right. I promise."

Rory looked at Hunter again, studying him as he used both his hands and his voice to gentle the horse. The more she thought about it, the more logical it seemed that this man really was Jared Slade. Why hadn't she seen it sooner?

The answer to that was as simple and uncomplicated as it got, she thought as the three men and the horse finally made it into the trailer. She'd been totally blindsided by lust.

And then she'd taken that long, slow tumble into love.

From inside the trailer, Lucky whinnied, this time as if in agreement and Rory glanced back at the road. The car was still about a hundred feet away, but it was slowing. She barely had time to absorb that before Hunter/Jared started down the ramp. He was halfway down when the car pulled to an abrupt stop right beside her.

She shifted her gaze to the driver. He wore mirrored sunglasses, and he had the window down and the sunroof open—in spite of the heat. Then she saw a man with a gun push himself through the open sunroof. After that, everything happened at once.

Hunter stepped off the ramp.

"Jared!" She had time to scream that one word before she launched herself at him.

The shot rang out, loud enough and close enough to make her ears ring, and her shoulder burned as if it had been stung by a giant killer bee. She absorbed those two sensations as she smashed into him. Then they fell, hitting the ground hard enough to knock the breath out of her. With the pain still singing right through to her bones, they began to roll.

HUNTER STOOD IN THE STUDY of the Wainwright house in much the same position as he had on his arrival—was it only two days ago? He ran a hand through his hair and shoved down hard on his emotions as he listened to Tracker making arrangements on the phone.

He couldn't afford feelings right now. A cool head had always served him well, and it was his only solution now. Rory was all right. Banged up, a bit bruised. The bullet had only creased the skin of her upper arm. But the blood…

Turning away from the window, he shoved the image ruthlessly out of his mind. He'd been able to stop the bleeding right away, and McGee was seeing to first aid. She would be well taken care of by him. She'd gotten to the Wainwright's butler just as surely as she'd gotten to him.

Shoving his hands into his pockets, he stifled the urge to pace. He was going to be cool and logical. He knew what to do when he wanted something. And he wanted the person who was responsible for hurting Rory Gibbs.

Tracker set down the phone. "The helicopter will be touching down in a few minutes."

"Her sisters will be on it?" he demanded.

Tracker's brows lifted. "Yes, sir, as ordered."

"Sorry. I just—I know I've been snapping out orders ever since we got back."

"Forget it. She's important to me, too. Natalie Gibbs is a very good friend, and she's not going to be happy that her sister got hurt. At least it wasn't more serious."

"Dammit, she tried to take a bullet for me!" Hunter whirled and paced back to the window as all the emotions he'd been suppressing bubbled to the surface. "She could have been killed."

"She wasn't," Tracker pointed out. "She's fine. McGee served in a medical unit when he was in the military. He says she likely won't even have a scar."

Hunter ran a hand through his hair. "I just keep thinking of what could have happened."

"Don't. Believe me, I've been in your shoes. If you keep letting your emotions rule, they'll cloud your thinking."

"Don't you think I know that?" Hunter said. Then he sighed, strapping down his control as he ran a hand through his hair again. "Sorry. You're right."

"Let's concentrate on getting the bastard who's behind this," Tracker said. "I got a license plate. My men are checking out the owners as we speak. My guess is that they'll find the car was reported stolen. Those men were pros."

"Alex, Michael and Denise—I pay them well enough that any one of them could afford to hire someone. But how did they know I was here? What did you get out of Lea Roberts?"

"Not a whole damn lot," Tracker said, disgust clear in his voice. "When I asked her where she got the information that Jared Slade was here on the estate, she said that Rory Gibbs had told her that in a phone conversation yesterday."

"That's a lie."

"Maybe."

"No. Not maybe. She's lying. Rory doesn't know **that** I'm Jared Slade."

Tracker studied him for a moment. "I'm afraid you're wrong there. Just before the shooter drove up in that car, she was interrogating me about why I was here and why I was so concerned with your safety when I was supposed to be protecting Jared Slade. Then do you recall that she called you Jared just as she shoved you out of the path of that bullet?"

Stunned, Hunter replayed the scene in his mind, but he couldn't remember what she'd called out. The whole scene was a series of flashing images and sensations—the man pointing the gun, the sound of the shot, the impact of Rory's body against his, and the fear that had iced him through to the bone.

He began to pace. "No, I don't remember. But if she did call me that, she'd only just put it together." He turned to face Tracker. "I have to see her. I have to explain…" What? That he'd lied to her, that he'd given her an interview with a man who didn't exist? How in hell was he supposed to explain that?

Tracker's cell phone rang just as Hunter heard the sound of the approaching helicopter.

"Yeah," Tracker said into the phone. "We're ready." When he hung up, he said to Hunter, "Your conversation with Rory will have to wait. I'd like to get you out of here as soon as that helicopter lands."

"I want to take her with me."

"I can understand that," Tracker said. "But I'm voting against it." He held up a hand when Hunter opened his mouth. "Hear me out. If we're going to get to the bottom of this, I could use your full attention on the problem. And Rory is safer here. I've called in extra men to protect her. Besides, you're the target. If you're not here…" He shrugged and he let the sentence trail off.

Hunter paced to the French doors and watched as the helicopter landed on the grass near the stables. Dammit. Tracker was right. Rory would be safer here with her sisters, and the best thing he could do for her right now was to figure out who had shot at her.

"If Rory didn't tip off Lea Roberts, do you have any idea why she showed up outside the gates?"

"Yeah," Hunter said. "She knew that Hunter Marks went to college with Lucas Wainwright."

"There you go," Tracker said, nodding.

"Can you confront her? Get her to admit what part she's playing in all of this?"

Tracker shook his head. "I'm not the police—and you don't want them involved. When I went out to the gate to speak with her, I kept it very friendly. All I had to do was ask her a few questions and she was making excuses about going back to D.C. We have no solid evidence that she's connected to either the shooting or the bomb."

"There's no solid evidence connecting anyone to the shooting or the bomb," Hunter said. The moment he heard the frustration in his own voice, he shoved it down. He'd built Slade Enterprises by being cool and logical. He was going to have to use those same skills now if he wanted to save it.

"It's possible Lea told someone about the connection between you and Lucas. Or it's possible that the person behind the threats is very smart and dug up the connection on his own."

"All three of our prime suspects—Denise, Michael and Alex—are very smart."

"We'll just have to be smarter. C'mon," Tracker said, leading the way out onto the patio. "Once we get to the Wainwright Building, I'll show you everything I've dug up. And I can protect you there until we can figure this out."

Hunter met Tracker's eyes. "I'm going to Oakwood. Whatever the hell is going on, it started there, and I'm going to end it."

Tracker sighed. "You're just not going to make this easy for me, are you?"

Hunter met his eyes steadily. "I know that you went there, looked at the stories in the local paper, talked to some people. But there must be something you've missed. Maybe I'll see it."

Tracker studied Hunter for a moment as they walked toward the waiting helicopter. "Okay, this is the way it will be. My men and her sisters will protect Rory. We'll stop at the Wainwright Building and take a look at my file. If we're lucky, you'll see something there and we won't have to go to Oakwood. If we have to make the trip, I'll be going with you." He raised a hand to stop whatever objection Hunter might have made. "It'll cause less notice if you cooperate, but either way I'm going."

RORY SAT AS CLOSE as she could get to the edge of the couch, concentrating hard on the patterns in the kitchen floor. She didn't dare look at the mark the bullet had left on her arm. The first time she'd looked at it in the ditch where she and Hunter had landed, she'd passed out.

"This is going to sting a bit, Miss Rory," McGee said. "But I have a pot of tea brewing. I know that you prefer coffee, but tea has medicinal benefits, and I made another batch of chocolate-fudge cookies this morning."

"I know the drill," Rory said, tensing. "A spoonful of sugar makes the medicine go down. The one thing that I always used to do better than my sisters was get hurt, so I'm used to it. Just do it. I want to see Hunter." Or whoever he is.

She hadn't seen him since they'd gotten back to the estate. She had a vague memory of him holding her in the truck, but she'd been drifting in and out. And the next thing she knew, McGee was bending over her holding smelling salts under her nose.

The kitchen was huge with a sitting area that boasted an overstuffed couch, a fireplace, and a patterned floor with white and black tiles marching along together.

"Ouch," she said as McGee swabbed her shoulder with something nasty. "That really hurt."

"Sorry. I promised both Mr. Tracker and Mr. Hunter that I could take care of this. But if you'd prefer, I could drive you to the emergency room in town."

"No. Swab away." She winced as he did just that. Mr. Hunter. Then she remembered. Not Mr. Hunter at all, but Mr. Jared Slade. That's what she'd been thinking about when the shooter had risen out of the sunroof. Hunter had to be Jared Slade. That would certainly explain why Tracker had been so upset that they'd left the estate to ride the horses, why he'd told them to take to the woods, why he'd come for them in a trailer.

And why someone had shot at Hunter.

A bomb had been planted in his hotel suite, and Mark Hunter, alias Jared Slade, had gone into hiding at his friend's estate. It all made horribly perfect sense.

"This will feel cool, Miss Rory," McGee said as he rubbed something onto her shoulder.

McGee was right. It did feel blessedly and deliciously cool. She just wished it could do something for the sick feeling in her stomach. For a moment, she closed her eyes and tried to think. "I need to talk to Hunter. Can you tell me where he is?"

"Mr. Hunter and Mr. Tracker are in the study, I believe. They're waiting for Mr. Lucas to arrive."

Mr. Tracker, Mr. Lucas and Mr. Hunter, she thought. Odd that everyone called Mark Hunter by his last name.

"I'm going to put a bandage on this now," he said. "And then I'm going to pour you some tea, and you'll eat some of the cookies you like."

Rory's stomach gave a lurch. Then there was a sudden noise that sounded as if a tornado had just touched down. "What on earth—?"

"It's just Mr. Lucas's helicopter. Sometimes, it's the most convenient way for him and Dr. Mac or Miss Sophie to get here."

As the noise suddenly stopped, Rory imagined how it was going to be. Mr. Hunter or whoever he was would be closeted with his friend Lucas forever. "Are you finished?"

"Just a moment," McGee promised as he smoothed down a bit of tape. "If you're very careful and massage the salve in every day, you won't have a scar. And now you can have some of those cookies."

"Thanks." Rory rose from the couch. "First, I need to talk to Mr. Hunter or whoever he is. I'll be right back." She made it to the door, but when she opened it, Natalie and Sierra rushed in.

"Are you all right?" Natalie asked, taking her hands.

"Is she all right?" Sierra asked.

"I'm fine."

"She'll be fine," McGee assured them. "I've treated the wound. The bullet just grazed her skin. Would you like tea? I've prepared some of Miss Rory's favorite cookies."

Sierra studied him for a moment, then smiled. "Yes. Tea and cookies would be perfect."

"We were so worried," Natalie said, studying Rory closely. "Tracker said you were all right. But we had to see for ourselves. He arranged for Lucas to bring us."

"I need to see Hunter," Rory explained. "Or Jared. Or whoever he is."

"Jared? Jared Slade is here? Tracker said you were interviewing this Hunter person," Natalie said.

"I was," Rory said. "But I'm pretty sure he's really Jared Slade, and I have to—"

The deafening noise of the helicopter starting up drowned out her words and suddenly her stomach lurched again. She turned, rushed to the kitchen window and saw her worst fears confirmed. Hunter, alias Jared Slade, head bent low, was running across the lawn with Tracker at his side. He hadn't even said goodbye. As she watched them climb in, she felt the same stream of sensations she'd felt years before when she and her sisters and mother had gone to the airport to say goodbye to their father.

Oh, Harry had said that he'd only be gone for a while, but it had been a lie, and she'd somehow known it. Men always lied to her when they were never coming back.

Behind her, Rory heard a cell phone ring. Then it rang again. Still, Rory ignored it.

"It's not mine," Sierra said. "Mine plays Chopin."

"Don't look at me," Natalie said. "Mine's on vibrate."

Rory whirled then and dashed to the table where McGee had set her purse. Hunter was calling her. "Hello?"

"I'll give you one hour. If you don't deliver those pictures to me, you're fired."

"Lea?"

"Yes, this is Lea—Lea Roberts, your boss, the one who sent you on a very simple mission—to get a picture of Jared Slade. Do you have the photos?"

Rory drew in a deep breath. "No. I traded them for—"

"Sex. Don't think I don't know what you've been doing. You've been holed up there with the man who now calls himself Jared Slade, and you've been sleeping with him. For your sake, I hope that he was as good in bed as he used to be because your little dalliance has cost you any hope of a job at *Celebs*. You're fired."

When the call went dead, Rory merely stared down at her cell phone. Whatever luck she'd once had—it had just run out.

13

"TRACKER SAID HE WANTS YOU to stay here until this is all cleared up," Natalie said.

"I can't," Rory said as she led the way up the stairs to the room where she'd been staying.

"You'll be safer here," Natalie said. "They don't know who's behind these incidents yet. Your apartment was searched, you know."

Rory turned to her sister. "No one told me about that."

"Tracker thinks whoever it was might have been after the photos. Please. Someone's already taken a shot at you. I'd like you to stay here where Tracker can protect you until this is over."

Rory lifted her chin. "I can't."

McGee knocked on the doorjamb. "I thought you might like tea up here while I pack your things."

"Yes…I mean no. I won't be taking any of these things with me." Rory took the pearls that she'd stuffed in her jeans pocket and dropped them on the dresser. She didn't ever again want to see any of the things that Hunter had given her. She certainly didn't need another dumping gift from Jared Slade, alias Mark Hunter.

McGee set a tray down on a glass-topped table near the windows and pulled up three chairs. "Things always seem a bit better after a cup of hot tea." Then he left.

"I totally agree." Sierra wrapped her arm around Rory's waist and lead her to the table. "And look at those cookies."

Rory sat down and let Sierra pour her a cup of tea. "I'm fine. Really."

Natalie took one of her hands. "No, you're not. I know just how you feel. I felt the same way when I came home from Florida last month and I learned that Chance had flown to England without saying goodbye. I wanted to kill him. But even more, I wanted to bury myself in a hole and never come out again. Men can be such jerks sometimes."

Sierra passed Rory the plate of cookies. "Chocolate helps. There's a lot of research supporting the fact that dark chocolate is a mood enhancer, especially for women."

"No, thanks," Rory said.

Sierra and Natalie exchanged a look.

"If you're not eating, you must be in love," Sierra said.

"No, I—" To her horror, Rory felt her eyes fill with tears. She rubbed away the one that escaped and blinked back the others. She never cried. Never. "I'm just not lucky that way. Even if I were, I just don't have… I'm going to be fine. I'll find another job and I'll…" What? Find another man? Not likely. Jared Slade had even ruined any relationship she could have with a fantasy man—because her fantasy man was him. "I'll…go home and just…"

Rory lifted her teacup and then set it down. She was thinking of doing what she'd always done. She was giving up and running away.

Suddenly, the advice her father had given her in his letter came back to her, almost as if he were sitting beside her, whispering in her ear. *Trust in your luck…stay in the game.*

Rory glanced around the room. This was the room where she'd seduced her Terminator—whatever his real name was. She'd driven him crazy. And she could do it again. She wanted to do it again.

"No." Straightening her shoulders and lifting her chin, she faced her sisters again. "I'm not going home."

"Good," Natalie said with a sigh. "I'll feel so much better if you stay here."

"I'm not staying here, either. But I'm not going to run away and start over—looking for a new career and a new man. That's what I always do. Lea Roberts isn't the only boss in the world, and *Celebs* is not the only magazine."

"Here! Here!" Sierra said, raising her cup again.

Rory was out of her chair and pacing. "And I'm not going to go looking for another man, either. Hunter—or whoever he is—is the only man for me."

Natalie and Sierra exchanged another look.

"You're right. She is in love with him," Natalie said.

Rory raised a hand. "Maybe. I'm not sure. I—"

"She's definitely in love with him," Sierra said. "The confusion, the fear, the fact that she's passing up food. Classic symptoms across cultures."

Rory clapped her hands over her ears. "I'm not listening. I'm not even going to think about that right now." Then moving to the door, she called out, "McGee?"

"Yes, miss," he said, stepping out of a nearby room with a suitcase in his hand.

"I changed my mind. I'd like you to pack everything, please."

Nodding, McGee followed her back into her bedroom. "I thought you might. Shall I pack the bubble gum, too?"

"No, I'll put that in my purse. And the cookies, too. Can you wrap them up, please? And one other thing. Why do you call Hunter Mr. Hunter?"

"Because that's what Mr. Lucas has always called him—even back in the days when they went to college together."

"Hunter might be his first name then," Rory said, turning to Natalie. "I'm going to need your help."

Natalie frowned.

Rory fisted her hands on her hips. "Don't give me that look. If Chance hadn't come back from London a few weeks ago, what would you have done?"

"She would have gone after him," Sierra said when Natalie hesitated. "You know you would have, Nat."

"You followed Dad's advice," Rory said. "Now it's my turn. If I don't take a risk, I may lose him."

Natalie threw up her hands. "Okay. What do you need?"

"I need all of your research skills and the equipment at D.C. Metro. I want to know the hometown of a man—first name of Hunter, I think. He went to Harvard with Lucas Wainwright and he was accused of embezzling from his family's bank about ten years ago. Can you get me that?"

Natalie smiled. "I'll try. But you'll have to help me out. You're the one who inherited the luck genes."

THE APARTMENT THAT TRACKER kept at Wainwright Enterprises offered a view of the Washington Monument and the Mall. But Hunter wasn't seeing it as he gazed out of the window. He couldn't get images of Rory out of his mind. Rory laughing in the sunlight as they rode. Rory, her eyes misted and locked on his, saying his name. Rory rushing toward him as the man standing in the sunroof pointed the gun at him.

He wanted her with him right now. His body was hard just thinking about her. And he was beginning to regret that he'd left without talking to her, seeing her. Touching her.

"Earth to Hunter."

He whirled from the window to find Tracker standing in the doorway to his office. "I've called your name twice."

"I never should have let you talk me into coming here without her."

Brows lifted, Tracker studied him for a moment. "You've got it bad, pal."

"What are you talking about?" Hunter asked.

Tracker grinned. "You've fallen in love with her. As a recent victim, I can spot the signs."

Hunter frowned. "What signs?"

"For starters, you've been staring out that window for the past ten minutes. You can't hear your name when it's called and you can't clear images of her out of your mind. Plus, you want her with you pretty much all the time."

Since Hunter realized he was presently experiencing everything Tracker had just described, he didn't comment.

"And even though you've spent your life doing just fine on your own, you're beginning to see that a future without her in it would be empty."

Was that true? No. Hunter sank down on the arm of a nearby chair. But hadn't that been the very direction his thoughts had been taking in the woods right after they'd made love? Hadn't he felt what it might be like to have her with him when they were old? And it had felt right somehow.

Tracker moved behind a sleek stainless-steel counter, pulled two beers out of a tall refrigerator, and handed him one.

Hunter twisted the cap off and took a long swallow. "Suppose all that's true. It doesn't mean I'm in love. I just never should have left without talking to her." He rose and began to pace. "She doesn't have a lot of self-confidence where men are concerned. She's probably already convinced herself that I've dumped her, that I won't come back. Hell, maybe she doesn't even want me back. I've lied to her right from the start. She'll think everything—everything we shared—was a lie." Turning, he found Tracker regarding him steadily, a sympathetic look on his face.

"I'm not…" Hunter began. "I don't…I never wanted to be this responsible for another person. I—"

Tracker lifted his beer in a toast. "Ain't love grand?"

"It isn't…" Hunter began. He wanted to deny that he'd fallen in love, but he was beginning to be very afraid that he had.

"I was in denial at first, too. I just didn't think that people as different as Sophie and I were could ever make a go of it."

"What happened to change your mind?" Hunter asked.

Tracker grinned. "She made me an offer I couldn't refuse. And you can make Rory Gibbs one just as soon as we figure out who's trying to kill you."

"Right." First things first, Hunter thought as he strode to the large oak table where Tracker had spread out the contents of a file.

"This is what I've got so far," Tracker said. "Michael Banks, Denise Martin and Alex Santos—our three prime suspects. I've run background checks on each one of them and I can't connect them to Hunter Marks. Plus, everything on their résumés checks out."

Hunter studied the faces of his three most trusted business associates. If he wanted to get back to Rory, he had to solve this problem first. "Okay. We've run into a dead end with who. Maybe we'll have more luck with why. This has to go back to the embezzlement scandal in Oakwood. He or she knows what I did and wants to expose me and perhaps destroy Slade Enterprises, probably for revenge."

"That may well have been plan A, in Atlanta and New York, but the threats got more personal once you arrived in D.C.," Tracker said. "The question is, why?"

"Lea Roberts was here. With her help, Jared Slade could be exposed in the press as Hunter Marks—because she was the one who originally broke the old embezzlement story."

"Why the bomb?" Tracker asked.

"A message to me along with the note that the exposure is only step one of the master plan."

"And if the bomb in your suite had killed you?" Tracker asked.

Hunter shook his head. "It wasn't meant to. It was set by someone who knew I was definitely out of the suite." Reaching down, he turned Denise Martin's picture facedown. "Which eliminates Denise. Now there are only two suspects."

"Okay. The note and the bomb are delivered to let you know that the threat is personal and serious. Next in the plan you see Slade Enterprises ruined because it's suddenly revealed that Jared Slade is none other than the embezzler who used to be known as Hunter Marks. Then you die."

"But the plan goes awry. Rory doesn't turn over the pictures on schedule, and her apartment is searched without success, and I go into hiding."

"Panic sets in," Tracker said. "And he goes to plan B— just shoot you. Which one of them is more capable of coming up with a complicated plan like that?"

"They both are."

"Pick a favorite," Tracker said.

Hunter stared down at the photos and finally shook his head. "I still can't see either of them doing this."

"Then we'll have to find something that links one of them with your past as Hunter Marks."

"You've checked places of birth?"

Tracker nodded. "Alex was born in New York City. I'm still checking on Michael."

"Maybe we're coming at this from the wrong perspective," Hunter said. "Assuming it is one of these two, they've been working for me for some time. I covered my tracks well, but one of them somehow made the connection between Hunter Marks and Jared Slade and applied for a job with Slade Enterprises. Why wait three or four years to get revenge?"

"You're wondering what happened to trigger the notes and the incidents in Atlanta and New York?"

"Yes." Then Hunter suddenly sank into a chair. "Of course. That has to be it. I don't know why I didn't see it before. Three months ago, I made plans to take over Marks Banking and Investments, my family's company. Both of them worked on the research."

Tracker nodded. "It started one of them thinking and they connected you with Hunter Marks."

Hunter met Tracker's eyes. "That's why I have to go back there. There's something that I'm not seeing, something that I don't know about. No one was supposed to get hurt or lose any money. That's why I let them make me the scapegoat."

"Ah, the deep, dark secret at last. You're not really an embezzler."

"I'm going back there," Hunter said.

"We'll be there when the bank opens in the morning."

"Damn!" Lea Roberts slammed on the brakes as she hit the bumper-to-bumper traffic that she'd have to battle all the way into D.C. She needed to get to her office and clear her calendar for the next few days. Her trip to the Wainwright estate had been a bust in all but one respect. She now knew that Jared Slade had been there. From the looks of the security, he'd been hiding out there. So there had to be some truth to the tip she'd received about the bomb in his suite at Les Printemps.

Frowning, she tapped her fingers on the steering wheel. So Jared Slade, alias Hunter Marks, was under siege. By whom, was the question. Of course, it had to be her anonymous tipster. But who in the hell was that?

As if to join in on the little discussion she was having with herself, her cell phone rang. She nudged her car into a faster-moving lane, and then pushed the button on her speaker phone. "What is it?"

"I want you to run the story proving who Jared Slade really is."

It was the same androgynous voice, and there was more than a trace of anger in it. Lea bit back her own temper. "No."

"Why not?"

"I still don't have the pictures."

The voice swore. "You always were incompetent. Even years ago, you didn't cover the story well. You covered up the harm that the Marks family did. You were on their payroll just like everyone else in town."

Even as Lea blinked in surprise, the call ended. So it all went back to the original embezzlement. And there'd been a cover-up? Suddenly, she knew where she might find Hunter Marks. If she was right, the story was even bigger than she'd originally thought.

OAKWOOD HADN'T CHANGED MUCH in the ten years since Hunter had last seen it. As Tracker drove the rental car down Main Street, he noted that most of the family-owned stores were still in operation—Maisie's Diner, Bob's Barbershop, the Law Offices of Thorne and Grayson. It had been Marshall Thorne Sr. who'd sat on the bank's board and advised his family.

The only new business he saw was an antique shop where Dennison's Jewelers used to be. When they pulled to a stop at the traffic light, Hunter glanced at the library first. The large redbrick building stood in the center of the block, flanked by parking lots on two sides. He wondered if Daisy Brinkman still patrolled her building, breaking up necking sessions in the stacks.

Even when the light turned green, he waited until the last moment to shift his gaze across the street to Marks Banking and Investments. The three-story structure stood at the intersection of Main and First streets. The solid look of gray stone and the clean lines of the Federal-style architecture projected security. How often had he stood in front of it as a boy and known that one day he would work there?

As they pulled into the curb in front of it, Hunter noted that the sign on the door was just the same. Come In and Bank with People You Trust.

Right. The last time he'd seen those words had been the night he'd left town, and he'd hurled a rock through the window, breaking the glass. One last hurrah to assuage the mix of fury and disillusionment that had been burning inside of him.

Odd, but he felt none of those things now. And yet nothing had changed, neither the building nor the reasons why he'd given up all ties to his family ten years ago. Still, just looking at the building had some of his tension easing.

Perhaps he'd changed. If he had, he owed it to Rory.

Firmly, he pushed her out of his mind. She was safe, and he'd see to it personally just as soon as he finished what he'd come back to Oakwood to do.

"I'll go in alone," Hunter said.

"No way." Tracker let himself out the driver's side and caught up to Hunter as he pushed through the glass doors. "Until we catch whoever's out to get you, just think of me as your guardian angel. You won't even know I'm here."

"I need to talk to my brother alone," Hunter said, and he was surprised to find it was true. He did need to talk to Carter and not just about who might be threatening him.

The building smelled just the same, a mix of lemon wax and old leather. The tellers still worked in little cubicles behind a row of brass bars. Miss Tolley, his father's secretary, still had a vase of fresh flowers from her garden on her desk. But when he shifted his gaze, he saw there was young a woman in a neat black business suit sitting at the desk that used to belong to his brother.

"Miss Tolley," he said as he reached the secretary's desk. He saw recognition flash into her eyes the moment she glanced up at him.

"Hunter?"

He grinned at her. "Still sharp as ever." His smile faded. "I want to see my brother."

She lifted the phone. "I'll tell him you're here."

Hunter strode toward the door behind Miss Tolley's desk, the door that now had his brother's name on it.

"I'll be right here," Tracker murmured.

For a moment, Hunter continued to stare at his brother's name on the door. Why hadn't Michael or Alex mentioned that it was Carter Marks III who was now running the bank? With his hand on the knob, he hesitated another moment, and then he walked into the office.

Carter rose from behind the desk, but he didn't move. As Hunter walked toward him, he saw a flood of emotions flash over his brother's features—shock, apprehension. And was there some guilt? He'd imagined this scene so many times in the first few years after he'd left home.

And then he saw in his brother's eyes what he'd never seen in his dreams—pleasure.

"Hunter." Carter circled his desk. "I'd given up. I never thought I'd see you again—or that you'd want to see me. Welcome back." He held out his hand.

Was it just that simple? When Hunter grasped his brother's hand, he felt his tension ease. "How are you?"

"A bit harried. Mandy, that's my wife—your sister-in-law—she's expecting twins in a week or so. The doctor says it could be anytime." He ran a hand through his hair. "There's other stuff—business. Someone's trying to buy us out, but we've been able to prevent it so far."

Not much longer, Hunter thought. Not with the sweetened deal that he was going to offer the board and the town council. "Where's Dad?" he asked.

"Dad hasn't been here at the bank for almost ten years."

Once again, Hunter wondered how this information hadn't been in the reports he'd been presented with. "What happened?"

Carter flushed a little. "He couldn't get the gambling thing under control, and so the board forced him into retirement."

Hunter studied his brother and saw what he wasn't saying. "You caught him with his hand in the till again?"

Carter nodded. "About six months after you left, Mother moved him to a nice retirement community in North Carolina. He still has his horses, but she holds on to the purse strings and sits on the town council. They visit up here twice a year, and she doesn't let him near the bank or any casinos."

"How about you?" Hunter asked. "Do you ever get the urge to gamble?"

Carter met his eyes steadily. "If you're asking if I visit casinos, no. The only gambling I've done in the last ten years was to marry Mandy. So far it's paid off."

"You're lucky."

"Yes, I am. Hunter, I—I'm glad you're here."

Hunter felt something inside of himself loosen. And although he never would have predicted it, he found that he was glad, too. But he wasn't ready to say it, wasn't ready to trust completely.

"I came because I have some questions."

"Sure. Sit down. I'll have Miss Tolley bring us coffee."

Hunter waited, happy for the reprieve as the coffee was served. Finally, when Carter was seated in the chair beside him, he said, "I need some information about what happened after I left. Did anyone in town lose money because of the embezzlement?"

"Absolutely not. I made sure of that."

Hunter studied his brother. Carter had been less than a year out of college when he'd taken over the bank. "You must have put in a lot of hours."

Carter shrugged. "I'd do it again."

"Why did you ever get mixed up in gambling and embezzlement in the first place?"

Carter shrugged. "In those days I did everything that Dad did. I figured it was the only way to really fill his shoes. And I didn't know about the embezzlement until you did."

For a moment, Hunter let the silence stretch between them. Then finally, he said, "Someone told me recently that the thing about revisiting the past is that you see it in a different perspective." Then taking a sip of his coffee, he refocused his thoughts on the problem at hand. "Are you sure that no one in town was hurt by the embezzlement?"

Carter hesitated for a moment, then said, "Well, there was Mike Dennison, the jeweler. He committed suicide the night before the story hit the papers."

"I was still here. Why didn't anyone tell me?"

"No one knew. The body wasn't discovered for three days or so. His wife claimed that he learned about the embezzlement and panicked. She always blamed us for his death. We never accepted the responsibility, of course."

"I thought the board and our attorney had the news sewn up tight. They were so afraid of a run on the bank. Who would have leaked the information?"

Carter shook his head. "We never found out."

"Would you still have a list of employees from that time?"

"Sure." Carter studied him for a moment. "This is important?"

"Yes."

Carter reached for the phone and instructed Miss Tolley to gather the information. When he finished, he glanced around the office again. "It'll be tight for a bit. There won't be as much money as you might expect, but there's room for you here. You can have a desk in here if you want. We'll move mine. There should be room."

Hunter frowned. "What are you talking about?"

"You coming on board. I've been trying to track you down for years. To tell you the truth we could use some help in handling investments. If we can strengthen that department, we can discourage any future attempts at a buyout."

Hunter's brows shot up. "You're offering me a job? You don't even know what I've been doing for the past ten years."

Carter met his eyes steadily. "You're my brother, and you took a fall for Dad and me ten years ago. I never should have let you do it. I wouldn't have if I could have figured out a better way to save the bank. I certainly wouldn't have let you do it if I'd known I wouldn't see you again. But what you did—it saved Marks Banking and Investments. This place is here because of you, so you have a job here anytime you want."

Carter held out his hand.

Perhaps it *was* just that simple, Hunter thought as he took his brother's hand and then pulled him into his arms.

When he drew back, he said, "There are some things I need to tell you first."

"About what you've been doing for the past ten years?"

Hunter smiled. "That, too." And Hunter began to fill him in.

_14_

IT WAS AFTER TEN when Rory pulled into the driveway next to the Oakwood Public Library. During the drive from D.C., she'd had plenty of time to debate where to start—the newspaper office or the library. When she spotted the latter first, she went with it.

At least she had a name. Natalie had found the name Hunter Marks and the small town of Oakwood for her within an hour. But it had taken Rory another three hours to gather all the information about the embezzling scandal she could find online. Then, since her sister hadn't been keen on her visiting Oakwood, she'd had to be sure that Nat was asleep before she'd sneaked out of her sister's apartment.

After parking her car at the back of the brick building, Rory climbed up the short flight of wooden steps to the back entrance. The moment she walked through the door, she found herself in a small room where a group of children, either sitting or stretched out flat on the floor, were listening to a young woman reading aloud. They paid her no heed as she moved quietly into the next room. Here, sun poured through immaculately clean windows, and she had to shade her eyes to see the woman behind the information desk.

As she drew closer, Rory saw that the woman was a perfect fit to the image she carried in her mind of a small-town librarian—tall and thin, wearing Victorian-style clothes, with gray hair pulled back neatly into a bun. At first, Rory guessed her age to be about seventy, but up close, she could see that the dark eyes held both intelligence and humor, and the welcoming smile softened the older woman's features in ways that shaved years away. Daisy Brinkman was the name on the little brass plate on her desk. It suited her to a T.

"Well, this is Oakwood's day for visitors. What can I do for you?" Daisy asked.

"My name is Rory Gibbs." She handed the woman a card and drew in a deep breath. "I work freelance for *Celebs* magazine, and I'm researching an article on Hunter Marks and the scandal that drove him out of town ten years ago."

Daisy studied her for a moment. "Hogwash."

Rory just stared at her. "What?"

"I said hogwash. You're lying. And you don't have the eyes for it. Plus, I read *Celebs* magazine. The Marks embezzlement is an old story, not at all the kind of piece your magazine would run. The editorial staff there likes its scandals current." Her eyes narrowed. "Unless Hunter Marks has resurfaced as some sort of celebrity in his own right?"

When Rory continued to stare, Daisy tapped a pencil on her desk. "That might explain why he's come back to town to talk to his brother after all these years. The return of the prodigal—now rich and famous, is he?"

Rory swallowed. "He's with his brother?"

Daisy nodded, her eyes sparkling. "Leona Tolley over at the bank called me not half an hour ago. And Lea Roberts, the reporter who broke the embezzlement story, is hanging out at Maisie's Diner. Add that to the mix and there's got to be a good story. She hasn't been back here in ten years. You working for her?"

"No." Rory studied the woman for a moment and then went with her instincts. "What I just said *was* hogwash. I don't work for Lea Roberts or *Celebs* anymore. She fired me. But I am here to find out everything I can about that old scandal."

"Why?"

Rory was beginning to think the tiny woman in front of her had picked the wrong profession entirely. She'd have made a good cop or P.I. And Rory didn't think she was going to get much information unless she came clean. "What if I told you that I'm trying to prove that years ago Hunter Marks took the blame for someone else?"

"Hmmph. Wouldn't surprise me a bit. The story that Lea Roberts printed in the papers had cover-up written all over it. But it saved the bank and the town. Why do you want to dig up that old scandal after all these years? Young Carter has done a fine job of running the bank."

"Because the truth might save someone's life," Rory said. "Hunter Marks's life. Someone is trying to kill him, and I'm pretty sure it's connected to that old embezzlement scandal. Can you help me?"

Daisy studied Rory for a long moment, then said, "What exactly do you want to know?"

"Who was hurt enough by the embezzlement to want to kill Hunter Marks?"

"Come with me," Daisy said, stepping out from behind the circulation desk and leading the way to a staircase. "I store files on the third floor. Now mind the railing. It needs tightening."

The narrow room that she led Rory into was dim and

almost airless. The light filtering through one low dormer window was thick with dust motes. One wall of shelves was lined with books, the other filled with storage boxes. Daisy threw a light switch and began to scan the boxes. "Here it is."

Rory helped her set the box on the floor and opened it.

"I kept a folder with all the stories. But you won't find much about the one tragedy that was linked to the rumors of embezzlement at the bank."

"A tragedy?"

"Yes. Ah, here it is." Daisy pulled out a file and flipped through it. "Very unfortunate. Mike Dennison who ran Dennison's Jewelers—the store used to be right on the corner where the antique shop is—he killed himself. His wife maintained that he got wind of the scandal and knew that he would be wiped out if there was a run on the bank. The Marks family was able to keep the suicide from getting much news coverage. Mrs. Dennison did file a civil suit against the family on behalf of her son and herself. It was settled." Daisy fished out another clipping.

Rory looked down at a yellowed picture of a stocky woman and a thin boy. "How old was the boy?"

Daisy thought for a moment. "Twelve or thirteen."

"Where are they now?"

Daisy's eyebrows shot up. "I can keep pretty good track of people while they're in town, but Michael and his mom moved out of town right after he graduated from high school. Rumor was young Mike got a free trip to the college of his choice as part of the settlement. When he left for his freshman year, she moved out of town, too. I heard she got married again."

Rory was still studying the picture. The story was interesting, but it didn't sound like the Dennisons had been hell-bent on revenge. "You don't happen to have a more recent picture of young Mike, do you?"

Daisy shot her a smile. "I keep copies of all the high-school yearbooks. Wait right here."

Rory knelt down to inspect the file again. All there was on the Dennison family was an obituary. She'd been so sure that she could help, but she had the feeling that she was following a dead end. No. She started through the files again. There had to be something here. All of her instincts told her that what was happening now had to be tied to this old tragedy.

"Here it is," Daisy said as she hurried into the room. "Michael was the valedictorian of his class, a very bright boy. Word was he was going to major in business."

As Rory studied the picture, she saw a blond young man, very preppy looking, and a little flutter of recognition moved through her. In her mind, she attempted to add on ten years, and the flutter grew stronger.

"YOU'RE SURE THAT NO ONE ELSE was hurt by the possible collapse of the bank?" Hunter asked.

Frowning, Carter shook his head. "You of all people know what the family did to keep anyone from being hurt, how quickly we acted. Dennison panicked."

Dennison. Hunter had only been able to come up with a vague image of the jeweler in his mind. The store he could picture, but at nineteen, he hadn't had any reason to go in or get to know the family. "How did he learn about the embezzlement? I didn't even know until the night before the press release. And that was the night he hung himself."

Carter nodded. "The widow claimed that it was her son who brought the news home."

"So the son brings home a rumor, and his dad kills himself before the truth comes out." Hunter shook his head. "That's a huge burden to carry around with you for the rest of your life."

"When we made the settlement, we urged Mrs. Dennison to move out of town and make a new start. But she wanted her son to remain in Oakwood." Carter sent him a troubled look. "I can't see any connection between Mike Dennison's suicide and these threats on your life."

Hunter couldn't, either. Tracker was having his men trace the mother and the son, but that would take time. A fresh wave of frustration rolled through him along with a feeling deep in his gut that time was running out.

There was a knock at the door. *Tracker,* he thought as he turned. But it was Rory who rushed into the office. Tracker followed, talking on his cell, but Hunter couldn't take his eyes off Rory. His first thought was that he'd conjured her up because he'd been wanting her with him ever since he'd left her at the Wainwright estate. She looked hot and sweaty and there was dust on her face and arms. Just seeing her made his mouth go dry.

"I think I know who's threatening you," she said as she placed an open book on the desk and pointed to a photo.

He didn't glance down right away because he couldn't stop looking at her. His heart took a long, slow tumble as he faced what he hadn't been able to accept before. He was in love with Rory Gibbs.

"Look," she said impatiently. "You have to imagine him with ten years added on. Do you recognize him?"

Hunter looked at the photo for a moment. Then, eyes narrowing, he leaned closer to study it more thoroughly. Finally, he straightened and turned to Tracker. "Mike

Dennison's son is my executive assistant, Michael Banks."

Tracker conveyed that information to whomever he was talking to.

"Where did you find this?" Hunter asked.

"The library. Daisy Brinkman was very helpful."

Carter's intercom buzzed, and he pressed the button and picked up the receiver.

"I have a question, too," Tracker said. "Just how did you manage to get away from both your sister and the man I had following you?"

Rory looked at him and shrugged. "I climbed out a window and cut through an alley to where I'd parked my car."

Hunter couldn't prevent a smile, but it faded when he saw the expression on his brother's face.

"Miss Tolley says that there's a reporter here asking to see you, Hunter. Lea Roberts."

"I don't like this," Tracker said. "If she's here and Rory's here, can Michael Banks or one of his hired killers be far behind?" He glanced at Carter. "Is there a back way out of here?"

"Right through that door over there." Carter dug in his desk and pulled out a set of keys. "Take my car. It's a beige SUV right outside the back entrance. I'll stall Lea Roberts."

"I don't want her to know that Jared Slade is really Hunter Marks," Tracker said.

Carter grinned. "Don't worry. I can handle her. I never did like her much."

"C'mon." Tracker urged them toward the door.

"I have a plan we can use to trap him," Rory said.

"Good. You can tell us all about it once we're safely out of town."

HUNTER SHOVED A BASEBALL CAP down low on his forehead and scanned the dining room of the Blue Pepper again. He didn't like Rory's plan one bit, not even with the revisions that Tracker and Natalie Gibbs had insisted on making. And he hated the onlooker role he'd been assigned in the little charade they were going to play out.

Of course, he had to admit that the others were right. If he got too close, Michael could recognize him, and that would spoil everything. Plus, it might put Rory in even more danger.

So he was stuck sitting at the bar while Rad, one of the owners of the Blue Pepper, escorted Rory to a table in the upper-level dining area. After a glance at his watch, he took a sip of the beer in front of him. Rory had called Michael, inviting him to meet with her because she had proof that he was trying to kill Jared Slade. She was wired, so they could hear and record everything, and if she could get Michael to admit what he'd done, then everything would be over.

Tracker had explained to him what they needed on the ride back to D.C. Even though they'd discovered that Michael might have motivation, they still had no proof tying him to either the bomb or the shooting. Hunter shifted his gaze to the dining room again as Rory took her seat. She was wearing the red sundress that McGee had purchased for her. And she'd told him that she was wearing the red thong just for extra luck.

He wished to hell that he had some of her confidence that this was going to go well. The fact that Chance Mitchell and Natalie Gibbs were stationed at the table next to Rory's eased his fears somewhat. But there were things that could still go wrong.

Tracker climbed onto the stool next to Hunter. "One of

my men just spotted our friend walking toward the restaurant. He's about a block away."

Instead of easing the knot in Hunter's stomach, the news only tightened it. Michael had taken the bait, but now the danger for Rory was real instead of theoretical.

"I still don't have a good feeling about this," he said.

"Chance Mitchell is the best. And the two other men I have stationed up there are top-notch, too. Ah, here's our boy now."

Hunter didn't move his head, only his eyes, but he kept them steady on Michael Dennison Banks as he walked up the stairs and sat down at Rory's table.

"HI," RORY SAID as Michael Dennison avoided the chair that Rad was holding for him and sat in the one next to her.

He said nothing until Rad was out of earshot. Then he pitched his voice low. "What kind of game are you playing? I had nothing to do with the bomb at Les Printemps. I don't even know anything about a shooting."

Her nerves were jumping so much that Rory barely kept herself from blowing a bubble. She knew what she was supposed to say. Tracker and Natalie had taken her through the script over and over. She kept the bubble gum tucked in her cheek while she said, "I went to Oakwood, Connecticut, and did a little research. I know about your father's suicide, but I haven't told anyone yet."

"So?"

The voice and the eyes were so cold that Rory barely kept herself from shivering. "So my sister Natalie is a cop with the D.C. police. There was a fingerprint recovered from the bomb. Once they discover it belongs to Michael Dennison, alias Michael Banks, how long do you think you can continue to play dumb?"

For a moment he didn't say anything. Once more, she had to stifle the urge to blow a bubble. He was thinking, weighing the truth of what she was saying. Rory remembered Daisy Brinkman saying that she didn't have the eyes for telling a lie. Could those cold blue eyes staring at her now see that?

She leaned toward him. "I can either tell them or keep your identity a secret. It's up to you."

"Tell anyone you want. I don't know what you're talking about."

"HE'S NOT ADMITTING ANYTHING," Hunter murmured. "He's going to stonewall her."

Tracker laid a hand on his arm when he would have moved. "Give her a few more minutes."

Hunter took another drink of his beer as he watched Rory reach out a hand to keep Michael from rising.

"I can understand why you did it," she said. "You blame him for what happened, don't you? Everyone in town knew that he was reckless, the black sheep of the Marks family. And he'd certainly lived up to his name—gambling and then stealing money to cover his losses. Stealing your father's money. Your money."

"She's off script," Tracker murmured. "But she's keeping him there."

Yeah, Hunter thought. But the bad feeling he had wasn't getting any better.

"You know nothing," Michael said.

"I know you lost your father. I lost mine, too, when I was ten. He died in a car crash. The driver of the other car was drunk. He never even went to jail. If I could have, I would have gone after him and made him suffer for taking my father from me."

Hunter stiffened then. "She's lying. She can't tell a lie to save her life."

"Wait." Tracker tightened his grip on Hunter's arm.

"Hunter Marks deserves to die," Michael said.

"See? She's playing him just right," Tracker said.

"I know just how you feel," Rory murmured. "How did you ever find him?"

"Luck. I had no idea when I went to work for Jared Slade that he was really Hunter Marks. I only put it together when he told me to do the research on buying out Marks Banking and Investments. He was actually going to buy them out. I've seen what he can do when he takes over a business. Within a year, he would have doubled their profits. And my father wouldn't be there to benefit from any of it. I knew then what I had to do."

Rory tried to suppress a shiver. She couldn't take her eyes off Michael's, and she was beginning to glimpse the madness just beneath all that ice.

"Oh, I would have found him eventually. I was saving every cent I made for that purpose. It was my mother's idea. She always told me that I would have to track him down and make him pay. That's why we stayed in town for so long. She was waiting for him to come back. And when I finally left for college, I promised her that I would carry out her wishes."

Rory licked her lips. "Your mother wanted you to kill Hunter Marks?"

"He destroyed her one true love. The two men she married after that never loved her the way my father did. She depended on me to get her justice."

"You changed your name."

"My mother wanted me to use the name of her second

husband. That way no one could ever connect me with the Marks family."

When he paused to smile at her, Rory did shiver. But she made herself ask, "What is Lea Roberts's connection to all of this?"

Michael shrugged. "She wrote the original story that told the truth about Hunter Marks. I thought she deserved to be able to write the final chapter in Marks's life. But she proved to be incompetent. I'll handle that, just as I'm going to handle you."

Rory felt something hard poke into her side.

"I've got a gun. Get up slowly and smile at me. Then we're going to leave the restaurant. If you try to signal anyone or give me any trouble at all, I'll shoot some of the other customers."

"Don't use the gun," Rory said as she rose. "You haven't killed anyone yet. And Hunter Marks isn't the monster you think he is. He'll help you."

"Shut up." He took her hand and pulled her closer, pressing the gun in his pocket against her side. "Don't you think I know that you're his girlfriend? He'll come after you, and then I'll finish this."

"EVERYONE STAY BACK." Tracker spoke into his mouthpiece. "That includes you," he added to Hunter.

"To hell with that," Hunter said as he got off his stool. "I warned you that he was smart. He wants me, so he's going to get me."

Tracker grabbed his arm. "Let him get out of the building. If he's that smart, he'll know that he can hurt you by killing her."

An icy knot of fear twisted even tighter in Hunter's

stomach as he edged his way through the crowd. It seemed forever before Tracker said, "He's out and moving up the street."

They began to move more quickly then.

"Can you keep your cool?" Tracker asked as they pushed out onto the street.

Hunter nodded. "I'm going to try to reason with him."

Michael and Rory were halfway down the block. Salsa music blared from the patio, so Hunter didn't bother to call out. He just broke into a run. He knew that Tracker had moved into the street on the other side of the parked cars, but Hunter kept his eyes on Rory. He was going to get her back safely.

When he was close enough to be heard, he called out, "Michael, it's me you want."

Michael turned then, but he kept his grip tight on Rory, and Hunter saw that the hand gripping the gun didn't waver. "I want you both."

Hunter raised his hands, palms out and prayed that the reasonable side of Michael Banks's brain was still functioning. "You can't have us both. The man in the street to my right will take you out before you can get a second shot off. It's either me or Rory. Which one would your mother want you to shoot?"

When Michael took his hand out of his pocket and pointed the gun at him, Hunter began to let out the breath he was holding. It caught in his throat when Rory threw all of her weight at Michael Banks and two shots rang out simultaneously.

"IT'S A DAMN MIRACLE you didn't get yourself shot," Hunter said.

"It was luck," Rory corrected. They were seated on the curb down the street from the Blue Pepper with a blanket wrapped around them. She hadn't been able to stop shaking after the shots were fired, so one of the policemen had dug a blanket out of his trunk. It was only after Hunter had joined her beneath the warm folds of cloth that she'd begun to get warm again.

Michael Banks was being loaded into an ambulance. Tracker and Natalie were talking with the detectives who'd arrived on the scene. Two uniformed policemen were encouraging the Blue Pepper patrons to go back inside and enjoy the evening.

Rory blew out a bubble, then sucked it back into her mouth. "My knees are like jelly now. I'm not sure I can walk."

"Yeah. I've got the same feeling in mine. Maybe we'll have to stay here all night. Are you warm enough?" He slid his hand up her side and drew her closer.

"I'm warmer now."

The doors of the ambulance swung shut and Rory said, "I feel sorry for him. He lost his dad, and he had a wacko for a mother."

"Seems that way," Hunter said. "I'm going to hire him a good defense attorney."

She turned to stare at him then. "You're the sweetest man I've ever met. You took the blame for your brother and your father all those years ago because you didn't want anyone to be hurt. Never mind that you lost everything."

Hunter smiled. "I haven't done so badly for myself. And my brother's done a good job with the bank. He told me today that the merchants in the town have rallied behind him to prevent Slade Enterprises's hostile takeover."

"Maybe it's time for the whole story to come out," Rory said.

"That's what Carter would like. But he stonewalled Lea

Roberts because I told him I happen to have this other reporter in mind," Hunter said. "She has good instincts, and I think she'll tell the story well." He lowered his mouth to hers, and then he said against her lips, "I'm going to offer her an exclusive interview if she'll give me just one kiss."

She wanted to laugh, but she was already sinking into the kiss, and his hands became very busy under the blanket. When one of them parted her thighs, she started to protest. "Hunter…"

"Shh," he whispered. "You're wearing the thong." He traced his finger down the little red lace triangle that covered her cleft, and she shuddered.

"I can never look at you without wondering if you're wearing this."

"You have to…" Stop. That was the word she should say, but he was moving his finger over her again, and she could feel her insides heating and melting.

"Do you know how long I've been thinking of doing this? That whole long drive back to D.C. with Tracker." He stroked his finger down her again, and Rory bit down hard on her lip. "And all the time that he and Natalie were prepping you, I was thinking that I just wanted to hold you in my arms like this and make you come."

She had to fight the moan back when he slipped two fingers into her, then curved them and began to rub them on the spot he'd found before.

"You…can't," she whispered.

"Yes, I can," he murmured against her ear. "And I can do this, too." He continued to move his fingers inside of her, while he found her clitoris with his thumb and began to rub that also.

Blending with the murmur of nearby voices and the

sounds of the salsa band at the Blue Pepper, Rory could hear her own breath coming in pants.

"I love to hear you breathe like that. You have no idea what it does to me," Hunter whispered.

A flood of sensations moved through Rory. She had a feeling that they were heightened by the fact that they were seated in the shadows between two parked cars. At any moment, someone could turn and look at them. "We're…on a public street."

She could feel his lips curve against her ear.

"That means you have to be very quiet when you have your orgasm," he said. "And you can't move, either."

She should stop him. But her body had become swamped by the pleasure he was giving her. The fact that she couldn't move, couldn't make a sound sharpened each response that was streaming through her.

As if he could sense the moment that the first wave of the orgasm moved through her, he took her mouth with his while she rode it out. Then he continued to hold her tight even after the last little shock wave passed.

It might have been minutes or hours before Tracker came over and said, "Hey, I've been sent over to break this up. They don't allow necking on one of the main streets of Georgetown."

RORY BLEW OUT A BUBBLE as she stepped off the elevator into the reception area of the offices of *Celebs* magazine. Hattie Miller, a perky blond receptionist who'd always been nice to her, beamed her a smile. "Ms. Gibbs, congratulations on your story."

"Thanks, Hattie." Her story on Hunter Marks, alias Jared Slade, had appeared in an edition of *Vanity Fair* that had hit the newsstands the day before. As she neared the desk, Hattie winked and pitched her voice low. "It's caused quite a stir around here. Some of the suits flew down yesterday from the New York office. Word is that heads are going to roll and you can name your price if you'll come back to work."

"I think Ms. Roberts is expecting me," Rory said.

Hattie nodded. "Yes, sirree. You can go right on back."

Rory walked down the short hallway to Lea's office. On the way, she passed her temporary desk. It looked the same as it had the last time she'd been here—as if it were just waiting for her to return to work.

The phone call from Lea had come that morning shortly after Hunter had left for Dallas on business. It had been thirteen days since Michael Banks had been arrested, and ten days since she'd sold her story to *Vanity Fair.* But the time had flown by, and Hunter had spent more time in Dallas and Oakwood than he'd spent in D.C.

That was beginning to worry her a little. Pausing before the door to Lea's office, Rory drew in a deep breath. She hadn't wanted to agree to meet with Lea. The old Rory never would have. But the new Rory had questions and something to say to her old boss that had to be said in person.

She raised her hand and knocked on the door, and the moment she heard Lea's muffled "Come in," she entered and closed it behind her.

Lea rose from behind her desk, and even though she was impeccably dressed and groomed, she looked older. And tired.

"Congratulations on your story," Lea said stiffly.

"Thank you."

"I don't imagine that my call surprised you."

"As a matter of fact, it did. I can't imagine what you want to talk to me about."

Lea's brows shot up. "You might as well can the act. I know that you're not nearly as naive as you make yourself out to be. The shit pretty much hit the fan yesterday when your story came out. My boss learned that you used to work for me, and he was unhappy that you didn't bring the story to us. When they asked why you weren't working here anymore, I told them you quit."

"I see."

"If you deny that, it will be your word against mine."

"That's why you wanted to talk to me? To tell me that?"

Lea circled her desk and propped a hip on one of the corners. "For starters. I also wanted to see what it was that I'd missed. I'm usually a good judge of people. But you really fooled me. I didn't expect you to double-cross me, and I certainly didn't expect you to sleep with Hunter Marks just to get a story."

Rory lifted her chin. "I'm not surprised that you believe that because that's what you did, didn't you? You had an affair with him in the hopes that it would help your career. And it did."

Lea smiled, but it didn't reach her eyes. "Touché. I guess we're even more alike than I thought."

"No." Rory took a step toward Lea. "I don't think we're alike at all. I would never have written that story ten years ago."

Lea's brows shot up. "It was news. The public had a right to know."

"He was in love with you, and you believed what you wrote, didn't you? You believed that he'd embezzled the money?"

Lea folded her arms across her chest. "Of course, I did. Everyone did."

"Did you even ask him if he was guilty?"

"No. He confessed."

"He needed someone to believe in him."

Lea stared at her for a minute. "Good Lord. Don't tell me. You're in love with him, aren't you?"

Rory felt the heat rise in her cheeks.

Lea started to laugh. "You little fool. Sleeping with him is one thing. But falling in love?" She shook her head. "Maybe I wasn't so wrong about you after all. You can't think that Hunter Marks is going to settle down with someone like you."

Rory said nothing. There was nothing she could say about what Lea was implying. She and Hunter hadn't had time to talk about the future. Or they hadn't made the time. Pushing the nagging worry out of her head, she said, "Why don't you ask me why I agreed to see you?"

Lea's smile faded. "That's easy. You have to know or at least suspect that *Celebs* wants to make you a job offer. I'm authorized to make it a very generous one."

Rory shook her head. "That's not why I came."

"No? Well, if you've come to gloat because you got the story and I didn't, forget it. I may not have broken the Hunter Marks story, but my bosses are pleased that I've landed an exclusive interview with Michael Dennison Banks. My agent is already shopping around for a book deal."

"Congratulations." Rory knew for a fact that Lea was lying through her teeth. Michael Banks's lawyer wasn't letting Michael speak to anyone until the trial was over, and she had the inside track for an interview once the verdict was in. For the first time since she'd walked into the room, she felt a little sorry for Lea Roberts.

"That's not why I agreed to see you, either. I came because I wanted to thank you for hiring me. None of this would have happened if you hadn't had faith in me and given me a chance here at *Celebs*."

Lea merely stared at her. Rory knew as she turned and left the room, she wouldn't forget the stupefied expression on Lea's face for a long time.

Nor would she forget the laughter. It was the second time that Lea Roberts had laughed at her.

So she was a fool if she believed that Hunter Marks would settle down with someone like her, was she?

Ha. She'd just have to see about that.

15

"GOOD LUCK." Irene Malinowitz took one last look around Silken Fantasies and Rory followed her gaze. Natalie was lighting the tall pillar candles that rested on nearly every surface in the store, and Sierra was unpacking the contents of a small picnic hamper and checking each item against a list she held in her hand.

"Not that I think you'll need luck," Irene added as she turned back to smile at Rory. "I think you and your sisters have the plan completely under control. When is he due?"

Rory glanced at her watch, then at her sisters. "Soon. You're sure you don't mind my using your shop?"

Irene smiled. "It's not my shop anymore. I'm just managing it during the transition period. Jared—I mean, Hunter—convinced me to stay on for a while. Besides—" Irene paused to wink at Rory "—you can't spend a large part of your life in the lingerie business unless you're a true romantic at heart. Have fun." She leaned closer. "And I hope you're planning on making good use of some of the merchandise."

Rory smiled at her. "Thanks. I've already picked up several of your red thongs. You were right that first time I came here. I've been getting pretty good mileage out of them."

"Good," Irene said. "I'll just let myself out the back way."

Rory watched as Irene slipped through a curtain behind the sales counter. Then she gave her gum two quick chews and blew out a bubble.

"Everything is here," Sierra said as she tucked her list back into her canvas bag.

Natalie lit the last candle. "When exactly is Hunter due to arrive?"

Rory glanced at her watch. "Any minute."

Sierra put the final touch on a tray of chocolate-covered strawberries, then turned to survey the rest of the room. "I think this is so romantic—to return here."

"Desperate times call for desperate measures."

Natalie frowned. "Desperate? I thought everything was going well between the two of you."

"Everything is just…" Rory blew out another bubble, then licked the burst bits of gum off her bottom lip. "It's just that… Things have been… For the past two weeks, since Michael Banks was arrested, we've both been so…"

"You've been busy," Sierra said.

"Yes." They had been busy. When she'd sold her story to *Vanity Fair*, the magazine had wanted a follow-up on the whole Marks family in Oakwood. And Hunter had been swamped, too, flying back and forth from D.C. to Dallas. They'd both gone to Oakwood when Carter's wife had delivered the twins. Rory shrugged and took the bubble gum out of her mouth. "We just haven't spent much time…" She waved a hand. "You know…"

"Alone together," Natalie finished for her. "In other words, you're sex starved."

Rory smiled. "Well, there's that. He's been gone for two days. Although we usually manage to fit in making love—sometimes in the oddest…" She thought of sitting on the street in Georgetown between those two parked cars.

"Places." Sierra finished the sentence this time as she stepped forward to take Rory's hands. "Have you told him yet that you love him?"

Rory felt a familiar jolt of panic and wished that she hadn't gotten rid of her gum. "No."

"Tell him," Sierra suggested.

"I'm planning on doing that tonight. But he has a way of distracting me."

"You'll do just fine," Natalie said.

Rory swallowed hard. "What if he doesn't want to hear it?" The panic had morphed from a jolt to an earthquake in her stomach. "What if he…?"

Natalie patted her shoulder when her sentence once more trailed off. "I'm in thorough agreement with Sierra on this one. Just tell him."

There was a knock at the door.

"Speak of the devil," Natalie said as she leaned down to kiss Rory's cheek. "We'll exit through the back door the way Irene did."

Sierra hugged her and whispered, "Remember Harry's advice. You can do anything you want if you just dare to take a shot at it."

There was another knock as her sisters disappeared through the curtain. Rory straightened her shoulders, turned toward the front door and reviewed her game plan. Two simple steps. First tell him and then seduce him.

She took one last look around the room as she walked to the door of the shop. Pushing her luck had never seemed this important before.

The moment she opened the door and saw Hunter, her

plan began to fade from her mind. He was dressed just as he'd been the first time she'd seen him in that lobby—sunglasses, black leather jacket, black boots, black jeans. Her Terminator and fantasy man all rolled into one.

HE'D HAD A PLAN. When she'd left him the voice-mail message to meet her at Silken Fantasies, the idea had sprung full-blown into his mind, and on the three-hour plane trip from Dallas he'd had plenty of time to hammer out the details. He'd even stopped at a jewelry store on the way from the airport.

But seeing her now, wearing the same clothes she'd worn in the lobby of Les Printemps…those damn red boots had his throat going dry. And he knew she was wearing the thong. Would it always be this way? Hunter wondered. Would she always stir up needs in him until his whole body pounded with them?

"Hi," he said.

"You brought me flowers."

He glanced down at the bunch of daffodils he'd picked up on impulse from the stand at the end of the street. He'd completely forgotten about them. "Here."

She took the flowers and looked at them as if they were dozens of red roses. Stepping into the shop, he shut the door behind himself and locked it. "I had this plan. I worked it out on the airplane." Perhaps if he stopped looking at her for a moment, his brain cells would resuscitate and he'd be able to remember it.

"Me, too," she said. "I mean about the plan. I had one."

He managed to tear his gaze away from her long enough to take in the candles, the champagne and the tray of food, and his heart took another tumble. "I think I'm going to like it."

"You are. But I'm already thinking it needs revision."

She moved to him, placed her hands on his cheeks and drew his mouth to hers. "Because right now I want to make love to you in that dressing room."

"Yeah," he managed to say as he gripped her hips and raised her so that she could wrap her legs around him. "We can do that." When she began to rain kisses on his eyelids, his cheeks, his neck, his mouth, he stumbled and wondered if he was going to make it. But he did.

"Clothes," he said as he pushed her through the door. She was already unbuttoning his shirt. "Let's lose them."

"Right." She allowed him to pry her legs loose. Then they went to work on what still separated them. Flesh to flesh was what he had to have. Her skin, already hot and damp, made his mouth water and his fingers fumble. Shirts, jeans, boots fell to the floor until finally, he was naked and she was wearing only the red thong. He could see all of her in the three-way mirror. Images of the first time they'd made love flooded his mind, and desire hardened every muscle in his body.

"One kiss." He barely recognized his own voice. "One kiss." That's what had started it all. But when he reached for her, she placed a hand on his chest.

"Time for another revision. Lie down on that bench."

He glanced at it in the mirror. "It's small."

"It'll be fine, but we have to move it first," she said, grabbing the end and angling it in front of the three-way glass. "Now, sit down on it."

He was never going to be able to predict her, Hunter thought as he sat down on the bench. His own plan had involved making love to her slowly, thoroughly, building the pleasure, layer by layer. Then when she was fresh from his loving, he would take out the jeweler's box.

"No. You have to sit back farther." When he complied, she straddled him on the bench, placing one knee on either side of his hips. His breath backed up and burned in his lungs when she rubbed her damp heat against his erection, and his fantasy of how the evening was going to go evaporated in the wake of the desperate need she was creating. All the urgency that had exploded in him when he'd first stepped into the shop bubbled up again.

"Now," he said as twin urges battled inside of him. He wanted to drag her mouth to his for that kiss. But his hands went to her hips instead. He couldn't get a handle on his hunger. He had to be inside of her.

"Look in the mirror," she urged as he dug his fingers in and lifted her. "Watch me take you in."

Hunter's head began to spin as he did what she demanded. He could see everything. As he lifted her a bit higher, he saw her reach down to move the thong aside and then he watched the two people in the mirror as he pushed himself into her and felt that wet searing heat grip him. He had to close his eyes then as bright explosions of pleasure ripped through him.

"Watch. Keep watching," she said as they both began to move.

And he did. The two figures in the mirror seemed to be two other people there in the room with them, matching their movements stroke for stroke. The woman had thrown her head back, and her nails were digging into the man's shoulders as she raised and then lowered herself to take him in again and again. He felt like a voyeur at the same time that he was experiencing everything he was seeing. The added thrill brought a dark, erotic edge to the feelings streaming through him.

"Hurry," she said.

He managed to drag in a breath as he turned his gaze back to Rory. Her slim, strong body moving faster now.

"Hurry. Hurry."

She filled his vision as his body responded to her commands. He thrust himself into her, feeling helpless and powerful at the same time. She obsessed him. Possessed him.

His mind and vision had begun to blur when she raised her head and gripped his in her hands. Then her eyes fastened on his.

"Come with me, Hunter. I love you."

Something snapped inside of him then, and he allowed everything that was him to pour into her.

WHEN RORY OPENED HER EYES, she saw that they weren't on the bench anymore. She was sitting on Hunter's lap in much the same position they'd ended up in the first time that they'd made love. She didn't want to move. She wasn't even sure she could.

But the seconds turned into minutes. She could feel his heartbeat slow under her ear, and he still wasn't saying anything. She'd told him she loved him. Not the way she'd planned, but she'd said the words.

When she couldn't bear the suspense of the silence any longer, she said, "Wow."

He ran a hand down her back. "I can second that. That was some revision. And it's all your fault that it was wham-bam."

"Sometimes I like wham-bam."

"Me, too. What was your original plan?"

Raising her head, she met his eyes. "I was going to strip for you, very slowly, all the time luring you back into this dressing room."

"Well, we sort of did that, just in fast-forward, and I helped with the stripping."

"The bench was something I thought up on the spur of the moment," she said. *But before I did all that I was going to tell you that I love you,* she thought. He hadn't said anything about that. Maybe he hadn't heard her.

"The bench was a very nice touch. You're beginning to convince me that even the best plans are meant to be revised."

Distracted by the compliment, she said, "No kidding?"

"I had a plan, too," he murmured as he leaned down to drop a kiss on her bare shoulder. "I was going to seduce you slowly—very slowly. And then when you were still weak and thinking only of me, I was going to show you something."

"What?"

"Are you weak and thinking only of me?"

She pretended to consider that for a moment. "Close enough."

He reached for his jeans and dug something out of his pocket.

Rory felt a tightness around her heart when she saw the small velvet box. A jeweler's box.

"Aren't you going to take it and open it?" he asked.

Her hand trembled when she did, and she nearly dropped the box when she saw the ring. "Wow…I mean…I didn't expect…" She met his eyes and then hurriedly glanced back down at the ring—a diamond surrounded by tiny rubies. "I…I need some bubble gum."

It wasn't the reaction he'd expected, but then when had she ever reacted the way he'd expected? He dug into his jeans again and pulled out two pieces of bubble gum and unwrapped them. The suspense, the uncertainty, had tied his own stomach into knots. Together, they chewed in silence for a while.

Rory blew the first bubble and licked it off her lips. "A ring. I wasn't expecting it." Rory pressed a hand against her stomach. "The gum isn't working."

Hunter tried a bubble. No, it wasn't, he thought as the knot of nerves in his stomach tightened. He turned her then on his lap and drew her chin up so that her eyes met his. "Look. I know you might feel that it's sudden. And I know we haven't talked about the future. But we've been spending so much time apart lately, and I don't like it. I want you with me. I want to start something with you. I—" For the first time in years, Hunter felt at a complete loss. He had to find the words and he wasn't sure he could. "Did you mean what you said while we were making love?"

Rory drew in a deep breath and let it out. "Yes. I love you."

The knot began to loosen. "Look, for years I didn't have a family. I didn't think I'd ever want one. But you helped me find them again." He paused again to search for the right words. "I want you with me when I'm old."

Her gaze remained steady on his. "Why?"

His lips curved into a smile, despite his jangled emotions. "A tough question."

"Uh-huh."

"Because I love you, too."

Rory took the ring out of the box, handed it to him and extended her hand. When he slipped it on, she said, "I want to be with you when we're old, too. I'll bet that by then you'll have no problem making love to me very slowly."

They were both laughing as he rolled her beneath him on the floor.

"Complaints. Always complaints," Hunter said as he made a place for himself between her legs. "I think I'll just have to work on my technique."

"For a very, very long time," Rory said as she took him in.

*Natalie and Rory have both found
their happily-ever-afters.
Now it's Sierra's turn.
Don't miss the final installment of the*
RISKING IT ALL
miniseries in
THE FAVOR
*by Cara Summers
Available next month.*

Here's a peek…

1

IN RYDER KANE'S mind, the Blue Pepper was a yuppie haven. And the kick of it was, he fit right in. Twenty years ago when he'd been fighting for survival on the streets of Baltimore, he'd never have imagined ending up in a trendy Georgetown bistro drinking a designer-label beer and wearing the kind of well-cut clothes that allowed him to blend in perfectly with the other well-heeled clientele. With a grin, he lifted his beer and toasted the profitable high-tech security business, Kane Management, that had played a major role in his transformation.

And thank God that computer security wasn't the only business that he dabbled in. While it amused him and put a great deal of money in his pocket, it was his other business, Favors For a Fee, that really intrigued him. Not that Mark Anderson, an investigative reporter on the *Washington Post,* was going to provide much of a fee. But the cryptic message on his voice mail had intrigued him. "I have something hot and political I need your perspective on. Meet me at the Blue Pepper on P Street, 5:00 p.m."

A glance at his watch confirmed that Mark was now half an hour late. Turning slightly on the bar stool, Ryder scanned the entrance area. There was no sign of Mark, but the tall blonde caught his attention. She wore her hair fastened into bun on the back of her head, and even though she wore a loose-fitting jacket and long skirt, he could see that she had that slender, Audrey Hepburn/Nicole Kidman kind of body. Sexy.

Tall women with mile-long legs were one of his weaknesses. Twisting his chair a little farther, he watched as she hesitated, then drew in a deep breath and straightened her shoulders before she pushed through the door.

His curiosity piqued, Ryder narrowed his eyes. She looked as if she were preparing to face a firing squad instead of joining friends for a drink in one of Georgetown's most popular watering holes. Was she meeting a man? If so, she didn't look as though she were looking forward to it.

She crossed the entrance area and climbed the short flight of stairs to the bar with a dragging hesitation in her step that he recognized instantly. He'd walked just that way on each one of his many trips to the principal's office in junior high. One of her hands gripped the large canvas tote she wore slung over her shoulder as if it were a lifeline.

He had a sudden urge to go to her and ask her what he could do to help. The realization, and the effort it took to remain on his stool, surprised him. Rescuing damsels in distress was not the type of work that either Kane Management or Favors For a Fee regularly engaged in. He might like women in all their various shapes and sizes, but he didn't often find himself with an urge to do the knight-in-shining-armor thing. Sam Spade, he wasn't.

Turning away, Ryder took another sip of beer and checked on the score on the TV hanging from the ceiling. The Orioles were tied at the top of the seventh. He didn't turn when she passed behind him, but he had to put some effort into it. That was why he only glimpsed what happened out of the corner of his eye. One of the men at the far end of the bar shoved another one and that one plowed into another in a rippling domino effect that sent the blonde stumbling backward.

Fate, he thought, slipping from his stool and catching her elbows as she struggled for balance. For one brief moment, as he steadied her, he caught her scent—tart lemonade on a hot afternoon. Surprising. And certainly not sexy, at least he wouldn't have thought so. But his body had different ideas. If he'd followed his impulse, he would have turned around, pressed her close, just to see what that would feel like. But Ryder Kane could be cautious when the occasion called for it. And something about this fragile beauty spelled trouble.

"You all right?" he asked as he set her away from him.

"Yes." As she turned, she gasped. "My bag."

Ryder glanced down and saw the canvas tote on the floor, its contents spread about. Dropping to his knees, he picked up the nearest thing. An inhaler, he discovered when he took a closer look. He reached out for the objects that rolled beneath his bar stool—a pack of blue note cards and a plastic bottle that held prescription pills. Sierra Gibbs was the name he noted and she was to take two as needed for migraines.

"Thanks." The voice was deep and just a little breathless. When he turned, she was on her knees facing him, and for an instant his mind went blank except for one word. *You.*

Ryder couldn't put a name to the feeling that raced through him. Not recognition. The first time he'd laid eyes on this woman was a few moments ago. Wasn't it?

This close, her face wasn't quite as perfect as it had seemed from a distance. But the sparkles of freckles across her nose and the faint scar on her chin made it more interesting.

Several long strands of her hair had come loose. Reaching out, he resisted the urge to free the rest and instead tucked one strand behind her ear. He heard her quick intake of breath and felt the instant tightening of his body when his fingers touched her skin. When she closed even, white teeth on her bottom lip, heat shot through him. He wanted *very* much to replace those teeth with his own.

Okay. Now he could name exactly what he was feeling. Lust. That he could understand. He might have even relaxed a bit if it weren't for the fact that he couldn't quite free himself from her gaze. Her eyes were the deep blue color of the water—lake water—the kind that tempted you to jump right in even though there was no telling what lay below the surface.

"You remind me of someone," she said in the same breathless voice that sent ripples of awareness along his skin.

"Really?" He watched her eyes narrow until she was looking at him as if she were determined to see everything.

She took a deep breath. "Have we met somewhere before?"

He smiled then. "Isn't that supposed to be my line?"

WHEN SIERRA CAUGHT his meaning, she felt the color rise in her cheeks. In a moment, she'd be beet-red. Her skin must already be flushed from that arrow of heat that had shot through her during those minutes when he'd held her against him. His chest had been as hard as a rock. And his hands. She could still feel the imprint of each of his fingers where they'd gripped her arms. She'd never reacted quite that physically to a man before. And he thought…she was coming on to him.

"I didn't mean…" she began. "I'm not trying to… It's

just that…I mean…" How was she supposed to explain that strange feeling of recognition she'd felt just seconds ago when she'd looked into his eyes. But she couldn't have met this man before. She would have remembered. "I—"

"Stop." He held up a hand. "I'd rather you didn't tell me that you're not trying to pick me up. My ego is very fragile."

The glint of humor in his eyes settled some of her nerves. "Somehow, I don't think so."

He was different from the men who frequented the Blue Pepper—they were either local merchants or the up-and-coming movers and shakers of D.C. He was also different from the academic types she ran in to in her field of work.

This man, in spite of his classic Adonis-like good looks, was…what? *More real* was the first phrase that came to mind. His skin was a golden brown that came from working in the sun rather than a tanning salon, and she bet the muscles she'd felt came from something other than a tri-weekly appointment with a personal trainer.

When he smiled, her gaze shifted to his mouth, and for a moment she thought of nothing at all—except how those lips might feel pressed to hers.

"Why don't we start over?" He took her hand, and though his fingers only gripped her lightly, she felt the pressure right down to her toes.

"I'll say I'm sure I've seen you somewhere, I'll introduce myself, and I'll offer to buy you a drink. And you'll say…?"

She couldn't say a thing. They were squatting down, leaning toward each other, their fingers linked, their knees nearly brushing, and she'd never felt this kind of intense connection with anyone in her life. In the part of her mind that hadn't shut down, she realized she wasn't feeling like herself at all. Around them, people edged past. Above them, faint noises swirled—glasses clinking, people talking, laughing. She barely heard them. All she knew was that she wanted this man—this perfect stranger—to kiss her. She couldn't recall ever wanting anything quite this much. What would happen if she just leaned a little closer, reached up and drew his mouth to hers? Her sister Natalie would do it. Rory would do it. Wasn't it time she started acting like the Sierra she wanted to be? Suddenly, the wanting, the need, was so strong that she felt herself swaying toward him.

As if he'd read her mind, he tightened his grip on her hand and his free hand moved to the back of her neck, steadying her. "I want to kiss you," he said.

Startled, she raised her eyes to meet his and the old Sierra reasserted herself. "You…can't."

His brows lifted. "If you don't want me to, offering a challenge isn't the best strategy."

She'd suspected he'd be a bit dangerous. But she hadn't expected the thrill that moved through her. "I'm not. But we're in a public place. We don't even know each other."

His lips curved again. "And your point is?"

She moistened her lips, and tried to focus her thoughts. What was her point? If she wanted to initiate a sexual relationship with a man, she had to start somewhere. Kissing this man would be…good practice. "I've never before wanted to kiss someone that I didn't know."

Something flashed into his eyes then, and it made her breath hitch.

"That makes two of us," he murmured as he took her mouth with his.

Oh, he was definitely more real, she thought, as a riot

of sensations moved through her. His mouth was just as strong, just as competent as she'd anticipated. It terrified her. It delighted her. The scrape of his teeth on her bottom lip, the clever side of his tongue over hers sent tiny explosions of pleasure shooting through her. She'd never been kissed like this—as if he had all the time in the world to take and take and take. Her blood pounded, her body heated until all the worry, all the anxiety that had been plaguing her for weeks seemed to evaporate. She should think. But how could she when her whole being seemed to be filled with him?

You. The word repeated itself over and over in her head as she gripped his shoulders and felt those tensed, hard muscles. Greed erupted in her. She wanted to touch more of him. She wanted to run her fingers through that golden blond hair. She wanted to press her palms against his chest, his back, his waist. And she wanted his clothes out of the way.

With a moan, she moved her hands to the back of his neck and pulled him closer.

RYDER FELT AS IF HE WERE going under for the third time. Worse, he felt as if he'd been sucked into a riptide. Her mouth wasn't soft and warm as he'd expected. Instead, it was as hot and avid and demanding as his own. Greed— his, hers, or a combination—rocketed through his system, tearing at his control. He could feel the beat of her pulse against his fingertips, the moan vibrating deep in her throat. No woman had ever set off this fevered combination of sensations and needs.

Needs? Even as a little alarm bell went off in his mind, Ryder felt a flash of intuition—this woman could shake up a life he was perfectly satisfied with. It was that thought and not the fact that they were in a very public place that had him grasping the reins on his control and pulling tight.

Slowly, he gripped her shoulders and set her from him. Her eyes were huge and that deep blue color had clouded. Her hair had fallen out of its knot and tumbled to her shoulders. She looked every bit as stunned as he felt.

"Are you all right?" His voice was ragged, and when he drew in a quick breath, his lungs burned. He'd forgotten to breathe. No woman had ever made him forget to breathe before. Ryder frowned. Just who was she that she could do this to him?

When she closed her eyes and sagged, he felt a sprint of panic. That was a first, too.

"Are you all right?" he repeated as he tightened his grip on her.

CLENCHING HER FISTS, Sierra stiffened her spine and wished for her inhaler. Taking a slow, deep breath, she said, "Fine. I'm fine." She would be in a minute. What had she been thinking? She'd kissed him. She'd let him kiss her back. And she'd do it again in a heartbeat.

She drew in another breath and pushed down the little ripples of panic that were threatening to turn into huge waves. She hadn't been thinking at all, and that wasn't like her.

"Here," he said, pushing something into the hand he'd been holding. "Do you need this? Or this?"

Opening her eyes, Sierra glanced down to see that he was offering her inhaler and the prescription pills she carried with her at all times. Reality check. This was Sierra Gibbs, she thought—a woman who suffered from migraines and asthma. She very much wasn't a woman who kissed strangers in bars. This time the deep breath helped. "No. I'm fine."

She used her inhaler, then steeling herself, she met his eyes. Concern was all she saw. Sierra swallowed her disappointment. This was a male reaction she was familiar with. All her life, she'd brought out the protective streak in men. Wasn't that what she wanted to change? She was tired of being the baby in the family—the one everyone protected.

Still, it might be better not to look at his mouth again. It was hard enough looking into his eyes. They were as gray as smoke, the kind that could swallow you up in a heartbeat. For the first time in her life, the thought of losing herself that way sent a little thrill through her.

"At least let me buy you a drink. You look as if you could use one. I know I could."

"Yes. Okay." The words were out before she remembered. "Oh, no, I can't. I forgot." Tearing her eyes from his, she glanced around. How could she have forgotten the letter and the mission she was on?

"You have a date?"

"Yes." She grabbed her bag and stuffed the pills and the inhaler into it. "Sort of. My sisters and I are having dinner." She grabbed the letter next. Then spotting her day planner under a stool, she reached for it, but he was quicker.

"Sierra Gibbs, Ph.D." He read the name off the card in the plastic pocket on the cover. "What's the Ph.D. in?"

"Psychology." She scooped up the letter and stuffed it into her tote.

"You're a shrink."

In spite of the interest in his voice, she kept her gaze averted. "Not in the way you mean. I don't have a private practice or anything like that. I do research mostly. And write. I teach at Georgetown." She was babbling.

"No couch?"

"No." She could hear that he was smiling, and she very much wanted to look at his mouth again. More, she wanted to feel it pressed against hers. For one moment she was tempted—so tempted to become the woman she'd felt like during that kiss. But she'd come here with a plan, and she always stuck to her plans. Scrambling to her feet, she said, "I have to go."

As he watched her turn and walk away, Ryder forced himself to stay right where he was. He was a man who went with impulse when the occasion warranted it. But this woman was new territory, and a smart man knew when to let caution rule. Still, it took more effort than he would have liked to turn back to his stool. Then he saw the blue note card lying beneath it. It had to have fallen out of the doc's bag.

Bending over, he picked it up and his gaze fell on the neat little list.

A five-step plan for initiating a sexual relationship.
Intrigued, he read further.

1. Attend speed-date at the Blue Pepper and collect data.
2. Study data.
3. Select a lover.
4. Select appropriate sex techniques.
5. Begin relationship.

Could this possibly be what it seemed to be? Eyes narrowed, Ryder read the list again.

What kind of a woman set out to have an affair with a to-do list in hand?

If you enjoyed what you just read,
then we've got an offer you can't resist!

Take 2 bestselling love stories FREE!

Plus get a FREE surprise gift!

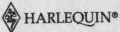

HARLEQUIN®

Blaze™

COMING NEXT MONTH

#189 INDECENT SUGGESTION Elizabeth Bevarly
It's supposed to help them stop smoking. But the hypnosis session Turner McCloud and Becca Mercer attend hasn't worked. They're lighting up even more. What a waste! Or is it? Since then, the just-friends couple has become a bed-buddy couple—they can't keep their hands off each other. In fact, it's so hot between them, why didn't they do this years ago? It's almost as if they've had some subliminal persuasion....

#190 SEXY ALL OVER Jamie Sobrato
She's going to dress up this bad boy in sheep's clothing. Naomi Tyler is the image consultant hired to tone down reporter Zane Underwood's rebel—and sexy—style. Too bad Zane is unwilling to change. Since her career depends on making him over, she's prepared to do whatever it takes...even if it means some sensual persuading from her!

#191 TEXAS FEVER Kimberly Raye
Holly Faraday, owner of Sweet & Sinful gourmet desserts, is thrilled to learn she's inherited her grandmother's place in small Romeo, Texas. That is, until she learns that her grandmother was the local madam—and the townspeople are hoping she'll continue the family business. And once she meets her neighbor, sexy Josh McGraw, she's tempted....

#192 THE FAVOR Cara Summers
Risking It All
Professor Sierra Gibbs didn't realize a speed date could lead to a thrilling adventure. Was it that earth-shattering kiss from sexy Ryder Kane that set her heart pumping? Or the fact that somebody's trying to kill her? Either way, Sierra's feeling free for the first time in her life... and she's going to enjoy every minute of it. She's going to make sure Ryder enjoys it, too....

#193 ALMOST NAKED, INC. Karen Anders
Scientist Matt Fox perfects the silkiest, sexiest material ever invented, but he knows nothing about business, even less about fashion. Yet childhood friend Bridget Cole sure does—she's a hot model with all the right contacts. Soon she's got a plan to get his material into the right hands, though first she'd like to get her hands on Matt....

#194 NIGHT MOVES Julie Kenner
24 Hours: Blackout Bk. 1
When lust and love are simmering right beneath the surface, sometimes it takes only a single day to bring everything to a boil.... Shane Walker is in love with his best friend, Ella. But no matter what he does, he can't make Ella see their relationship any other way. It looks hopeless—until a city-wide blackout gives him twenty-four hours to change her mind....

www.eHarlequin.com

HBCNM0605